CW01214239

The Champion's Lord

TRAIBON FAMILY SAGA
THE FALL OF ASHTON BOOK 1

THE CHAMPION'S LORD

AWARD-WINNING AUTHOR
V.C. WILLIS

The Champion's Lord
Copyright © 2024 Valerie Willis. All rights reserved.

4 Horsemen
Publications, Inc.

Published By: 4 Horsemen Publications, Inc.

4 Horsemen Publications, Inc.
PO Box 417
Sylva, NC 28779
4horsemenpublications.com
info@4horsemenpublications.com

Cover by Autumn Skye
Typesetting by Valerie Willis
Edited by Tilda M. Cooke

All rights to the work within are reserved to the author and publisher. No part of this publication may be reproduced, stored in a retrieval system, or transmitted in any form or by any means, electronic, mechanical, photocopying, recording, scanning, or otherwise, except as permitted under Section 107 or 108 of the 1976 International Copyright Act, without prior written permission except in brief quotations embodied in critical articles and reviews. Please contact either the Publisher or Author to gain permission.

All characters, organizations, and events portrayed in this novel are either products of the author's imagination or are used fictitiously.

All brands, quotes, and cited work respectfully belongs to the original rights holders and bear no affiliation to the authors or publisher.

Library of Congress Control Number: 2024937855

Paperback ISBN-13: 979-8-8232-0506-1
Hardcover ISBN-13: 979-8-8232-0507-8
Audiobook ISBN-13: 979-8-8232-0509-2
Ebook ISBN-13: 979-8-8232-0508-5

Dedication

This is to all my readers and friends who helped me find the courage to write my own MM Romance, putting up with me reading to them, or begging for them to tell me what they think. Look what we created together!

Table of Contents

Dedication 5

Chapter 1
  Newcomers and Invaders 11

Chapter 2
  The Difference Between Tea and Wine 16

Chapter 3
  The Weight of a Soul 21

Chapter 4
  Le Denys Familia 26

Chapter 5
  The Man Before Me 31

Chapter 6
  The Things We Might Regret 35

Chapter 7
  Value is in the Eye of the Beholder 39

Chapter 8
  Facing the Past 42

Chapter 9
  Building an Alliance 46

Chapter 10
  A Future with False Hope 50

Chapter 11
  The New Council of Grandemere 54

CHAPTER 12
The Scarlett House Regulars 59

CHAPTER 13
The Art of Watching 63

CHAPTER 14
Valet de Chambre 68

CHAPTER 15
Down by the Bay 74

CHAPTER 16
Looking the Part 78

CHAPTER 17
Taking a Seat 82

CHAPTER 18
Cutting Threads 87

CHAPTER 19
The Marriage of Desire and Despair 91

CHAPTER 20
A Broken Creature 96

CHAPTER 21
Back to Calm Waters 101

CHAPTER 22
Sowing the Seeds 105

CHAPTER 23
Home of the Wayward Soul 110

CHAPTER 24
A New Phase 114

CHAPTER 25
Grandmama's Insight 118

CHAPTER 26
Blood Ties to the Gods 122

CHAPTER 27
Master of my Lord 128

CHAPTER 28
Apples, Apricots, and Assholes 132

CHAPTER 29
Fever Dreams 138

CHAPTER 30
Healing and Helplessness 142

CHAPTER 31
A Place to Breathe 146

Chapter 32
What Drives Us 150

Chapter 33
Stabbing and Shielding 155

Chapter 34
The Bridge to Nowhere 159

Chapter 35
The Traibon Truce 163

Chapter 36
Even Tame Beasts Bite 169

Chapter 37
Run Him into the Ground 173

Chapter 38
The Bruising of Pride 177

Chapter 39
The Significance of Threads 181

Chapter 40
The First of Many Battles 186

Chapter 41
Blood and Threads 190

Chapter 42
The First Champion Supreme 195

About the Author 201

Book Club Discussion Questions 205

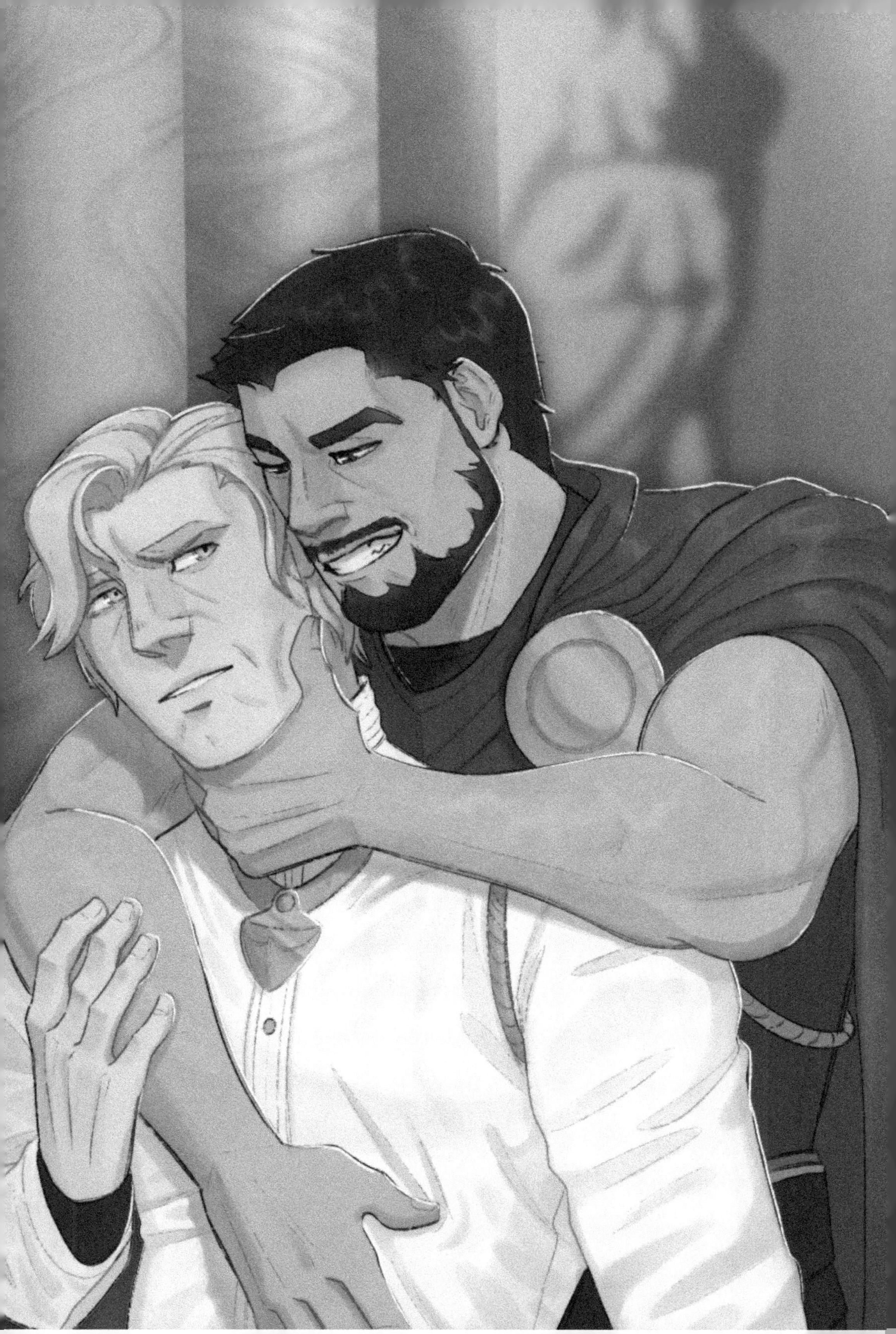

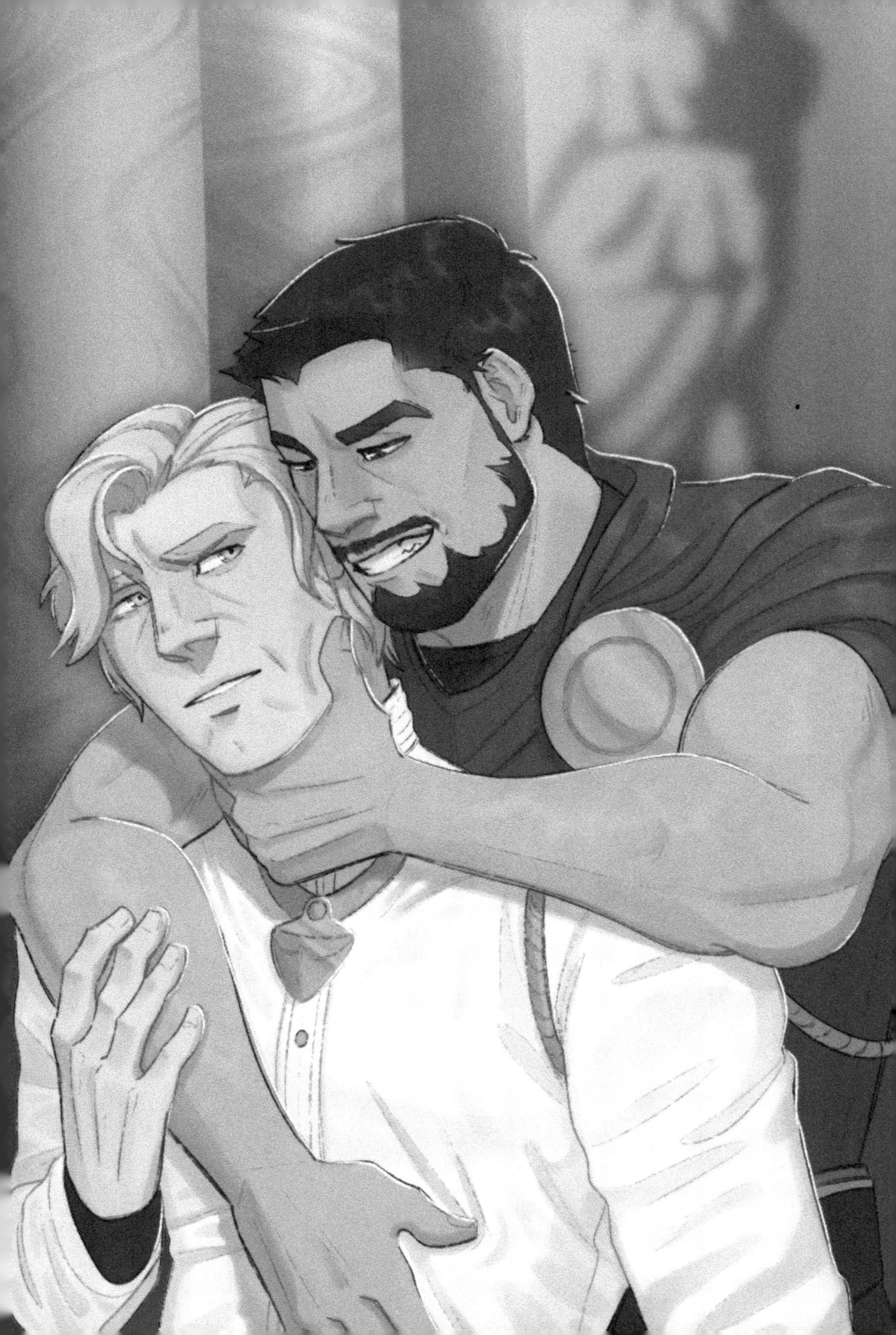

CHAPTER 1

Newcomers and Invaders

I'd never seen someone so frail and stubborn as Raphael Traibon the day he marched onto our field and demanded my father's council. Unlike the other invaders, he hadn't been part of the group who had come to Grandemere to attack, steal, and enslave my people, the daemonis, who had made up most of the population since their arrival a year ago. Instead, he wanted to be "civil" and talk out the agreement as if we were on "equal" standing.

Fool. Only a madman or a stubborn mule walks into enemy territory with nothing more than the clothes on his back. I paused my work, leaning on the hoe as I glared at him. His blue-eyed gaze seemed to find itself struggling not to stare at me, wandering down and up my body as he sucked on a cheek. I knew that glance well. I stood there with nothing but my sweat-soaked blouse and trousers on, and I smirked. *He's got good taste, at least. Perhaps, at the center, they're not that much different from us. He's a little shorter, but fit and athletic. Strong jawed and those eyes, mmm, human, weaker, but much to be desired.* I licked a fang, returning with my own bounce in gaze.

"We relocated this far north to give you land and you dare enter our new home and demand more of us?" My father, Germaine Thompson, was clan chief. He didn't stop breaking the ground as he criticized the young foreign noble. "Does your greed know no bounds?"

"That's not why I'm here," Raphael said sternly. "I'm here to learn from your people and even hope to live amongst you. To make an alliance with you so we may help one another with the rising tide at our backs, no?" His words were sharp and straight to the point.

Scanning behind him, he had no one with him despite his attire and braid to announce his station. *Something's off. Where are his servants? His guards?* Completely alone, he had a pack hanging off a shoulder, a weapon at his side, a wagon with a few chests back on the road, and a scar across his left cheek, still bright pink and new. *He's been fighting and surviving alone.* His dark blue attire seemed loud against the brown of the farm and the green of the encompassing forest. *We're in complete isolation here. If we were to kill him—did he even think this through?*

Originally, we had lived west of the capitol, Captiva City, where my father served as a councilman, and I spent my days as the bachelor of high society for many a decade. Our farms were taken from us when we lost the battle in the east, so we went north. Here we had to start again, where winters were longer, the dirt filled with rocks, and the wilds full of fangs and claws. The Forest of Wayward Souls, a dangerous dark forest, is just on the other side of the Fate's Tears River from the farm. The river runs south to fill the lake called Willow Waters just north of where we once lived west of Captiva City. *No one dares enter there. You can't find your way home, at least if you don't know how to navigate in the darkness of towering evergreens.* To the east, a village had started, filled with daemon and humans alike who had been run off their lands to the south. *It's only a matter of time before they take this too from us and force us to the sea, or worse, to freeze to death in the Perines Mountains farther north.*

Looking over the golden markings and emblems adorning Raphael's clothes, I finally found what I was searching for and spoke up. *I recognize that emblem from the books. He's asking for trouble waltzing in and revealing who he is like that.* "What's the heir apparent to the Old Continent doing here instead of ruling over our lands with his thieving people?" My words cut harshly, earning me a glare from both Raphael and my father.

"Ashton, hold your tongue," hissed Germaine.

"Come now, Father." I smirked as I cooed. "No one can tame my tongue. Ask the girls and the stable boy."

"Ashton," admonished Germaine, face mottling in embarrassment. "Do you have no shame?" he muttered to me.

I shot Raphael a look, arching a brow before licking a fang. *Surely, he wasn't looking me up and down for no reason, but if this insults him enough to walk out... win-win.*

"Is that so? I'll take your word on that, Ashton." A grin crested Raphael's face, a sparkle in his blue eyes. "I see you are well versed about the Old Continent as well. This is a refreshing change from the others I've encountered. There were rumors—"

Newcomers and Invaders

"Rumors get people killed," warned Germaine as he gave up on breaking the ground. "Let us go inside and talk in private, Lord Raphael."

"Raphael," he corrected with a look of disdain painting his face in reply to the honorific. "I've brought tea to offer as well as rare wine. I heard that was customary when discussing such important matters that impact both parties."

I shot my father a glance before he waved me on. "Ashton, take him to the house. I'll hand this work off to someone else until we've finished our talk. I will hear you out, boy."

"Thank you, Mister?" Raphael bowed his head, a golden braid slipping off his shoulder as long as anything I had ever seen with 18 knots. *So, he's so daring to just accept he is the emperor of the Old Continent, even though Fallen Arbor now rules his land. I mean, the emperor's dead, and he is the only actual blood to the late emperor, despite his mother not being the empress herself. Ha, but that was the reason why they fell, wasn't it? So, what good does it do now?*

"Germaine Thompson." Father wiped the sweat from his forehead and cleared his throat. "Ashton, please take our honored guest to the house and pour us a drink of your choosing. We'll need it for what I imagine the topic is about." Father gestured for my hoe.

I narrowed my eyes, reluctant to even agree to it all. "My pleasure." Handing Father the hoe, I motioned for Raphael to take the lead to the only house, where his wagon waited. "After you, Raphael."

Raphael was broad-shouldered despite being shorter and, overall, less bulky than me. His hair fell in golden threads, which seemed to glimmer in the sunlight as it swung in a braid down his back. I couldn't resist gliding my gaze across his every fiber, curious about his slender waist yet thick thighs. *What a peculiar physique. I'd love to see him naked.* His skin was tan, cheeks mildly blemished, and his hands were covered with callouses. *He's been living outside and on the move for some time. Is he homeless? I wonder what sort of offer he intends to make with us knowing this much. Does this man have anything to offer besides himself? What could he possibly say that my father can't say no to?*

As if he felt my eyes on him, Raphael glanced back with an air of curiosity as he cast his stare over me. "Ashton, was it?" he inquired with a soft, honeyed tone.

"That's right, sweetheart," I teased, curious about how he would react. *Will he play along or be offended like so many others of his kind?*

"That's a new one." He chuckled, rubbing the back of his neck. "So, what's your position in the tribe, if you don't mind me asking?"

"Next in line to be the chief if my father has his way." I guffawed, rolling my eyes.

Nodding, he paused long enough for me to catch up, then walked side by side with me. "It seems we share similar fates."

"I doubt that, Golden Boy." Snorting, I added, "I didn't invade another continent with a gang of vile men who hold nothing but ill-intent for strangers and the original holders of a land new to them." *I want him to know exactly how I feel about him and his people, just as they've made their distaste known.*

13

"Not all of us agree with the majority," Raphael replied, cool and calm, as we left the field and inched closer to the side of the house. "Some of us came here to disappear, but it seems they followed us."

I grabbed his arm, furrowing my brow at his words. "Are you implying you've been here on our land long before they appeared?"

His gaze locked with my fist full of his sleeve before following it up my arm to linger on my chest. "Yes." His voice was quiet now, the loneliness and despair loud in his eyes as he finally met my gaze. "I've been living in the wilderness for some time, two, maybe three years. I tried my best to keep this from happening, but..." He pushed my hand off and I let him. "As you see, even I couldn't convince them there was a better way, and I hope your way. Your clan rivals, the Farrows, have recently joined forces with the Vendecci family."

"And why should that matter to us?" My father's voice made us both flinch and turn.

Clearing his throat, Raphael stepped back so he could cut a path between us. "Because they intend to subjugate every tribe under their rule."

"Ambition leads to annihilation," barked Germaine. "They'll destroy one another before long. Why should we throw ourselves in the crossfire?"

"A-agreed that they might take one another out, but..." Raphael started his walk once more alongside my father now while I lingered behind, curious what this hardened man had in mind. "I have some power and allies in the derelicts who have followed me here, but if I had my choice, it's your tribe that's always intrigued me the most. I fear leaving these two to conspire with one another may do damage that may bring Grandemere to its knees."

"How so?" Unlatching the door, Germaine paused as his maroon-eyed glare measured the stranger before him. "What could we offer you that none of the others have in order to oppose them?"

Raphael smiled, leaning back on his heels, as he proclaimed, "Are you not the family which has the true guardian bloodline, as well as the wards of your people's history?"

Every nerve tightened as I flew between them. *How does he know?!* My fingers wrapped around his throat as I marched him into the house, the tips of his boots scraping the floor as we went. He wheezed for air, hands trying to pull and push me off, failing to grab the door frame. *I should kill him here and now, where no one can see!* The difference in our height and strength made was loud and clear as his eyes bulged; he was barely able to draw a breath under my grip. *But first, who betrayed me? I want their fucking name now!*

"Whose loose tongue told you this?" I snarled.

Behind me, my father closed and locked the door. "Ashton, release him."

"Why?" I tightened my grip as I slammed Raphael against the wall as if a wolf unwilling to abandon its prey.

Newcomers and Invaders

"Because I sent your sister Lillian to find someone worthy to ally with." Father's words were enough to pull me off Raphael, leaving him coughing and gasping where he landed on his ass.

"Why didn't you fucking tell me?!" Father cut me with his eyes, and I snapped my mouth shut.

"You see, I was aware of what was unfolding between the Farrow and Vendecci families, but we can't do this without knowledge of their ways. Isn't that correct, Raphael?" Raphael still sputtered on the floor. "I sent your sister to do some digging and spying. She's easily dismissed, unlike you, who'd rather waste his time in the Scarlett House." I winced at his words, unable to refute the truth thrown at me.

Wheezing a moment, Raphael rasped, "I brought the books. In the wagon, as she requested."

"I demand answers." My anger rose, muscles twitching with the rise of heat filling me as my blood boiled. "Why was I not informed at the least of this? We both know that I'm the one carrying that bloodline, and it matters when someone knows my secret!"

Chapter 2

The Difference Between Tea and Wine

My father smacked my forehead, a scowl across his face before demanding, "Go pour us wine!" He turned to Raphael and helped him off the ground. "Forgive my son. He's rather sensitive about the threat we face."

Raphael cleared his throat, rubbing his neck as a bruise began to form. "Completely understandable," he croaked, giving me a fiery glare. "My mistake for not realizing how," he struggled with breathing and speaking for a second, "sensitive a fact this is for you."

"You get tea!" I pointed to Raphael and looked at my father. "I will not drink wine on this matter." *This is serious and requires a sober audience. How dare he take my situation so lightly and with an invader!*

A smirk crossed my father's face. "Then tea it is, though a first for you, Ashton. I thought you'd choose wine for such a topic. What was it you told me last time? There's nothing wine can't resolve?"

"Keep your musings to yourself," I spat. "Where is your offering, Golden Boy?"

"Wagon," Raphael rasped, looking to the door. "You dragged me in before I could grab it." He added insult to injury, and I shot him a disapproving glare.

He's bold. Waving a hand at him, I marched for the door and escaped Raphael's burning gaze. At the wagon, I took in his meager belongings. *I see no pack or hint of food or drink anywhere, just these damn old chests. Is this really the entirety of* what he owns? *Ridiculous.* A padlock kept me from prying inside the two traveler's chests, large and battered, and I scoffed. *Not like that's ever stopped me.* Pulling one closer, I spun it and gripped the chunk of metal. With a tug, it broke and rendered the padlock useless. Flipping the lid open, I found a canister of nutty-smelling tea, dark and pungent. In an unopened, Old-Continent-marked, green glass bottle was wine. The handwritten label was done in the language of the Old Tongue. *Why'd I have to choose tea… I bet this is some legendary wine that only nobles get to sample once in their lifetime. Why did he mention the bloodline for the Sacrificial Daughter? Does he not know enough of my religion to not tiptoe on the matter? How ignorant is this man?*

Grumbling and muttering to myself, I shut the chest with the offerings and books inside. The weight of it made my arms ache and burn, but I'd lifted heavier and didn't slow my entry into the old cabin. Dropping it at Raphael's feet, I could see the rage in his eyes, though he held his composure with practiced skill. *Oh, a temper does lay inside that pretty little head,* I mused to myself. Locking the door, I returned to the table in time for my father to lay out the cups and bring the kettle of hot water from the hearth. *This should have Father happy. He rather enjoys tea, but I am already regretting my decision to stay sober.*

My chair screeched loudly in the silence as we glared at one another. Raphael cleared his throat before bending down to pull a key out of his pocket. I watched him, a smug expression on my face, waiting for him to discover I had already gone through his things. *Surely, he'll say something of it. Make a scene and give me a reason to shove him out the door and be done with this farce.* Raphael paused, blinking at seeing the padlock gone, and I could see a flush of red hit his face. Turning slightly, he aborted, looking my way and I flinched. *Did he catch on?*

Instead, he opened it, saying nothing of the matter. "Tea, was it?" Raphael's voice was smooth once more when he spoke. "I believe that was your decision, Ashton." My name fell from his lips in such a way it sent a shiver through me. "Was that right, Ashton?" His tone was an astute and stern thud as his tongue pressed on his teeth, an accent slipping out when he called me a second time, then thrice. "Ashton?"

Now he met my gaze, and from under the table, out of the view of my father, I saw it. *Oh, he's pissed.* The fire in those brilliant blue eyes, the fleck of an eyebrow as he bit his lip. *He's very attractive angry.* I lost myself. *Oh, this will be fun.* Raphael's eyes dipped across me again, the eyes lingering, and I closed my thighs. *What was that?* Blinking, I knitted my brow and smiled. A smirk fought to appear across Raphael's plump lips, and I looked away, turning myself to face my father. *He's fucking with me.*

"I was rash. Tea or wine, Father?" My heart fluttered, and for the first time in a long while, I felt the heat of desire in earnest. "I've swallowed my temper now," I announced, marveling over this useless crush burning at my core.

Germaine narrowed his eyes at me, his mustache twitching before he waved a hand. "No, no, Ashton. You said tea, and we shall take this meeting serious and sober as you so intended it to be." He shuffled and sat in his seat as Raphael slid the canister across the table, where my father snatched it up, smelling the leaves. "Mmm, this is quite delightful and fragrant! Is this a black tea? From the Old Continent?"

"Yes, I personally harvested this before winter." Raphael winked at me, and I rolled my eyes. "I managed to get it to take root, though it was quite the learning curve that first year I was here."

"A farmer at heart," remarked my father, opening the teapot to prepare to start seeping the nutty, fragrant tea.

"We'll find out at the risk of our tastebuds," I drawled. Then a nudge hit my knee under the table, the bottle of wine pressing against it. *He's definitely going to fuck with me.* Stealing a glance under the table, I cast an annoyed glare at Raphael and I lipped, "What's this?"

"Yours," he lipped before also adding, "take it."

"No," I lipped, shaking it off my knee as he still crouched under the table, pulling items from his chest.

"Oh, may I keep what tea is left after this pot? It smells divine, Raphael." My father seemed in a better mood now.

"Absolutely," answered Raphael as he pressed the bottle, and I refused.

"Wait, this calls for better cups." I watched in horror as my father abandoned us for the kitchen cabinets, fully distracted.

"Take it," whispered Raphael, looking at me over the tabletop.

"What's the matter with you?" I remarked in a hushed voice.

Raphael disappeared under the table once more, and I slapped my hands on the table in alarm. Before I could stand, the bottle of wine was shoved forcibly between my thighs as my father returned. I straightened in my chair. Puffing my cheeks out, I was at a loss. *This cheeky bastard of a human Lord!* Popping back up, Raphael placed a stack of books on the table, a grin of victory on his face. My father had returned, scooping leaves into the filter with far too much excitement. A second bottle slid behind the first bottle, and I caught his wrist under the table. *This asshole…*

Smiling at my dad, who gave me an arched brow, I suddenly blurted, "Let me help with these books! Seeing as they are the reason he's here and taking so long." I growled, ducking under the table, and threw his wrist back at him with a heated glare. *He's having the time of his life! Look at that fucking shit-eating grin on his face! He thinks he's being funny!*

With a smile across his face, Raphael handed me a book. "Thank you so kindly, Ashton. Perhaps, after this meeting, we can become friends."

"Did your horse kick you in the head?" I seethed, pushing the second bottle back to him.

"The other?" Raphael whispered, gesturing he was at last willing to take it from me.

The Difference Between Tea and Wine

Narrowing my eyes, I replied, "This one stays with me." I slapped the book onto the table. "Any more of your tomes? Shall I retrieve the other chest?"

"We'll start with this much." Father intervened, sliding cups of tea in front of us both. "Now, to business. Sit, sit."

"What is this about?" Staring at my reflection, my eyes carried a glow to them. *Yeah, I'm pretty annoyed and pissed off right now.* "You had Lillian sneak out, you invited this man to our home, and all I can see is that it's over some dusty old books." I plucked one up and started to flip through it. "Written in … the Old Tongue and occasionally Ogrean."

"You can read that?" A sparkle of excitement hit Raphael's voice, but my glare snuffed it out. "Right, I should have expected that much from such a prestigious family." Raphael rubbed his neck before taking a sip of tea. "You do know your tea. I couldn't have made it better, Germaine."

"Flattery will get you nowhere, Raphael," reprimanded my father. "Right, but these books, they hold accounts and possible evidence of Fallen Arbor planning everything that's been happening here and on the Old Continent for a few decades, correct?" My father blew on his cup of tea. "They are pulling strings worldwide, and I believe it's because there's something they want from both of us, Lord Raphael." Germaine shot a hardened glare across the table at Raphael as he sipped his cup at last.

"They had started with coming to hunt me down directly, but it stopped, and before long, the invasion and battle unfolded last year." Raphael stared at his cup, fingers drumming on the tabletop.

"What makes you think they even stopped? One doesn't win at the game of corruption without corroding from every corner." Father hummed, delighted in the tea now. "Wonderful and astringent. Lillian must have told you what my tastes were in teas."

"She was kind enough to answer my questions when I asked." Raphael heaved a sigh, pondering my father's words before he spoke further. "So why follow me to the wildlands of the New Continent? I thought being out of their way would suffice. That was what I kept asking myself over and over again before someone I trust sent these journals to my doorstep." His forehead wrinkled, a hint of crow's feet in the corner of his eyes. "I was good as dead to them."

"Greedy men will grab for gold, no matter the cost. Especially for the prize they value the most." I echoed a saying my father had said many times over to me, granted over my own conquests. "They aren't just after you. They want Grandemere, too. Whether they want your standing as heir apparent by proving you are indeed dead or want something else from you, it still doesn't answer their fascination over us, the daemonis." Placing the book down, I spun it and pointed to a page written in Ogrean script. "Someone's been doing research on Ogre culture, specifically the weapons the clan leaders hand down to one another." I shot a harrowing glare to my father, the only person in the room as well-versed as I was on the matter. "Someone is trying to find a means to recreate this. Someone wants to bring magic back."

Placing his cup down, he slid the book closer, and we watched as he read page after page. After several minutes, he waved for another book. With a long sigh, I began diving into more books, searching, and Raphael sat drinking tea and refilling our cups as he gave us all the time in the world. The outside world seemed to no longer exist as time froze for us to search for answers among the pages of a stranger who seemed angry and bitter at times. *Does Raphael not have a sense of alarm on the matter? Could it be he's not aware of what this means?*

This could destroy not just someone's life forever but become a scourge to the world if they manipulate something that took centuries to even master. No one should ever dabble in arts where souls are at stake. It's written by the Fates that they took it from this world to provide peace and rid the world of its plagues and corruption. Magic was locked away, stripped from the minds of all, and, more importantly, forbidden by the gods themselves. What good would come from going against the gods themselves? And could it mean they know about our greatest secret and our beloved Fates? May the Mother of Life continue to give, the Sacrificial Daughter mend, and the Devoted Sister protect us all…

Chapter 3

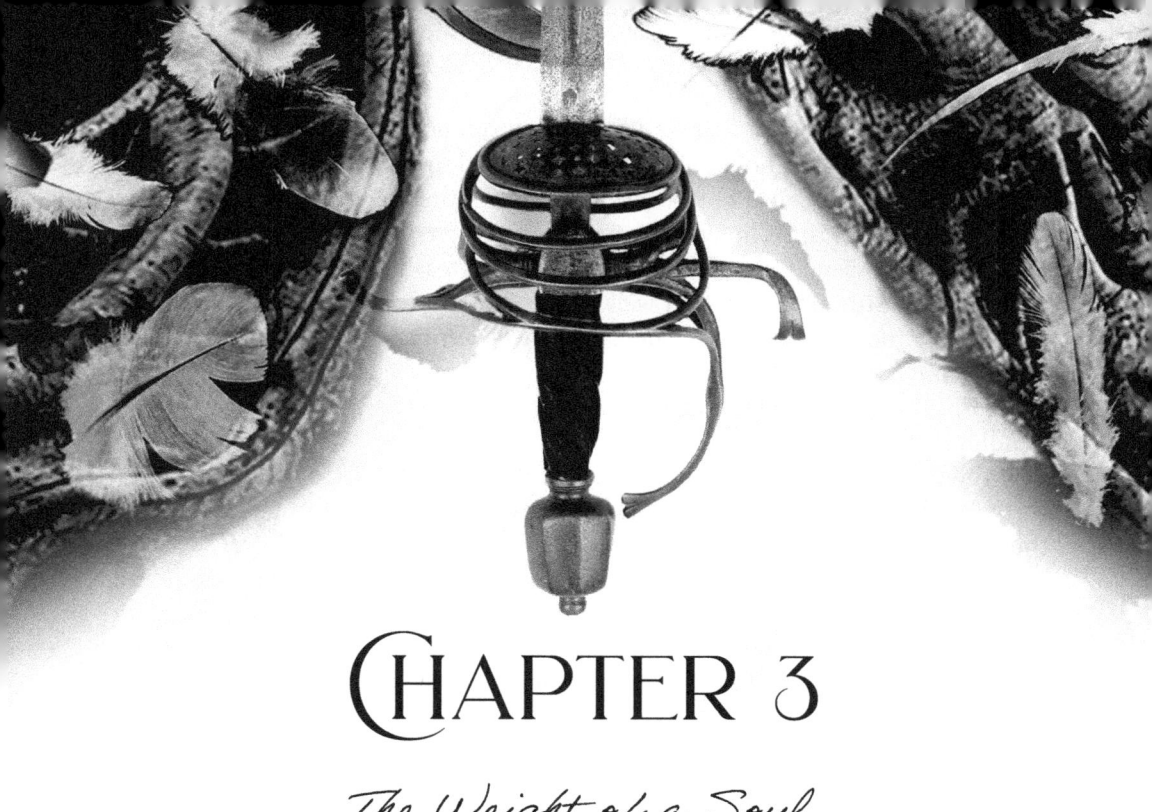

The Weight of a Soul

The sun had long set, another round of water heated on the fire as the three of us read through the books. There's so much research from all over the world. He's comparing similarities in magic, gods, and more. At some point, we had crawled through the cellar to the hidden door and retrieved books on various subjects, along with the other chest full of books from the wagon. The notes that unnerved me the most were the ones that acknowledged the connection between the gods and our souls and how we siphon magic from them. *This can't be right.*

Meanwhile, Raphael remained in the cabin, waiting with utter patience. He ended up fetching water from the pump to bring back. Outside the sky was still dark and aimless through the windows. My eyes found matches of information verbatim in our own sacred texts and the mysterious researcher's notes. *He's seen our works or even owns copies of some of our more sacred texts. This comes from a book passed down in my family; only a few of the other families even know about it. How is that possible?*

"Here." I slid it to my father to show him the thing I had wanted to confirm. "Soul weapons. That's what they're after."

"I figured that was the aim." Father waved a hand at me, and I slapped it, earning an annoyed sigh from him.

"But he's manipulating it and adding in information from our people, here." I pointed to the research notes, allowing him to read them before swapping to one of our very own historical books. "It's verbatim, Father. He's seen this book, or a damn good copy of it. Who would have that?"

"The Farrow clan." Father sat back and sipped his tea, his stare on the flames now.

"But this journal was written well before they came." Frantically, I searched on, reading more as my chest ached. *They've been chasing down the connection between the Fates and daemons.* "This madman wants to use souls or even break them open to gain forbidden magic from the gods. The world is not made to handle such power."

"Then where does the daemonis come into the fold?" Raphael at last joined while he slaved over the woodstove. "If that's the case, then I might know why they chased me down."

"In my religion, the books talk about why the Fates cut ties to other gods and the Old Continent after they managed to lock away magic. It's even forbidden for anyone to pass down knowledge of magic outside the history books under our family's care." I swallowed as my eyes hit a note in the journal that shook me. "He has a formula or ritual of some kind here. One that could pull out a perverted version of what the Devoted Sister bestowed unto the Le Denys clan with her own blood."

Raphael cut between us; bowls of stew set before us. "Eat. Let me share something about what I know about the information and how I have my own connections to the gods. Or at least where my own bloodline shares a similar tie."

Looking at the stew, I swirled it with a spoon before staring Raphael down. "Quite hospitable, are we?"

"Just patient, seeing as I interrupted supper time, I shall take a moment to make amends for that." Raphael gave a half-hearted smile as he sat and poured himself a fresh cup of tea. "Where I come from, there's been a new religion building for a few generations, and it caught on like wildfire thanks to the alliance between the first headmaster of the church and Emperor. Admirably, it comes with its share of mixing myth with history, but I can't tell you how much truth is under it all."

In short, Raphael and I both carry blood ties to our gods. It's only a matter of time before they come knocking at my door to drag me off. Whether we join forces or not, we need to be prepared for what comes next.

Raphael offered to refill my cup, and I turned it down. "They believe in a Holy Trinity of their own making, which includes the Divine Father, Knowing Mother, and the Anointed Child. Unfortunately, when my ancestors helped establish this, they put a target on my family's heads by claiming we come from the blood of the Anointed Child. Whether this was a god or half god or just a man with power, I can't say. I vote the latter," he said reassuringly.

"And what of the old gods?" pressed my father, eating a fingerling potato from his bowl.

"Well, the author of these journals started their journey praising Nuen." Raphael pointed at a book. "There, Nuen is praised a few times, but it didn't last long. Whoever this person is, they definitely believe in the gods and even seems to have a connection to one later on. It's quite … disturbing since they even describe them as a person, almost or living being."

Nuen was refusing to help him, so they went with a different god who was willing to approach. It's rare for a god to show themselves, but when they do, calamity will soon follow. In every account, entire families, countries, even the land itself, is devastated. Swallowing down a bite of food, I pointed my spoon at the book. "What's an old god of the Ogre clans have any business being praised in what clearly is written in Old Tongue and not their language? If he thought he would reply to that, it's a huge insult to Nuen and even his counterpart, Utash. Any god, really."

"Ah, see, that's what had my interest piqued." Raphael sat his cup down and grabbed a different tome. "Normally, someone will worship both Nuen, the male god of the night and the perversions of the world, alongside his counterpart, Utash, the female god of day and justice of the world. Instead, he only worshipped this one god before abandoning him for the Quisling Spirit. Granted, his flipping between Old Tongue and Ogrean only leaves me to think—"

"—they might be an ogre? Who converted religions?" Taking the book from Raphael, I thumbed through it and dropped my spoon. "Wait, here." Flipping back a few pages, I laid the books open at the center of the table. "He was close enough to sketch the ogre leader's sword. He must be related or even a disparate, half-ogre/half-human since he's multilingual and has access to more than the two ogre patrons. Perhaps in a position like ourselves, a prince or son of an important official?"

"Ah, and who is this other god you speak of?" My father sipped the broth from his bowl. "I am not familiar with that one, though I knew a little of the others."

"The Quisling Spirit is both old and new." Raphael covered his mouth, contemplating as he took in the sketch of the sword with a look of recognition.

He's seen this sword in person some place. I suppose, as a prince, he would encounter the legendary ogre warlord Sebastian l'Ifrit, or was it he who sent Raphael these tomes in hopes of uncovering more with our help? He hasn't lived the last two centuries for naught. I mean, the books say he's favored by both of his gods and, worse, has uncanny instincts. I wonder. Narrowing my eyes, I scowled at Raphael as I questioned how much he knew. *Did Sebastian tell him to seek out the Thompson clan specifically, and when Lillian approached, he ran with it?*

Catching my gaze, Raphael added, "He's known in the old texts as a traitor to them and was named *Tombré*. I suspect Fallen Arbor implicating they are the saplings under his command, but that's assuming gods exist."

"It's foolish to assume they don't," I warned, and Raphael hmphed to himself. *So that's it. He's a non-believer and dismisses magic and gods, trying to see this without any of those elements. If he only knew what I knew of the Fates…*

"As for the new religious texts, he's painted as a jealous trickster. I can't say if this entity is more like the Anointed Child where someone or a bloodline performs godlike duties or if he's really a living, breathing ancient."

"Or a real god," I added. *What's that saying? Don't turn the eyes of the gods to you or suffer endlessly as their plaything. I wonder, does Sebastian fall under this saying? I'll have to ask him if I live long enough to cross paths with him.*

Raphael ignored me and slid the book closer. "This is a very accurate drawing of this sword, but why such deep interest in this weapon?"

KNEW IT! My heart fluttered at the confession, but a thought hit me, *He's met Sebastian. By the Fates, I'm jealous and wonder if he's as striking as they say. Ever since I read his stories in the books from the Old Continent, I have imagined finding favor with the Fates and going on adventures in their name. Ha! How foolish I was, and short-sighted. Now, I know no glory comes from that, and when the gods look your way, their power will make the world around you barren of destiny and choice. You will know no love, no death, and no life when they are finished cutting and knotting your thread to no means. There was something in the ancient daemonis that said one could become a god themselves, eventually, but they pitied the fool who would give up their destiny to take on such a miserable burden.*

"How much do you know of the oldest race of the world, and in this case, the ogres, Raphael?" My father stood, making his way to the stove to refill his bowl.

"Honestly, I read a lot, but retained nothing," Raphael answered, exasperated. "Even then, if I were to be truthful with you, gentlemen, I don't necessarily trust my upbringing that much anymore. It's not the reason I'm still alive. That much is for certain."

"The leaders of their clans pass down their knowledge," I announced, drumming my fingers on the table. "But that's only upon their death."

"How is that possible?" Raphael's forehead wrinkled, and his features seemed more pronounced in the fire's light.

"You see, that sword is the last surviving relic from the time of magic. Granted, soul weapons were a skill for ogres specifically, or a custom, to be more accurate, and it might still be possible or used by them." Tapping on the drawing, I lowered my tone and emphasized, "This is a soul weapon, the last known one in the entire world in today's age. There used to be six in total, one for each clan." I pulled the wine from between my thighs and popped the cork. "They don't just pass down knowledge and skill. The former clan leader gives the full weight of their departing soul into the blade of the new leader. They say this sword had hundreds of souls inside it before Sebastian held it." I took a swig of the wine straight from the bottle, the sweet dryness of it painting my tongue with each swallow before I let go. "In short, whoever this is, they've been praying to every dark god they can think of, starting close to home first." Wiping the wine from my lips, I gave him a dangerous look. "But this betrayer god, Tombré, must have made him a bargain." I pointed to a specific book, the ritual circles etched into my memory like everything else I've ever laid my eyes upon. *I need only to see it once to memorize it.* "He knows how to make the perverted version of a soul weapon. One rune. One shift in the rune from willing to unwilling participant in the sacrifice of a living being turning into a weapon." Another draw of wine, and I kept going, spilling what I knew no one could piece together so accurately or as well read and remembered as I could. "Normally, the initial weapon is someone's soul and body turned into their soul's form. The way he's changed it, according to the notes here, he can lay a sword on the table and make someone's soul go into it. He's willing to kill someone and force this fate upon them for the sake of getting some sort of magic pull from the gods themselves, and Tombré told him how to do it."

Raphael balled his hands into fists. "I think it's bullshit; some god told them how to siphon magic from the other gods. I don't believe in the gods because…" The anger building in him broke the calm façade at last. "Where were they when I…" Raphael shook his head, covering his mouth to keep his anger inside.

He's guilt-ridden. I, too, feel such self-hatred for the death of… I swigged the wine to keep the thought from finishing in my head.

"Settle down." Sitting back at the table, my father sighed as he spoke up. "You see, he's found a means to force a soul open, then. Whether he pulls the full weight of a soul into a weapon or simply enough to cut the chains, we will have to wait and see. If the ritual is on paper, then it means it's already happened. He's figured it out if someone was able to steal away all this research."

"He?" I arched a brow.

My father pointed at a few books. "Ogrean. It's characters change depending on who the writer is. Men use a more masculine version of the letters versus when a female writes. We know that our enemy is male from that much. Old habits die hard, and it shows he grew up in an ogre clan at the very least, and perhaps, if by some twisted fate, we find means to meet Sebastian, we can ask him about it."

"Regardless. He's killing people with any connection to the gods and willing to lay waste to entire countries." I glared at the sketch, trying to picture what it might feel like to have that sort of prison. "He's imprisoning people's souls inside weapons in servitude for the rest of their days."

Raphael's chair toppled, hitting the ground with a loud clatter. "We need to stop him!"

Glaring at him, I finished another swig of wine and patronized him. "And who is it? Who are we looking for, exactly?"

"I…" Raphael bounced his eyes between my father and me before picking up his chair. "I see," he admitted at last. "We can't do anything without … knowing," he said bitterly. "To know all the damage and lives lost over foolish desire for magic, something that doesn't exist."

"That does exist," I corrected, the wine sour on my tongue. *They took out a long-standing empire over this.* A shudder rolled through me, and I glared into the fire. *My family and world are smaller in comparison; they would burn it down in a blink of an eye, surely.*

Chapter 4

Le Denys Familia

Raphael lowered his brow, anger biting at him. *He definitely denies or doesn't believe in the gods.* I shifted in my chair, unsettled at this idea. *Does he know he's only asking for them to bring calamity upon him? They will make him believe by the time they bring him to death's bedside.*

"You see, this is where this gets dangerous." Father topped off his tea, swirling it with a touch of honey this time as he admired the steam drifting from it. "We will have to put ourselves in competition with these fools dangling from Fallen Arbor's puppet strings. Whether we join them or call their blades to us, we need them out of the shadows to figure out who this man might be. I don't think he's the leader of Fallen Arbor, but he's close to the top."

"I don't think it is safe for the family to even get involved." I shook my head, waving my hand in disagreement. "We can't join this farce that involves fucking with the gods. It's asking for the Fates to strike us down."

"Nowhere is safe for the family." Father shot me a look, and I closed my mouth. "But now we know our duty, not only to our kind. The task we promised the Sacrificial Daughter and Devoted Sister is upon us. Was it not written that we mend and protect against such threats?" I cast my gaze away, unhappy he would use my devotion against me. "We must act, but we should do so with every resource at our disposal."

"Fine." I banged the wine bottle on the table. "What would you have us do, Father?"

"We accept servitude under the young master here." Germaine motioned to Raphael as he spoke. "He has the most clout regarding the former throne, and with us under him, it will surely rock the alliance between House Vendecci and the Farrow clan. Whoever this person is," Father nodded to the books on the table, "he has connections through the Farrow clan for certain."

"Ah, and they clearly have had a connection with House Vendecci, which can trace this back to the Old Continent. I can confirm they've aided Fallen Arbor in the past." Raphael took the wine from me and stole a swig before shoving it back. "That means they haven't really been exiled from the Old Continent like the other families."

"No, they were sent here to take over," declared my father.

"But what proof do we have?" I rolled the wine bottle between my palms, agitated and angry. "We can't even fight back, nor do we have a target."

A knocking at the door made us jolt, the wine bottle tilting before spilling across the table. I looked back at my father and Raphael, both shaking their heads. *They knew of no one coming.* Another knock, slower and in a pattern I recognized. The tension left me, and my father sat down as he muttered curses under his breath. Raphael gave me a confused expression. I motioned for him to sit. He did so, though his hand stayed on the hilt at his hip.

"Do you want her to enter?" I glared at Father as my hand lay on the lock.

"Let her in. I take it she has news of her other assignment." My father waved his hand.

Upon unlocking the door, she slammed me between it and the wall as she rushed in. "Is he still here?!" I heard the familiar woman shout.

"By the Fates!" I cursed, slamming the door shut and locking it again. "When will you learn to enter a room with some dignity and grace?" I growled. "And why do you always forget to knock correctly?"

"Says the man who was caught with the stable boy bent over the—" My sister was quick in reply, her tongue sharp as ever.

I slapped a palm over my sister's mouth. "Lillian, we're having tea." Removing my hand, she scowled at me, pulling a lock of her stark white curly hair from her lips. "Either leave or read the room."

Clearing her throat, she turned her attention to Father. "I see you are still negotiating with Lord Raphael." She nodded her acknowledgment to him, and he dipped his head in return. "Would you like for this other matter to be discussed in private, Father?"

"What other matter?" My temper rose at the idea there would be more I wasn't aware of. *Why am I being left in the dark on this? It's clearly about the fact that I come from the blood of the Fates and have shown signs of carrying it. Why do I not get a say in how I want to handle this?!*

Father heaved a sigh, taking down the last of his tea before he spoke sternly. "I don't need your permission to protect *our* people."

"I don't understand how you want to pressure me into the role of taking over as clan chief when you croak yet continue to go behind my back when—"

"—If you'd keep your belt buckled, you would have been home long enough to be here for the more urgent matters," quipped Lillian, her maroon eyes glowing with her rising ire.

My stomach twisted. Y*es, I had snuck out a few nights before and chased some fun with the stable boy. And the maid from town,* I thought bitterly. *Lillian clearly saw me; she came looking for me only to find me hilt deep in Jeoffrey and...* Anger was replaced with the weight of regret. *I'm busy fucking around while Father is over here trying to decide to fight or flight with the changing tide.* I caught the look on Raphael's face, his glare burning through me. *And now I'm the dick in the room.*

Throwing up my hands, I relented. "Fine. I get it. Ashton, the asshole, fucked up again and can't keep his dick in his pants. But I'm here now. I even chose tea." I threw my arm out at the kettle. *The prince may not realize the weight of that custom, but Lilly should...* Her expression softened. "Well?"

My father had defaulted to that expression he infamously wore on occasion that revealed no emotion as he poured himself more tea. "Go on, Lilly."

Raising her chin, Lillian pushed me off to the side before she announced, "The Le Denys survivors have been reached, and they wish to have a meeting with all parties involved."

"Le Denys?" I shot a look to Father, a panic building at my core. "Haven't they been through enough?" My mother's pale face, laid on the very table in front of me, set my anxiety off, my throat tight. *What is he thinking? He already feels guilty about her death, and why would they trust us after that failure of a battle? We lost all of my mother's family last I heard.* "I don't think it's right to ask them—"

Father held up a hand, silencing Raphael, who seemed equally as alarmed over the matter, and me, motioning that we take our seats at once. "Let me now share my thoughts on what it is I had decided long before seeking Raphael or even Le Denys." His teacup thudded loudly in the sudden silence, sounding as heavy as an anvil. "We've tried running, we've tried staying neutral, and we've tried standing our ground." The fire popped and shifted, prompting Lillian to walk around to toss another log in to bring the flames to light the room better. "But we can no longer sit here and pretend this is working. There's no point in it." Steam from his tea danced in his exhale as he drew in another breath. "We're at a turning point, one in which we must decide if we would rather be the cornered animal or the one which turns its predator into prey."

"But the Le Denys," I pleaded, trying not to unravel in front of Raphael. "They were the warriors, the sword and shield of our people. When they stood their ground on our behalf, we lost Captiva City." Balling my hands into fists, I pressed, "We're lucky they even let us inside our own city, but it's only a matter of time before—"

"As the wardens and keepers of the guardian bloodline, we must keep our promise to preserve our people's history and heritage at all costs," he reminded me with a dangerous glare.

"I know. We were given a gift and duty by the Sacrificial Daughter and Devoted Sister on behalf of the Mother of Life." Shifting, I couldn't make the crawling sensation leave me, feeling like a stranger in my own skin. *There's something unsettling about the pact we made all those centuries ago with the gods.*

"In short, that is how we protect our people. Diplomacy was our weapon. Knowledge our shield, was it not?" Father turned to Raphael, motioning to him. "We will fall into servitude under Lord Raphael."

"This is dangerous." Raphael's voice cut across the room. "Becoming my servants only makes you lesser and no longer equal among the other invaders the moment you do this," he warned, his body tense with the emotions this plan invoked within him.

"In actuality, we're already seen as lesser. That changes nothing." Tapping the table, Father continued revealing more of his plan. "We know this is a partnership. You don't conquer an empire or army without a team effort. We will do this together." Leaning back in his chair, he rubbed his forehead. "That being said, we will need allies. The Thompson lineage is only about five or eight families strong with maybe three or more of blood and the rest workers from elsewhere or no clan blood at all."

"And I'm only one man," added Raphael. "There's a chance I still can pull an alliance with one or more depending which families are on the council, but we'll have to bring some monetary value or information to persuade them we are the better ally of the options available."

"There's a chance the Le Denys might join," offered Lillian, where she squatted, stoking the fire.

Father grunted at her words. "We'll have to find a means to catch everyone's attention. Clearly, we'll never have the numbers to do so." He pulled a journal to him as his mind spun its webs. "Whoever wrote these journals had connections and not just any contacts. They would have links to both Grandemere and the Old Continent. In order to uncover who he is, we will need our own network, but perhaps alliances aren't quite the right answer." He snorted to himself and nodded, reconfirming "We need trustworthy contacts that we can trust not to do us harm, or at least, that will be willing to give us a heads up on danger."

"Well, back in the Old Continent, it was Fallen Arbor's spy and assassin network that brought down the houses one by one." Raphael leaned an elbow on the table and covered his mouth before adding, "Do you think we can beat them at their own game?"

A smirk crossed my face. "If anyone can go blow for blow on that matter, it would be my father," I reassured Raphael. "There's no such network on that level, but it wouldn't take long to build."

"The Le Denys survivors are few, but they'll be itching for work in the shadows," Lillian added. "There is a chance we can hire some stragglers to get the ball rolling. I mean, they specialize in combat on top of it, so this seems quite doable in a short amount of time to beat Fallen Arbor."

"Don't underestimate them," warned Raphael. "They didn't come here with a single purpose. For them to know I was here living in Grandemere means they have daemon spies and allies already established."

"Even the journal seems to reveal that much." I slid the journal in question across the table to Lillian, encouraging her to see for herself. "To have exact information means they've been here longer than Raphael, don't you think, Father?"

"Indeed," he mumbled, still thinking, before letting his gaze rise and land on Raphael. "Now, the question is, are you ready to make it clear you're back in the standing to be the new emperor of this new land, First Crowned Prince Raphael?"

Raphael closed his eyes tight as if pain shot through him. *Why does he not answer? He came here so eager and excited to join forces, but now nothing. What else could he possibly want from us? Or is it a reminder of where he failed his own family? After all, they're all dead while he sits here, still alive and breathing.*

Chapter 5

The Man Before Me

Raphael grimaced once more as my father pressed again, "You must stop running, turn around, and declare your right to the throne. Can you do that much, Raphael? If you can't, speak now, because this is our best chance."

All eyes weighed down on the foreign noble. His eyes were shut tight, a solemn expression as he leaned back into his chair with a heavy sigh. Everything about him was tense and agonizing. The silence enraged me, though I bit my lip in contempt. *Did he not expect this to be part of the plan? Was this fool really hoping to hide away in the woods after dumping this matter in our laps, as if we had the power to do something about it by ourselves? Honestly, if we had any control over our own destiny, my mother would be among the living, and I'd be back in Captiva City, spending my downtime at the Scarlett House.*

"You're right," he relented. "As much as I hate having to bring myself out into the open, it's not as if hiding away has been working for me, either." Raphael tilted his head back, eyes open and staring at the ceiling. "Do you really intend to fight, push back if this goes south? Or will that be the moment you choose to run?"

"I will gladly spill blood for my blood." Rising to my feet, I towered over the room.

Raphael didn't move, not even a glance. "They're here not just for me, but because they want something from your family. Secrets? Blood? Who knows anymore what power and dark arts Fallen Arbor intends to master." My gaze fell to the bruise painting Raphael's neck, my finger marks pronounced even in the dim light. "If you find yourselves backed into the corner as they have pushed me, would you be able to fight back no matter the cost, I wonder?" With this, his head tilted down and his eyes struck my own.

He's asking this of me, I thought. *Why would he direct such a question to me?* I opened my mouth, but Raphael spoke before I could.

"We do not make any decision without counsel," Raphael announced, turning his attention back to my father. "You've gotten this far without me, so I will follow your lead moving forward, Germaine. I've nothing left to lose but my life, and frankly, I don't even know if I'm worth saving anymore."

My stomach knotted at his last words, but I focused on the matter at hand. "So, Father will take the lead, counsel with me, Lillian, and Raphael," I offered.

"There will be others, but if something dire comes up, I will keep it to just us three." He pointed to Raphael and me.

"Father! What about me? I can be of help. I got us this far. Did I not?" protested Lillian, a scowl across her face.

"Precisely why I need you out there and not stuffed up in a cabin poring over books." My father waved at the room and the piles now covering the floors, chests, and table. "I need someone I can trust keeping eyes and ears on everything and bringing it back here to us." He leaned in, gripping her shoulder. "I need an advisor, not another councilman. In this way, you get to choose what information we need to consider, what choices you recommend, and will guide us where we are most blind. Even then, I need someone out there who can make a solid choice in the heat of the moment."

Her eyes widened and a smile crossed her lips. "I see. It seems I'll be the one with the most liberties in the end."

"Exactly!" Germaine patted her shoulder.

"I must confess." Raphael leaned onto the table once more, brow high as he spoke. "You knew more than I realized. I'm not equipped to face this threat alone, that much was clear, but I didn't know where to even begin." He gazed upon my father with almost a sense of respect and affection. "You've already taken the first steps without me. So, yes, let's make this alliance official. I'm in. Even if I have to put myself in harm's way, I'll gladly die for your cause, Germaine."

"How could you phrase it that way so easily?" I spat, his words grinding against my emotions. "No one should ever offer to die in someone else's place. Especially for a stranger and someone not even—"

"Ashton," my father barked in a stern voice. "Still your tongue."

I clenched my teeth, the force of it making my jaw ache. *My family and I are about to join his fight despite already losing so much, yet he's willing to toss his life out like a scrap heap. What little of my mother's people remain are going to be asked to be in harm's way for our people, and for him. How much more will I lose? How many more must die before anything positive begins to blossom?* I started pacing the cabin, their words mute to my ears as I seethed on the thoughts boiling within.

The Man Before Me

Does this man realize that all I have left are my sister and father? An uncle and some cousins I haven't befriended in years won't replace them if one should fall under a swinging blade! I can't. I can't do this, not again. I can't let someone who holds no value on whether they die on the battlefield hold my world in their hands only to watch it crumble!

I darted for Raphael, fistfuls of his coat as I yanked him to his feet, yelling, "I can't allow this!"

Raphael gazed at me, but unlike the first time I snatched him up, his will to fight was gone. A chill rolled over me, and I shook him. *Where the fuck did that will to live go?* Lillian moved to stop me, but Father stopped her. It wouldn't matter. *The last time I beat a sod half to death, no one could pull me off. Shall I repeat it until you find your will to live, to survive, comes back?* I searched those blue eyes; the luster to live was completely gone from them. *What's the matter? Too busy hating yourself to live? Did we remind you of the lost family and shame and...*

"I can't be okay with this," I snarled, our faces nearly touching. "Let's be honest! None of us are okay with this! You know! We've already lost our homes, lost family—" Something shifted in Raphael's glare, an anger that matched my own as he gripped my arms until they stung.

"I lost it all while running!" Raphael tugged me off and roared back, the fight back in those eyes making me feel relieved. "Imagine choosing to run and losing it all, anyway." His palms smacked hard against my chest, but I didn't budge. "Imagine leaving behind everything you love, alienating yourself, and even leaving the fucking continent only to discover they wiped them all out just because they could! Every fucking trace of you burnt and bloodied!" Raphael hit my chest again, his face red with the efforts of his outcry. "So, if I could be back here standing at the table again, yes. I would pick up my blade and fight back." Eyes bloodshot, his tears began to fall from the glassy portals to a broken soul. "I would gladly die for them, bleed for them, just to have some kind of chance to protect them at any cost, even if it meant I would die instead of them!" He spun on his heel, marching to the hearth to stare at the fire as he bit a knuckle.

My father took a sip of his tea, eyes on Raphael as he spoke. "Exactly. If I'm to lose any more of us, I want to be in the position to at least die trying to save them."

An ache filled me, my own tears fighting to be let loose as my throat tightened at Father's words. Lillian's face buried into Father's side, and I couldn't say I envied her for being able to do so. The faint smell of blood called me to return to Raphael. Still biting down on his fist, a small, dark line crawled down his arm. The tears had stopped as quickly as they had started, but I could still feel the burn of where he hit me, the rage and anguish. *He stood there and I have to make this same choice. But will it end any differently?*

"In that case, I will draw blood to protect blood." Swallowing, I caught their attention with my words. "If I have to be, I will be the wall that keeps the frontlines of this battle divided." I waited for Lillian to look up at me before adding, "Not because you wish this of me. I am doing this because I desire this the most."

33

The Champion's Lord

Raphael spun, his expression a bittersweet blend of regret and nostalgia. *This man before me, he stood there and made a very different promise to himself. It haunts him, and now, we will have to wait and see if I will later wear that very same expression for myself.*

Chapter 6

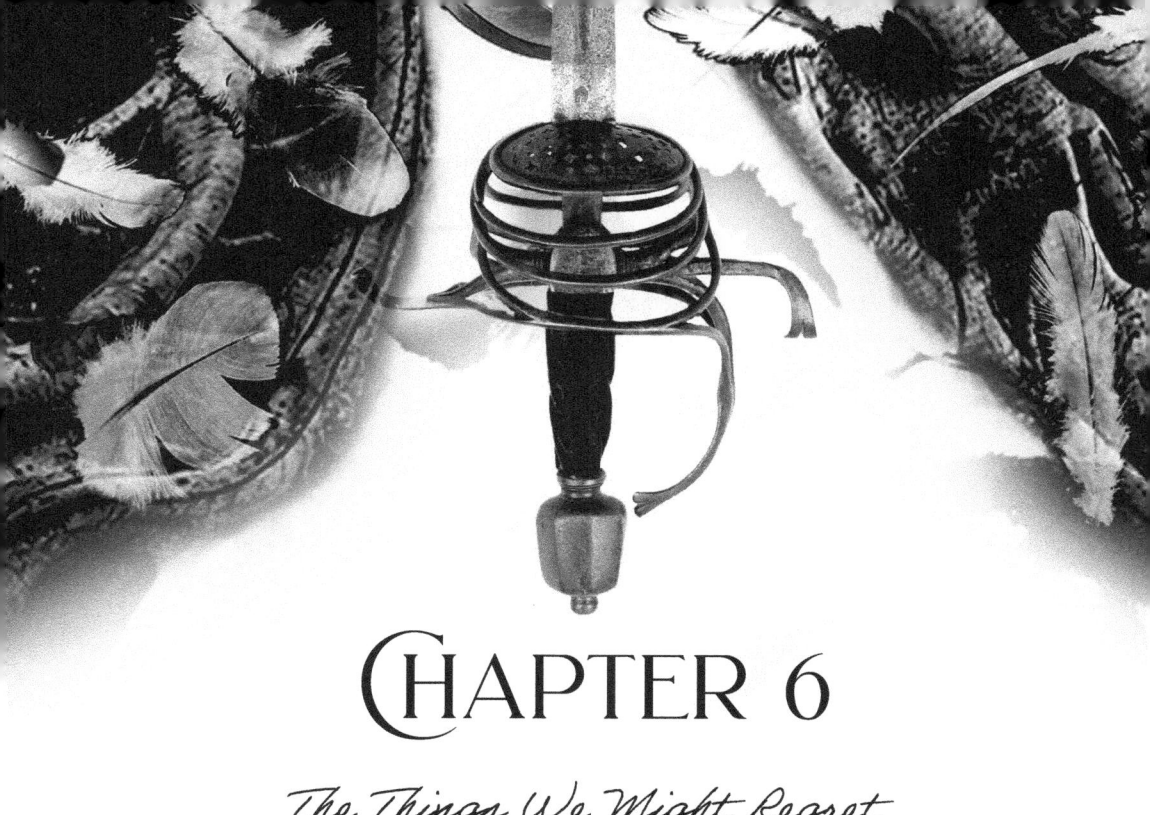

The Things We Might Regret

There is no way to describe the weight of regret that poured from Raphael. "I chose to run, and I lost everything," he reminded me more sternly.

He had sat here for hours, not eating or seemingly to drink a drop of anything. This was someone who had hit rock bottom. Even his own life held no more value to him in comparison to the brokenness haunting his every thought. *I hope to the Fates I will never come to know what he feels, what it feels to be at the point of losing all value in life. Fighting is always an option, isn't it?* I looked at my hand; my resolve wavered for a fleeting moment. *Perhaps I should aim to master all that I can. I've always been good at everything I set my mind and body to, haven't I?* My breath caught to see Raphael's eyes still burning into me. *He faced all of this alone. It must have been much for one man to carry, especially when he's willing to fight for my family.*

Lillian and Germaine were whispering amongst themselves now. *They're planning for the next move.* Again, I found myself drawn to Raphael, who had turned to glare at the flames dancing in the hearth. *He came to a new continent, abandoned his family in order to protect them, only for it to fail. It must feel as if he did nothing to save them, to even protect them. No, I don't want that for my family, for myself.* Swallowing, I turned away from them all to not let my face betray the dangerous thoughts I set loose, the dark promises I was willing to make to my own soul. *From here forth, I will never feel regret for the choices I make. This body of mine will be the wall I place between our enemies and everything I love and care for. Even if it comes down to sacrificing myself to the gods and the Fates themselves and walking this wretched world for all eternity, I'm willing to do anything to gain the power I need to do so.*

Walking to the door, I smacked a hand on it and looked back to the startled faces. "So, this is the decision then?"

Father nodded, and I glanced at Lillian, who did the same.

Raphael replied, "So be it. We will *draw blood to protect blood.*" He repeated my words back to me, casting a wary expression.

The heat of my temper spurred me to march out of the cabin. In the wilds, wolves howled, miles off from the farm but near enough to send chills up my spine. Aimless, I found myself crossing the fields. Clouds blackened the sky; not even the stars or moon could bring warmth to the coldness that bit at me. *Indeed, even the world feels murky about what I've decided for myself.* I couldn't hold my emotions in check nor hide them away. *We have decided to die sooner, not later, far as we all know,* I thought bitterly. Another wave of anger added to the first. *I made a decision, but why the hell do I feel like it's done nothing to fix anything?!*

The barn had a dim light casting shadows across the ground and I marched in to find it empty. The horses huffed and neighed softly, the shuffling of hooves announcing their surprise to see someone so suddenly. The chores were done; the stalls were all locked, and tools were washed and gathered in their place. Even the loose hay had been swept up and floors cleared, made ready for tomorrow's hustle and bustle. Momentary relief filled me. *At least I won't have to explain away anything to Jeoffrey.*

"Fucking pull yourself together," I blurted, grabbing an entire bundle of hay and throwing it at the far wall.

The twine snapped. Hay exploded in a flash, the force of impact sending it all over and knocking a saddle stand over. A flash of Raphael's disapproving face made me tense. Pulling the leather string from my ponytail, I shook my hair loose. Tossing my shirt off, I laid it over a stable door. My skin pimpled as the cool night air blew a breeze over me, but I refused to shudder. *I need to cool off.* Redoing my ponytail, I reached for the pitchfork. *I can't leave this place a mess.*

My shirt moved, and I warned the chestnut Percheron, "Feran, don't you take my shirt. I'll eat you if you do." The horse snorted and curled its lips at me. "Yeah, well, you know I'm big enough to do it by myself. Don't tempt me."

With each skid, scud, and toss of the hay, I could feel a calm trying its best to take hold. The horses whinnied and danced, excited for the extra round of hay. My mind spun, replaying the things I had read in the journals, the words of my father, and the look in Raphael's eyes. Skid, scud. *I'm decent at hand-to-hand combat.* It was a weak attempt at changing the conversation with myself. Skid, scud. *But I need to circle back to swordsmanship. I got lazy—*Skid, scud—*Fuck me. It was the* sword jokes to woo my next conquest before Auntie got tired of my shit. *Let's be honest, I've been a spoiled shit all my life.*

The last of the hay sent me spinning back to swap tools for a broom. My muscles were tight as I listed the regrets and things I could have mastered, that my mother had tried so hard to beat into my thick head. *Sure, I know and understand the principles, but what good are they without experience? Do I really blame my parents for giving me so many liberties while growing up? Not like I wasn't punished enough times to have tried to do better. I just didn't care to do better.* "Built like a bull and just as stubborn," Grandmama used to mutter at me.

Leaning on the broom, I started my plan. *I remember much of the books and tomes. Perhaps I first finish reading the teachings since Le Denys are scattered. It'll take some time to find a teacher who isn't recovering or seasoned enough to do it. Perhaps even asking Lillian or Father*—I shook my head, sweeping the last of the floor with a skeptical laugh. *No, let's not rely on them. Besides, I'm built like Grandpa Le Denys. I alone carry the last of a great lineage that made the daemonis fighting force possible. By the Fates, I'd devote my fangs to whoever can give us a fighting chance against these invaders!*

A flash of Raphael's hardened face as he said, *"This is dangerous,"* and I groaned.

Why can't I get him out of my head? Placing the broom into its spot, I went to the water barrel and dunked my head into it. Cold water swallowed me as the world deafened at last. Pictures of his smaller, leaner build were back yet again with the infatuation of leg muscles and the sword at—I burst from the water barrel, the horses reprimanding me with startled neighs and head bobs.

"That's it," I muttered to myself. "Why learn from what I already know when I have a chance to learn about the fighting styles of the invaders?"

My thoughts flew as I wrung my hair out. *Mother and the clan came back with wounds like nothing we had ever seen. Their weapons varied as well. Thin and twig-like to chains and even a sword so broad, it could double as a shield. What did they call it? Ah, the claymore. Lord Raphael might know of someone who can train me in the styles of his people. I want to master them all. Am I even capable of learning them?* Rage at the idea I would consider failure soured my mood. *I'm Ashton Le Denys Thompson. Why the hell would I fail*—my stomach knotted.

The pale grey flesh of my mother's death-face made my entire frame shudder like a horse trying to brush off a fly. I leaned on the barrel's edges, staring at the darkened silhouette it cast. *Can I really outrun my own death? Even she failed.* A sharp pain burned in my chest, squeezing my heart in a wretched reminder of the grief I tried to keep hidden. *I was supposed to be there with her that day.* I crumbled, elbows on the edges now as I held my head, eyes glowing in the wobbling reflection as my self-hatred rose hot like the flame of hell. *Mother had asked me to be her shield, to help guard and I, I told her…* "Following in the steps of family was foolish."

Covering my mouth, I sank until my knees hit the dirt floor and my head pressed against the side of the barrel. *I marched off like a spoiled brat, the size of a bull, and left her to the wind like a branch. Why did I think she would be back like so many other excursions with nothing more than a scrape and bruise? They were fighting invaders.* The tears began to fall, and I grew angry at my body's betrayal. *The one fucking moment I needed to be… that they needed me to be the man I had been trained and raised to be, I abandoned them.* Drawing an unsteady inhale, I tried to fight the stinging of my lungs and the heat in my eyes. *It was simple. Fucking be there. Fucking take a hit if I have to and bleed alongside my family… but I was a coward.*

Swallowing, I banged my head against the water barrel with a thud. *Raphael walked away from his family to protect them, but can't see how much he needs to—*I stood, splashing my face with water, desperate to wash away my pain, my guilt, and even the memory of that moment… *The smell of the flowers in the field, the crunch of a branch underfoot, and those words she muttered will not let me forget, ever.*

"It's ok if you're afraid; so am I, my son."

Chapter 7

Value is in the Eye of the Beholder

Another splash and I could breathe again. *I wanted to fight. At one point, I couldn't wait for the day to come. There it was, and I didn't have the heart to be honest about it. She knew. The moment she saw my face as I walked up, she had known what it was I was intending to say.* Again, the regret on Raphael's face made me scowl and I tugged my shirt from Feran's mouth.

Another curl of lips and I scoffed, "You're a dead horse." Taking a closer look, I confirmed holes had been chewed into it. "I can't even use this to dry my face, asshole." Feran snorted, bobbing his head and thumping a hoof in agreement. "Never will I understand why Mother loved you the most," I spat bitterly, half-admitting the idea about myself. *Mother had horrible tastes, it seems.*

Turning, I snuffed out the lantern and headed out the open door in a rush. I slammed into someone, sending them stumbling back a few steps. Before they could regain their balance, my hand was around their throat. A growl rolled from me, feral and wolflike. Blue eyes bulged in surprise before I recognized Raphael. Dropping him, I turned away as he coughed and sputtered on the ground behind me. With a hand on my hip, I covered my mouth; my fangs were elongated. *Fucking Le Denys blood-rage. Didn't he see my eyes glowing? Doesn't he know what that means?*

"What the hell are you doing?" I admonished, hiding my eyes and fangs. "You shouldn't be wandering in the pitch dark."

"I was looking for you," Raphael rasped, coughing a few more times.

"In the dark?" I looked over my shoulder. He was standing, rubbing his throat now. "I thought your kind sucked at night vision."

The remark brought a smile and a laugh before he nodded. "Yeah, we do."

Licking my tongue against a fang, I remarked, "Why haven't you left?" *Dammit, go away, fangs.*

"Because I can't see in the dark," he offered, taking a few steps closer. "And I was thirsty and offered to fetch more water."

Turning to face him, I closed the gap and leaned to meet his eyes. "They sent a man who can't see in the dark to fetch water in the dark with not even the moon to light his way?"

Raphael's brow creased, his thoughts keeping him silent until he hesitantly replied, "Your father did."

"My father's humor knows no bounds." I grabbed his arm and tried to lead him toward the spout. "Come—"

"Wait." Raphael gripped my wrist and tugged me closer; again, we found ourselves almost touching noses. "Actually, I wanted to check on you and it seemed a good enough reason to allow me to leave the cabin." His eyes linger on my lips before falling to my bare chest. "What happened to your shirt?"

"A horse ate it," I drawled, arching a brow.

Again, those blue gemstones flashed upward and my heart fluttered. "Why did you let a horse eat your shirt? You should have given him hay," he jested.

"I tried, but he didn't take the hay." I smirked, body tensing as I fought to swallow the want building inside me. *He's funny. And quick to reply. I like that… no. I can't do this. How is this any different than what I've been doing as of late—*

Raphael glanced at the barn. "You were making such a ruckus. I was a little afraid to walk closer for a while," he confessed, releasing my wrist at last, leaving my skin burning. "I just wanted to say, I know how it feels. To be the next heir, to have your entire family's survival all weigh down on your shoulders." I could almost hear his heart thudding loudly in his chest, and fought the desire to move. "I wanted to tell you that I'm here and will put my life on the line to protect your family. That was my intent, but…"

"Because you couldn't do it for your own." My words cut deep, and his lips scowled, the hurt striking as the muscles in his cheek tensed. "Look at me," I demanded.

"You're right," he whispered, unwilling to turn his face to me. "I'm only trying to relive this moment through you to ease my own guilt. A second chance to see if…" He choked on his words, swallowing before he forced himself to say, "…to see if choosing this path would have been better for them. For me. I'm a coward."

"Don't say that," I hissed, my temper rising at his words. "You don't have the right to call yourself that." With a finger, I turned his face to me so he could see

Value is in the Eye of the Beholder

the glow of my maroon eyes as my anger filled me once more. "I'm the only one who gets to feel guilt, carry regret, and be called a coward."

My body moved against my will. Our lips met. My finger guided my hand to cup the angles of his jaw as he responded in kind. His lips parted, tongue twisting with my own, hot as silk. I dropped my shirt and pulled him into me. *Tall but not tall enough.* Pulling him to his toes, I turned and kissed deeply from another angle, again his tongue dipping into my world and exploring the fangs before I broke it off.

"When you go back to the Old Continent, after we win this, I will fight for you." My heart ran like the hoofbeats of horses galloping. "I want to be the reason you value your life once more."

Raphael's face flushed red, his hands cupping my face. "You're the most maddening creature in all the world, Ashton," he declared, searching my expression as if some grand secret lay there. "What makes you so certain we'll survive this?" Raphael gave a heartbroken expression and my temper flared.

Leaning in, I whispered into his ear, "Because I will make sure, no matter what happens, you will know why I forbid you to have what is mine and mine alone to carry. You shall never know the weight of regret with me by your side. What you've done, what you've survived, does not make you a coward."

Turning away, I left him alone in the dark. Holding my lips, the taste of him lingered in my mouth as I headed through the trees. *Fuck me. What have I done?* My heart wouldn't slow. *I'm jealous that he wants to feel those emotions. But what the fuck was that?* I followed the footpath out of memory, heading for the old spring hidden way up the hill. *Didn't I sense it for a moment, though? That he came out there to soothe me, but the way he looked at me… what the fuck am I thinking?!*

Stopping, I leaned on a tree trunk. *We are the same… he's joking, right? I'm an adrenaline-lust-loving lone wolf. A stallion who can't stay inside his field and chases mares the moment they catch my scent.* Pushing off the tree, I continued my ascension. *Meanwhile, he has the patience of a… of something I've never seen the likes of. To get this far, I mean, I wouldn't be able to do it and keep going if I lost everything.*

"Ah! Now's not the time to loosen your belt buckle!" I fussed at myself. "If I didn't walk away, I am certain Jeoffrey would have come back to see… what the fuck is wrong with me?"

But he kissed back! I reasoned to myself, hoping to salvage some sort of positive aspect of what had transpired. *This temper always is led by the wrong head. Maybe if I go to the Scarlett House, I can blow this off. I can't get distracted and what do I get from chasing after the Heir Apparent of an emperor? I don't even want my role as the clan chief's son.* Stopping at the edge of the spring, I huffed. *I guess I should keep my distance until we go to Captiva City to put this plan into action.* Leaning forward, I let myself fall into the spring, drowning the emotions that had brought me there. *I can't do this now…*

Chapter 8

Facing the Past

I trailed behind everyone, happy to be back in the bustling streets of Captiva City. Here, I could lose myself and distract myself from the thoughts I couldn't seem to shake from my encounter weeks prior with Raphael. We walked down the main road, passing the larger businesses—taverns, blacksmiths, textile merchants, and more filled the shops and streets. Vibrant flashes of fruits and vegetables were only matched by fresh-cut meat and the assortment of fish laid out from this morning's catch. A few vendors waved acknowledgments to my family or me. Unlike for Raphael, this used to be home not so long ago before the invaders took it over.

We had a long errand list to attend to, from meeting with Le Denys leader to declaring Raphael as our master. *Many heads will be turning today before we're done. Being the talk of the town has always been a favorite pass time.* Father, Raphael, and Lillian were chatting amongst themselves, but I couldn't bring myself to meet Raphael's gaze during the entire wagon ride here. *Why should I feel so damn guilty for that kiss that he clearly wanted?* The heat in my cheeks was a mixture of my rushing temper and embarrassment. *Definitely going to the Scarlett House to blow off steam when we're done with our errands.*

"Ashton, what are your thoughts?" Raphael's words jolted me from them.

"I need to get laid," I blurted, locking eyes with him.

Raphael stopped dead in his tracks, looking away to hide his expression from me.

Facing the Past

"Ashton," hissed Lillian. "Must you always declare where your mind wanders to?"

My father groaned as he kept walking without even a flinch.

Walking past Raphael, I didn't bother to give him a side glance. "Don't worry. It's not like you have to come with me."

"I want…" He started, taking a few steps to catch up and walking by my side; we fell behind my family. "Scarlett House afterward, then?" he confirmed.

"Where else would one get laid?" I smirked, catching the red flushing on his face before he threw up his hood. "We go together then?" I chuckled, enjoying this strange exchange with him.

"After," he mumbled before returning to keep pace with everyone in front.

The rest of the walk was uneventful until we took a terrible turn in the apothecary shop. Covering my mouth and nose with my sleeve, I took in the tightly packed shelves filled with jars and baskets of dried plant materials. *Ugh, this place reeks and fucks with my sense of smell. Why do I have to have such a sensitive nose?* An old man at the counter was giving Lillian instructions, and before long, we were zigzagging through the maze of shelves, the entrance long lost.

"You've always had a touchy nose." My father looked back at me, and I found myself annoyed that I had fallen in line behind him and not Raphael. "What's the matter with you as of late?"

"Nothing that concerns you," I muttered, looking away from his glance in order to hide my emotions from him. "You should stop prying in my business, old man."

Much to my annoyance, he chuckled, nodding as he lowered his voice to say, "So, even you find Lord Raphael charming."

"You're full of it," I declared, trying to snort the sour odor of an herb from my nose. "This place is as vile as your mind."

"Just don't break yourself," he warned, looking away. "You take after your grandfather Le Denys so much, I worry at times whether you'll ever be able to swallow your pride and narcissism in time to achieve your full potential, Ashton."

"Gee, thanks, Father," I drawled, pissed at the fact he'd even say it to my face, let alone choose now to say anything at all about my pride. *I lost my pride the day we lost Mother, but you already know that, don't you?*

A bookshelf shifted in front of Lillian, and I rushed past Father and Raphael in alarm. *If it falls on her, she'll be crushed!* By the time I slammed Raphael into the shelf to push ahead, I met the pointed end of a blade. Following it to its master, I met the assassin who held it where the shelf had moved to reveal a doorway. They blinked maroon eyes a few times at me before looking at Lillian and putting the sword away.

"What is your problem?" Lillian shoved me behind her.

"I thought the shelf was falling and…" Stepping back, I bumped into Raphael, who grunted.

Raphael grabbed my shoulder, rubbing his chest in pain before whispering to me. "Please be a little gentler with me in the future." Clearing his throat, he added, "I bruise easy."

I refused to look at him, stepping forward to jerk my shoulder from him. "You should eat more. You don't eat enough."

"Follow me," demanded the assassin, their face, black like the cowl and robes they wore, covered. "The guild master is waiting."

We fell in line, silent as we spiraled down the old steps and soon found ourselves in a hallway deep underground. The torchlight fluttered and more assassins watched as we traveled through their secret world. Taking in the details of the walls, the worn path of the stones underfoot, and the musky smell added to my unease. *This has been here for a long time. How long has Father been aware of a secret group operating underground? Is it just our city, or could they be from the Old Continent? No, they're daemons, so they have to be part of one of the clans. Which one? Or is it one I'm not familiar with?*

They stopped us. The thick oak door opened up and we were waved inside. Lillian walked in, her body language portraying she had been there before, and an uneasy sensation rolled in my gut. *Why does she seem so at home here? More so than the farm?* She was older than me by a long shot. Her mother was from the Farrow clan, their famous stark white hair a telling sign. It was said they resembled the Mother of Life, whereas the Thompson clan was more in the likeness of the Sacrificial Daughter, the goddess with which my ancestors had made a pact.

The room was dark, save for some lanterns dimmed to hide the corners of the room. An old woman sat behind one at a desk, books lining the shelves behind her. She had an arm missing, and despite the stitched wounds across her face and neck, I recognized her immediately.

"Grandmama," I breathed, heart in my throat as her eyes cut through me. *Coward. That's what that look says. Does she blame me for Mother? Am I even considered family anymore?* I thought she, too, had been lost at battle.

"Guild Master Le Denys." Father dropped to a knee and bowed his head to her in complete servitude, something I had never seen him do in all my decades. "I am happy to see you are among us still."

"I'd rather see my precious Edwidge," she sneered, eyes glowing with her rage. "She deserved a better death and more children."

My father winced at the words.

"You came to our village, and like the fool we've come to know you as, you won her over." Grandmama rubbed the nub where her arm once had been, a grimace on her face giving away the pain it brought her. "If she had a warrior, a fighter for a husband, perhaps she might be here still." Her fiery eyes met mine, and I looked away. "Even her son—"

"Did I not win her through battle with her father, the clan chief?" blurted my father, stealing her rage from me.

My temper flared as I balled my hands tight. *I deserve what words she would use to lash me for my sins. Stop getting in the way, always taking my beatings for me.*

"Indeed, you did." Grandmama narrowed her eyes at my father.

Facing the Past

Germaine looked up to meet her gaze, a slow smirk cresting as he flicked his eyebrows. "There were no rules against it."

Grandmama banged a fist on the desk. "You fed him wine until he passed out and never woke!"

"You dragged his body to the fight the next day, but no one would let me or him draw our swords," he recalled. "I was ready to fight!"

"The only sword he had drawn was the one that rises with the sun in the morning!" At last, she started to laugh. "He was so angry he had been bested before the fight. He never stopped talking of it and never drank a drop of wine after that."

"Indeed. I miss him as well," confessed my father. "Know that I would gladly have swapped places with my beloved Edwidge." A long sigh escaped them both before he bowed his head once more, not to avoid her but to submit all of him to her and any rage she had for him. "Forgive me, as much as I wish to reminisce of happier times, I came to take responsibility for the losses Le Denys incurred that fateful day the invaders came."

"And what else, Germaine Thompson?" Her fingers tapped on the desk, something she had done in order to show she was willing to sit, listen, and spare you her patience for a change. "What has spurred you to finally crawl out of your potato fields and grovel before me?"

"We ask of you a favor, a request that I have no right to ask after your family has suffered so many losses because of the foolish decisions of myself and the council."

"We both know you were the only one against fighting them," she heaved another sigh, mulling on her thoughts before adding, "And you're the only councilman, besides myself, to take responsibility for what happened to the clans and their lands."

"I should have fought harder to turn the horns of the bull of war," he pressed.

"And why have you brought the heir apparent of the enemy into an assassin's den?" Grandmama arched a brow, her gaze shifting to Raphael, and I tensed.

Raphael fell beside Father, kneeling; his resolve strong in his voice. "I am here to make amends for what my people have done at any cost, even my life."

Rage filled me. *How dare he threaten to toss away his life here and now in front of me! Did I not make it clear it was mine to have?*

Chapter 9

Building an Alliance

Grandmama shifted in her chair, leaning forward. "We will not be making an alliance with anyone ever again."

Raphael flinched.

He's blaming himself, again, I thought angrily. *Lillian and Father didn't react, so they already came here knowing this would be the answer. What plan did you have for this, Father?*

"Glad to hear this," confirmed my father as he glanced up with a look of relief. "All I ask is if we may … pay for your services."

She lunged back in her chair rubbing her forehead. "You knew my answer beforehand. So does this mean my daughter divulged the plans of what we would do if we had failed?"

A grin on Father's face said it all.

"Of course she did," she guffawed, shaking her head. "We gather information, we sabotage, and we will, on occasion, at our own discretion, assassinate." She shook her head. "What plan do you have? I imagine now that the council has been disbanded or beheaded, but you have no desire to bother with those old fools who kiss the boots of our enemies."

Building an Alliance

"I want to protect our people the way I know best." Father stood, motioning for Raphael to do the same. "We have come to an arrangement with Lord Raphael Kristr de'Traibon."

"Yes, Grandmama." Lillian stepped forward. "We plan to leave here to register the Thompson clan into servitude under the heir apparent and take claim of the land deserving of his station. With this, we can begin to reclaim a large portion of land for our people while gaining a seat amongst the invaders to help sway votes in our favor or at least stop the destruction of Grandemere."

"And without us as your guardian, whoever shall be your warrior?" Grandmama tapped a finger, alarm rising in her voice. "Germaine, you do not intend to put the last of her legacy in harm's way without a sword and shield to protect them!"

"I will!" Rushing past everyone, I smacked my hands on the desk with such force I dented the tabletop like a hammer. "I will protect them," I seethed, meeting her gaze without shame but with determination like never before.

She laughed, and I tensed as the ridicule came at me without hesitation or deflection to protect me now. "He who dodged his hand-to-hand combat lessons," she hissed. "Did you even pick up a sword other than pleasuring your own?" She bashed me with her truths. "A lustful, flawed, no good for nothing—" she seethed, eyes on fire with rage "—I can't even see you as family!"

"Good!" I roared, claws digging into the wood as I matched her fiery gaze with my own. "Then let this dog be collared, kicked, and beaten until all he knows is to bite the enemies of his master!"

"Ashton!" barked my father.

Hands had been trying to tug me back. My father, Lillian, and Raphael clawed at me, but I would not budge. A growl grew from me. My muscles were tight, flexing with the fire of my temper. The door behind me slammed open, footsteps flooded in, and soon hands were replaced with the points of blades. They dug slowly deeper into my flesh until Grandmama raised her hand and they froze. The pain still couldn't cut through the anger overriding my instincts. She searched my face.

"I will not be responsible for mistaking a wolf for a tamable dog." She turned to Father, a wary look as her heartbeat fluttered in my ears. "He is too much like his grandfather, is he not?"

Looking back, I caught my father's expression before he dropped his head to hide it away.

"I see." Another wave of her hand and the blades retreated, and I turned away. "I will not teach you," Grandmama warned.

"I'm not deaf," I snarled, my shirt painted with the blossoming petals of my wounds. "I will find another way." I started for the gaping door.

"Ashton, do not take this path." Now, for the first time in a long time, I heard Grandmama's softer voice, the one from my youth as her grandson, for one last fleeting moment. "It will not bring your mother back nor close the hole of despair you dug for yourself on that wretched day."

Pausing at the doorway, I looked over my shoulder, still riding on my wrath. "You're mistaken. I do not wish for it to close."

There were shouts for me to come back, to calm down, and be reasonable. All those pitiful words did nothing. I had received the lashes I had so yearned for and the denied promise of the blades that had left insignificant marks. The assassins let me pass without a second glance, startling a patron in the apothecary's shop. I could breathe again by the time I made it onto the street under the burning sun. I stopped, leaning on my knees as my stomach knotted. I looked at the red badges on my shirt; the cuts were healing already.

"Fuck the Le Denys blood," I cursed under my breath.

My anger had, at last, let go as I pulled the shirt off, tossing it in a trash heap nearby. *How careless. I can't go to the castle in a blood-soaked shirt.* I turned back to face the shop; my sister's sour expression made me wince. Lillian shoved a clean shirt into my chest and crossed her arms without a word. *She's so pissed.* Soon after, Father and Raphael came pouring out the door. Blue gemstones paused, seeing me in a new light as if this was the first time acknowledging exactly how different I was, even amongst my kind. *That's right, Golden Boy. I'm a wolf, like she said. One with no master.*

"Put your shirt on." Father didn't even look my way, his tone a mixture of hushed anger and concern. "We'll discuss this matter at home."

"Yes, Father," I answered meekly. *Shit. I better just avoid going home for a while if he's not even looking my way.*

Raphael opened his mouth to speak, but I turned away to follow my father. *I don't want to be consoled by anyone, especially not you.* Pulling the shirt on, I didn't bother to tighten the strings or tuck it into my pants to be presentable. *I'm here to take a hit. What does it matter what state I'm in? I've already proven I'm a fucking mess today. Why put on airs anymore?* Only Raphael would glance back on occasion to make sure I was even following anymore. A few more turns, and we were in front of the main gate of the castle.

"Halt." The guards approached and my father lowered his head. "What business do you have at the castle?"

"We are here to register servitude." Father stood straight, explaining, "I am the clan chief for the Thompson clan. We wish to declare allegiance and sign the proper documents."

The guard nodded. "Alright, but which House are you signing up for?"

"House Traibon," my father said with a calculating tone.

"Traibon?" The other guard sounded confused. "I think you're mistaken, old timer. You can only declare servitude to a noble house, not anyone that tickles your fancy."

Laughter broke out between them, the first guard adding, "Either you thought you were slick, or someone is pulling your leg."

"I am Lord Raphael Kristr de'Traibon." Raphael sounded angry as he stepped forward. "The head of House Forestier can confirm this."

Building an Alliance

"I'm sorry, who are you?" The guards shook their heads, unable to recognize the title and name.

They know nothing of the Old Continent high houses. Grunting, I watched. *That's done on purpose, though, to keep anyone from gaining root here.*

"Fools," burst my father, making everyone jolt. "Do you not recognize the name of the one true heir apparent and blood of the late emperor?!" he roared, shaking his fist to the sky. "If I had any say, you'd take lashes for how rude you've been to his lordship!"

I rolled my eyes. *He loves it when he can be dramatic. Crazy old man... and this is where he reminds me that we are alike in some ways. Center of attention is definitely something I come by naturally.*

"I, uh, heir apparent?" The one guard paled, elbowing his friend. "Go get someone who can identify the heir apparent from the Old Continent."

"Last I heard, he was dead," he drawled, pushing his elbow off.

"You can't declare an heir apparent dead without bringing their head or their token back." Raphael pulled a pocket watch out, holding it before them with the golden lion emblem of the emperor, complete with sapphires bejeweling its eyes. "Now bring me the head of House Forestier," he commanded.

The first guard smacked the other guard's arm. "Go get the pudgy one. He's the one we want."

"Y-yes, sir." He pushed through the guard's gate on the side, and I watched him march through the courtyard behind the gate.

Turning back to us, Father flicked his brow high. "And now, we wait."

Remembering how long it took to run from the gate to the council room, I leaned on the large planter off to the side. Raphael watched me with confusion, and I snorted. *Should I tell him that the guard is probably going to drag ass and take hours? Nah, let's see how much endurance those legs have.*

Chapter 10

A Future with False Hope

The sun had started sinking by the time some sign of anyone coming back through the courtyard and toward the gates had emerged. A peachy hue painting only half the sky was being chased by the lavender and dark blue of the night blossoming in its wake. Standing, I yawned and offered my father a hand. He slapped it away without even looking at my face. *Yup, still pissed. Not coming home tonight.*

Close behind the guard was a short, round man of sorts. He had glasses and a dapper mustache as he hobbled to keep up with his guide. Trailing behind him, I recognized Henri Pomeroy, tall and thin like the orchard trees he grew to the east of the city. His ebony skin was like the coals in a fire, but Grandemere owed the Pomeroy clan much thanks for their heritage in carpentry. They were responsible for the blueprints of buildings and ships alongside specialty items, from children's toys to the tools the hatmakers and tailors relied on.

"Is this Forestier man your ally?" I whispered, standing close to Raphael's side.

"I suppose close enough." Raphael eyed me a moment before adding, "He's someone who is honest and honorable. Though, put under pressure, he will give away all he has kept secret and be the first to run."

"So, he's just a key to other doors until it breaks," I snorted.

A Future with False Hope

"And do you know this man with him? Is he an ally?" Raphael pried, a smirk on his face. "He's twice the old man's height and from the way he walks, you'd think he held a higher station than his master."

"That's because he does." I leaned into Raphael's ear, enjoying the way his face flushed and posture tensed. "Henri Pomeroy controls every grove and orchard. In fact, there's not a piece of wood he doesn't have some control or money tied to, including the specialty toys at the Scarlett House, or so I've heard." I could hear his heart flutter before adding, "You've seen them, yes?"

Palming my face, he cleared his throat. "You assume me an innocent sort, and sadly, you're mistaken. Though, you, on the other hand, are something that knows no shame, as your father has already confirmed more times than I can count in the short time I've been in your presence, Ashton."

Shrugging, I gave him distance as I jeered, "What can I say? I enjoy a good time, night or day, woman or man, cock or—" Lillian gut-punched me.

"Still your insolent tongue, Brother," she growled as I coughed and sputtered.

"Breasts," I wheezed, rubbing my stomach. "I was going to say breasts."

"How is that any better?" Lillian sneered after me, shoving me in reply.

The gate creaked open, calling all our attention to it. A look of recognition followed by surprise on the fat man's face said it all. The shorter man waved Henri, who had already raised a hand to greet us, closer. Henri retreated the action as he leaned down so they could whisper. Another look of surprise and a pang of jealousy showed in Henri's eyes as they fell to Raphael, who turned away and slid to look at my father. *The man can declare himself the heir apparent, after all. Will Henri allow it, though? He'd always been at odds with Father on several fronts when they served on the council together.*

"R-Raphael?" The large man pushed through the gates and approached Raphael with sheer awe. "We thought you dead, your majesty." He took a knee, kissing Raphael's hand before waving Henri over to do the same. "Where has the Divine Father been hiding you for the last few years?"

"That's a story far too long to stand here to tell and, alas, would need much wine to tell." Raphael motioned for the man to rise. "How are you, Winston? It's been quite some time since I found myself a mere pupil of history under you, hasn't it?"

"Indeed." Winston Forestier inhaled deeply, holding it there before he released it in admiration. "Come, let's get you in here and…" It was at that moment that he met my gaze and paled. "My, what a pack of animals you have chosen." Henri choked, leaning down to whisper into Winston's ear, and he added, "The traveling here must have been a long and rough journey. May we provide some food and libations? Perhaps even some luxuries such as baths and," he lowered his voice, "pleasures of the flesh, my prince."

Raphael patted Winston's shoulders, cooing, "All of that sounds wonderful." Raphael shot a look at me, and I narrowed my eyes, confirming, *Yes, I heard that.* "But first, let's get my servants registered. By the way, is it okay to call me prince and not Lord or viceroy here? Forgive me. I'm not well versed in the new government you and your fellow councilmen have started without me."

Winston's face paled. "Well, I am not sure, your majesty." He fumbled on his words for a while as we entered the front entrance to Captiva City's castle, the Tower.

"I see," hummed Raphael. "I suppose we will have to see how I fall in the pecking order."

"Most certainly not," Winston blurted. "You're the only one who has the emperor's bloodline in your veins." Henri shot a look at my father, who smirked in reply. "Besides, the rest all fall from the empress line, who, by our laws, fall behind anyone of immediate blood of our late emperor. They all know that."

Inside the receiving hall, a pang of nostalgia stung in my chest. Unbeknownst to these invaders, many of my peers and I had once played as children here while our parents, in the room overhead, drove the needs of Grandemere and its people. My last memories here were riddled with preparation for war. Soldiers and armored guards had never been a need or the norm when this building was nothing more than a place to house council business and records for the city and country. All around were the statues chiseled and carved into the stone and wood of the Fates themselves.

For the first time, guards stood to block the main stairwell to the upper floors of the castle. *This is no longer a place where the people come to seek aid or help. It's only for those with deep pockets and control over that which doesn't belong to them. Disgusting.* Overhead, the high ceiling was as white as sun-bleached whale bone, with embellished touches. *I used to spend hours just staring aimlessly at these ceilings and statues. Now I feel like they look at me with a sense of betrayal.*

The guards let us up the stairs. I followed closely behind Raphael, and Lillian brought up the rear of our group. After a few flights, we were at last on the same floor as the council room and stood in the heavily guarded receiving hall. I winced; the chairs and tables that had once made space for the public to meet with officials and review business were all gone. In their place were gaudy paintings, tapestry, and even brightly colored tufted chairs. All along the walls, guards were stationed, standing at attention, making it a prettier rendition of the assassin guild's dungeon walk.

"Wait here, your majesty." Winston motioned to a cushioned couch. "This will only take a moment. Henri, entertain them," he added and rushed off to disappear behind the council room doors.

"I see you are still breathing, Germaine." Henri pulled my father in for a hug before gripping his shoulders. "I was wondering if I was the last standing clan chief."

"We both know I'm too stubborn for nonsense such as death." My father waved a hand. "Speaking of which, did they not accept them, or was it a far more dangerous call?"

Henri's eyes fell to the ground, a sense of guilt crossing his face. "They were buried properly, at least. I managed that much for them."

A Future with False Hope

My heart caught in my throat as a dangerous thought crossed my mind. *Will they let Father live then?*

"I won't let them." Raphael's words caught me off guard as he placed a hand on my shoulder, whispering into my ear. "Leave this part to me, my wolf. Your Golden Boy will protect all that is yours with a flick of my tongue." Chills rolled over me as he walked away, offering a bow to Henri. "Forgive me. I don't think I've ever introduced myself fully to you, Mr. Pomeroy."

Henri scoffed, letting go of my father, and crossed his arms. "Here I thought you nothing more than a hermit from the Old Continent."

"I was until some not-so-savory events forced me to return." Raphael offered a hand, and after much contemplation, Henri shook it. "If you hadn't been so kind to me in the start, I would have been a goner, Mr. Pomeroy. I owe you much."

"It's no different than what my family has done for all people in Grandemere." Henri sighed, glancing at Germaine. "I take it you boys came here on a mission? This will certainly ruffle some feathers."

"What exactly has been the current state of affairs here?" Germaine had lowered his voice.

"Well, House Vendecci wants to be the leader or make a monarchy, but many are opposed to this. It seems among the inva—" Henri cleared his throat and redirected his intent "—nobles, that some have come here looking to be their own emperor and empire. Others see no reason to change the system since it has done far better and keeps them on equal footing with one another."

"I see, so it's as I had predicted, then?" Germaine arched a brow. "I'm shocked they haven't started a mass excommunication of daemonis from within the city walls."

"Not without several attempts. I've done what I can to stave off the worse of it." Inhaling deeply, he looked at Raphael. "I can't believe the Old Continent's emperor has been here living amongst us for so long."

"There is no empire, and it makes me the poor sap with a blood curse." Raphael scoffed, "They'd rather see my head on a platter than take claim leading them."

The doors opened and a servant ushered them in. "Please enter." We all took a step forward, and they panicked. "No, pardon me. Lord Raphael, Lord Henri, and the clan chief for the Thompson clan are all they asked for."

"Ah, excellent." Raphael exchanged a glance with Father, both nodding before he hit me on the back with a sugary smile on his face. "After you, Ashton." Before I could refuse, Lillian and Father were shoving me into the room alongside Raphael before its doors thudded behind me.

These wretched fools. They'll pay for this! What plans did these fuckers make without telling me again?!

Chapter 11

The New Council of Grandemere

Gripping Raphael's sleeve, I growled low into his ear so no one would hear me. "What is the meaning of this?"

Those blue gemstones only met my raging glare before his lips crested into that smile, whispering back, *"I want to be the reason you value your life once more."*

My words slammed into me from the other night, and I bit my tongue. *This is not the time to let my temper loose.* I turned my attention to the room; the large stone circle table still lay intact. The center was hollow but filled with the Fates back-to-back as they judged those who sat to decide on Grandemere's fate. The Mother of Life held a ball of string that twisted with others tangled in her needles, and in the hands of the Sacrificial Daughter were scissors in one and a knotted loop in the other. From there, the string twisted around where it tied to the Devoted Sister's hilt before swooping back to rejoin the ball of string. *These fools don't even realize the significance of the women before them who give, mend, and protect the lives of all.*

"Welcome, Raphael Traibon," Welcomed a gaunt man with grey hair in a long braid over one shoulder and grey eyes. "What can the council do for—"

"Prince," I interjected, my temper getting to me. "I expect you to address my lord with an appropriate title. Unless you prefer First Crowned Prince, his former standing, or even his current title, Emperor."

The New Council of Grandemere

There were whispers and rumblings. The shuffling and tugging of buttons and sleeves was enough to indicate that they were very aware that they were not dealing with someone of the same station anymore. Looking over the room, I picked apart my prey. Henri Pomeroy served under House Forestier, so that didn't leave much doubt as to whom lay in the other seats. The Farrow clan twins stood in the room, one to the right of the greeter and the other by a human, who had skin like stained walnut. *And the bitch, Madeleine Farrow, is in the ear of House Vendecci. This is going to be a hell of a fight. That means Henri was fighting against her and her push-over brother, Philippe, who will do anything to stay out of her warpath. She will not take us joining lightly.*

Raphael opened his mouth to speak, but my hand grabbed his arm and I warned the room more sternly, "I expect you to greet my lord properly and show him respect in front of this council."

Raphael's brow rose high, a smirk on his face as he met the heated glare of the head of House Vendecci and Madeleine Farrow. A collective shift occurred as we stared back at them while they whispered to one another. House Vendecci's hand had balled into a fist. A chair slid, and the other man, House Regius, spoke up despite Philippe Farrow's tugging on his arm not to dare acknowledge what I had offered. *We will see who among them still follows the system of the emperor.* My eyes measured his braid as he stood and slung it behind him as if to hide it away. *14-knots. Viceroy. Good to know not everyone is brave enough to push their luck here. That's the highest any non-royal can go, other than Royal Guard.*

"House Regius welcomes you, Prince Raphael!" The man's words made House Vendecci cringe.

Raphael whispered in my ear, "I didn't know you knew of our customs. I'm impressed you knew what my 18-knots meant. When did you notice it?"

Ignoring his musings in my ear, I opened my mouth to push further. "Thank you, Viceroy Regius." I bowed, cursing the untucked shirt and loose laces before standing straight with a grin. "Forgive me. I'm not yet acquainted with everyone's name here."

"No, no trouble at all." The head of House Regius cocked his head. "I'm impressed. How long did it take his majesty to teach you so much about the empire's ways?"

"Enough!" blurted the head of House Vendecci, waving Madeleine off him. "Forgive me, Prince Traibon. We weren't finished with prior discussions before you intruded."

"Forgive me, Viceroy Vendecci." Raphael knitted his brow, his voice giving away no sense of emotion or reaction to the events unfolding. "I am certain the servant said you were ready for us." Raphael gestured at the guard, who shuffled uncomfortably. "Was he mistaken in summoning us? Shall we wait outside again?"

"No, Prince Traibon!" Winston spoke up, scoffing at Viceroy Vendecci. "You said you wanted him to enter, Cruza."

"I did, didn't I? How did you teach him so thoroughly, I do wonder?" Viceroy Vendecci turned the focus back off himself with ease. "It's rather suspicious, considering the battle we endured a few months ago with these savages, and you were nowhere to be seen."

I arched a brow, looking at Raphael, who nodded and gestured for me to answer for myself. "I was educated in these very walls by the best scholars available both in Grandemere and the Old Continent. You may think of me as a rival prince to your prince, who stands beside you." Madeleine's eyes glowed with rage, the fanged sneer on her face signaling I hit the nerve I had aimed for. "You will find no other who knows and recalls knowledge as deeply as I do. Any page that has ever graced my eyes is forever among my memories, Viceroy Vendecci." Licking a fang, I paused to give the old men of the invaders time to think and gossip before adding, "Surely you have scholars and nobles with a memory such as mine? Perhaps Viceroy Forestier or Viceroy Regius have such talent within their own families?"

"My, what a flatterer, this one!" Viceroy Regius rose a goblet of wine high. "Indeed, my son, too, has a memory like a trap. I'll drink to talent, to you… you…" Faltering, his laughter paused and inquired, "who are you, exactly?"

"Ashton Le Denys Thompson." Madeleine's voice cut across the room like ice. "A traitor among traitors, my dear council. He is the son of the man you seek even now, Germaine Thompson, and worse, his mother led the attack that day." Her eyes glowed as she offered me up to all their hate and desires. "How dare he talk to this council in such a way?"

"Is this true?" The grin on Viceroy Vendecci's face said it all. "We should discuss the fact you bringing our enemy into this most sacred place is unforgivable, your majesty," he riled, straightening in his chair as he attempted to take back the majority mindset in the room.

Now it was Raphael's turn, and I watched him with intrigue as his smile never faltered. "Viceroy Vendecci, I am honored you recognize me as your superior."

"I did not!" Cruza Vendecci jumped to his feet, and Madeleine turned, walking away from the man.

"You did call him 'majesty' just now." Winston nodded, looking to Viceroy Regius. "Did he not, Ahmed?"

Viceroy Ahmed Regius chortled, "So is he your emperor, and we need to be making some changes—"

Cruza shrieked, "He is nothing more than a glorified Crowned Prince of a dead—"

"Watch your words," warned Raphael; his smile was gone, and a fiery expression filled with wrath was in its place. "I demand here and now you all swear allegiance to your Crowned Prince. On your knees."

The speed with which Winston and Ahmed fell to their knees made me flinch. *Who the hell was he before coming here? This is respect and obedience on a level worthy of an emperor, indeed. Why did he even need to run away in the first place?*

I looked at the annoyance on Raphael's face as he matched gazes with the reluctant Cruza.

Dropping to a knee beside him, I enticed, "Say the word, Master, and I will slay any enemy who stands before you."

"What will it be, Viceroy Vendecci?" Raphael signaled for me to follow, and I did so, silent and glaring like a pet wolf heeling. "I've tamed your biggest threat while you, the coward of the century, ran from my father and opened the door for his enemies to slay him. Was it not you who made a pact—"

"Enough!" Cruza barked, falling to a knee before proclaiming, "I swear allegiance to no country. We are equals here." He sneered with a wild grin. "Reviving the empire is a greedy man's quest."

"And you seem to chase your very own monarchy here among already taken seats." Raphael signaled for all to rise. "Rise. As of this very moment, I will bestow you all equal partners." There was a look of confusion on Winston and Ahmed's faces, despite the tension falling from their shoulders. "But I will also be joining." Reaching into his coat, Raphael pulled several papers out, unrolling them and a map of Grandemere. "Let us reassess the boundaries and divide these lands evenly. Here is the proposal. Please take your time reading it." He slid it across the table in front of Cruza before adding, "Don't worry, I've made myself a copy for safekeeping if it happens to fall to a flame."

Turning, Raphael walked through the door, and I followed. Not even exchanging a glance with one another, we passed the guards with no more tribulations. Once in the receiving room, we found my father and sister gone. I kept my composure as my eyes darted around. *No signs of a struggle. Were they escorted back to the gate? Or thrown in the dungeon below?*

Raphael whispered to me, "They went home."

"How do you know? I thought we were going back together," I hissed back disapprovingly.

"They said you didn't plan on coming home, anyway," he answered.

My brow folded and I huffed. "I suppose that wasn't untrue, considering how today unfolded."

"Your majesty!" Winston shouted after us as we descended the stairs. "Please, stay here for the night! We can make arrangements for quarters and entertainment!"

Raphael looked to Winston, then me. "Doesn't matter to me. Which do you prefer? Bath and pleasure here or at the Scarlett House?"

I searched his expression before shouting back up the stairwell, "My Lord wishes to go home tonight. We shall return tomorrow, and you can ask him once more tomorrow."

"Y-yes. Very well!" Winston had made it to where we stood, face red and panting. "We will prepare for your stay tomorrow. Thank you."

Raphael tilted his head, narrowing his eyes at me. "We look forward to it."

We managed to leave the castle and get out the gates, returning to the safety of the streets. Night had fallen, the streetlamps were lit and were casting shadows among the bustling streets. The wares had shifted from food to trinkets to alcohol and other pleasure buys. Couples, drunks, and more filled the road as we walked back the way we had come through Captiva City.

"So, home, is it?" Raphael spoke at last.

"Oh no, we're going to the Scarlett House." I threw an arm around him, poking his chest. "The secret is, you go to the Scarlett House first, since they're rowdier and more skilled. The next day you spend with the castle's Scarlett men and women, since they are more civil and perfect for nursing you after a wild bender."

"Why do I get the notion you've done this before?" Raphael laughed as we walked together.

"Because I have," I laughed as we spotted the Scarlett House up ahead.

Now, the question is, will he share a room or insist on a private room? What if I told him that watching him bring that room to its knees was quite attractive and only makes me want to bend him over under me that much more?

Chapter 12

The Scarlett House Regulars

My heart thudded loudly in my ears and down to my fingertips as we closed the gap between Scarlett House and us, where busty women and half-naked men shouted to those below. It wasn't just the excitement of coming back to the pleasures of flesh I knew awaited me, but the idea I might get a chance to experience the man beside me. An arm still across his shoulders, we kept talking about what we had just experienced.

"So, the white-haired woman, Madeleine, was it?" Raphael's smile had fallen away at this point. "What's with the murderous intent?"

"She's always been like that." I retreated my arm and rubbed my forehead. "Take it from me, that one's got a bloodlust that's not natural."

"Likes to fight like you?" We paused in front of the Scarlett House as I met his gaze.

"I have a temper. That one, she'll kill everything because she has the power to do it." Swallowing, I pressed, "Is that how you see me? Someone who lashes out without knowing his target?"

Raphael huffed, sucking on a cheek as he looked away.

"I'm just impatient," I offered, waiting for him to look back my way.

Closing his eyes, he shook his head before walking past me, saying, "I just wish you'd stop making yourself the target."

The Champion's Lord

The words cut deep as I followed him into the Scarlett House. Inside, we were met with strong aromas of herbs intended to enhance one's sexual desires and sensations. All around were women in loose attire, if any at all, alongside men in a similar state. Mixed among them were clients of all kinds, from servants with their day's wages to noblemen coming to indulge secret desires. One woman stood out among them, fully clothed, fan fluttering, with her corset laced tight. They called her Madame Scarlett, though no one really knew who she was behind the layers of makeup and wigs. She cut through the riffraff the moment she spotted us, just as I had gripped Raphael's shoulder.

"Well, isn't this an interesting moment?" Madame Scarlett snapped her fan closed and pointed at each of us with it. "Did my regulars finally find one another out in the world?"

"Excuse me, what?" I blinked, the music obscuring her words.

Raphael reached out and took her hand, kissing it as he replied, "That seems to be the case. We have found ourselves partners in business and politics at this time, haven't we, Ashton?" He looked at me, and I crossed my arms, reassessing every assumption and thought I had created in my head about the snake before me. "Madame, since you are most familiar with both our likes, could you make arrangements on my tab?"

"A group bath it is, then," she chuckled, opening the fan and fluttering it. "You two make me jealous. I may have to swing by and check in for my own secret desires." She snapped her fingers twice, and a Scarlett woman with sizable breasts appeared. "Lady Ursula, these two will be indulging us tonight once more. See to it they receive fresh attire as a thanks for their continued support of the Scarlett House."

"A regular?" I finally looked at Raphael, and he smiled at me, following the girl down the hall. "How long have you been coming here?" I asked.

"Long enough to have seen you come and go on occasion." Raphael shrugged, waving to two women lingering in the hall. "Good evening!"

"Raphael and Ashton?" marveled Jen.

"Good evening, Jen and Beau! Will you be joining us in the bath?" I arched a brow, licking my lips at them.

Beau tsked. "Do you really have to ask? Our two favorite boys are coming to get clean and dirty. Of course, we're coming!"

"In more than one way," added Jen under her breath before they started cackling and fell in line behind us.

The busty girl leading the way stopped at a door; the hallway was cramped and filled with groping and sweaty bodies all around. Jangling keys soon unlocked the door, and when it swung open, steam rolled from it. She waved us in, and we piled in as she slammed the door shut. Pushing past, she headed to the lantern, making it brighter to reveal the large stone tub filled with steaming water. Shelves held an assortment of herbs, bottles, and more. A chair and table tucked in the opposite corner were perfect for anyone to watch or simply sit for a drink, with wine and goblet waiting.

"Will two be enough?" Lady Ursula motioned to Jen and Beau before looking at Raphael.

"For now," answered Raphael. "Thank you, Ursula, as always."

"Very well, Master Raphael. Good to see you back." Walking between us, she added, "And you, too, Mister Ashton. The girls could use a bender with a stallion of your endurance." Slapping my ass, she left through the door.

With my hands on my hips, I licked a fang before meeting Raphael's amused expression. "It almost sounds as if you own the place, seeing that you know all their names and the way the staffers straightened themselves when we turned the corner."

"Very observant of you, Ashton." Raphael pulled off his coat before grabbing the chair, twisting it before sitting to stare at the tub. "Go on. Let's see this wild bender I've heard so much about from you and the staff."

"You joining?" Tossing my shirt off, I gave a grin as I tugged off my belt and grew hard at the desires champing at the bit. *I finally get to have a little fun with the golden boy!*

"Oh no, he likes to watch." Jen wiggled her dress down and off her hips.

"He what?" Again, I found myself blinking. *Watch?*

"He likes to watch," reassured Beau, helping pull off my boots as Jen loosened my pants.

Raphael smirked, leaning back in the chair and kicking off his boots. "I *love* to watch."

With that, the girls pulled my pants down and off. "Seems like no fun to me," I retorted, groping Jen's ass before slapping it, making her yelp. "But if you want a show, I'll give you one." *I'll make you want to join me before the night ends!*

"Promises." Raphael reached over, opened the wine bottle, and filled his goblet.

"Let's clean up before we start, ladies." I ran my hand into the water before easing into the steaming heat. "I don't think I've ever bathed in this one or been in this room."

"Of course not." Raphael's eyes soaked me in as he sipped his drink. "It's invitation only, and my personal room here."

Sitting, the tension in my muscles cut loose. Jen and Beau's hands wandered over my body, sometimes scrubbing, other times exploring for their own fun. I dunked under the water, the moment of muted world inviting and resetting my thoughts as I let go of all my emotions. *I'll feel better once I release.* Coming up for air, my eyes landed on Raphael, his intense gaze never faltering as I pulled Jen closer and deeply kissed her. Pulling Beau to my other side, her breasts pressed firmly against my body. Both women were busty, Jen's hair short and auburn, while Beau had longer locks unfurled from her braid. There was no gauging what class any Scarlett man or woman was outside these walls.

The Champion's Lord

Beau's hand gripped my cock, stroking it as my tongue twisted with Jen's. My eyes were on Raphael's as he watched my every move. I could see those blue gemstones follow my hand down Beau's spine, over a hip, and between her thighs until she moaned as I slipped inside her. He sipped his drink, silent and shifting slightly in his chair.

How long will he be able to simply watch? How many times has he seen me in these very halls and in open rooms fucking the men and women of his Scarlett House, fantasizing about getting me where he could see just me and only me?

Chapter 13

The Art of Watching

As I pulled myself up to sit on the ledge of the stone tub, my heart fluttered to see those blue eyes gazing upon me. Jen and Beau knelt in the tub at each leg, licking and sucking my hardened cock. The cool expression on his face as he sipped his goblet added to the eroticism of the moment. *I've been here numerous times before, not fretting over even needing a room to relieve and enjoy the pleasures even if someone were to watch. 'Let them!' I have thought to myself time and time again. But tonight, it's different. My heart beats against my chest louder than ever at the very thought he may even touch himself watching me fuck someone. But dammit, I wanted to fuck him!*

Now the girls took turns pulling my shaft deep into their mouths until I knocked the back of their throats, neither able to swallow me to the hilt. Each time, the muscles across my body would tense with the pleasure it brought. I shifted my legs and used my knees to force them to divide themselves outside my legs. *If he's going to watch, he should get a good view of the parts I want his gaze to focus on.* Raphael's eyes slid from my own and down my torso to take in my world. I grinned, excited that he wanted to watch me as badly as I wanted his gaze there.

The girls transitioned once more, their tongues licking up and down my shaft, making it jump as they rolled over the underbelly and the tip. From the dark corner, I couldn't tell if this aroused Raphael, but I was curious to see if it invoked a rise from his own cock. *Will he pull it free? Perhaps abandon his wine to reach in and stroke?* Raphael reached over and refilled his goblet. *His ability to seem indifferent all the time is maddening,* I spat in my thoughts. Another shift and Raphael leaned forward on his legs, his eyes returning to my face. Taking in several gulps, he slammed the cup on the table and sighed. *Agitated? Jealous?*

"Tell me more about Madeleine," Raphael demanded.

I frowned, scorning him. "You aim to ruin my mood?"

He smirked at this, saying, "I doubt someone with your talents and drive would disappoint these ladies any time soon, even if the conversation displeases you."

Scoffing, I relented. "I assume they executed her mother and left her and her twin brother the Farrow clan leaders. Rumors said she would divide it between them if she were to die."

"Indeed, they have culled the former leader, but it looks as if she's the sole leader." Raphael paused, watching as Jen pulled me into her mouth, shaking her head to attempt to pull me deeper, and I moaned.

I can't tell if it's him watching me or Jen's aggression making me edge closer.

He blinked and added, "I didn't anticipate her brother being under Viceroy Regius. What are your thoughts on that?"

"Philippe is at his sister's mercy," I grunted as Beau took her turn, the two Scarlett women competing to see who would get more of my cock down their gullet or be the one to push me over the edge. *Oh, it's getting harder to talk.* "Madeleine has always been bloodthirsty. We used to joke she was." Another moan escaped me as Beau pulled a hard suction and left my cock with a pop of her lips. "She was too bloodthirsty to even pass for a Le Denys." Clearing my throat, I tried to refocus despite the hands rubbing up my abdomen and squeezing my inner thighs. *No fair. Jen and Beau know how to set me off.* "Madeleine would destroy everything just for the thrill," I choked, biting my lip as one circled a tongue on the tip and the other began licking my sack, breasts pressing against me. "Of squashing out life," I blurted, and gripped the side of the tub to regain my composure. "Despite any consequence to herself or her own family, she would burn it all down to the ground for fun. Farrow is the largest clan, so there's a chance they were divided between the twins, so the key—" Another grunt and the familiar rush of heat and tingling was building as I teetered at the breaking point. "Fuck you guys are good! Ah, I didn't want… fuck!"

"The key?" Raphael teased.

I moaned as tongues licked from hilt to tip once more, my cock stiff and hard. "A wedge," I blurted. "The key is to drive them apart." My voice waned as Jen dipped down and I knocked her throat again and I pushed through it, eyes watering as I fought the urge to cum. "The twins don't really see eye to eye when you get them away from… mmm… one another."

"I see." Raphael's eyes lingered on my rock-hard cock as his Scarlett women devoured me.

The Art of Watching

"Tell me more about Cruza Vendecci," I demanded, gripping a fistful of Jen's hair. "I hope you're hungry," I cooed to her, shoving her down onto my cock as I peaked, and she swallowed. *Fuck me...* Through my heavy-lidded gaze, I could see him shift.

Raphael sucked on a cheek as he watched me pull Jen off, the last spurt and jolt lapped up by Beau's tongue. "Yes, Cruza." Raphael was distracted for a moment before blinking and looking back at my face. "He was the one who sold my entire family out to *Arbre Tombré*. I'm positive *Fallen Arbor* is at play with recent events."

Sinking back into the tub, I announced, "He saved me the trip to the Old Continent, then." Twirling Beau's wet locks only goaded her to grab my wrist to guide my finger into her mouth, sucking and wiggling her tongue. "Forestier is an ally, and normally Henri is a hardass," I stumbled on my words as Jen suckled my ear, the girls knowing full well I could keep going and coming as much as they could take it. *I suppose that's the advantage of a male daemon, no downtime like a human.* "Henri is on our side. With Le Denys out of the mix, it will be difficult to balance against the Farrow twins. From the way Madeleine could argue with Cruza, she has already won leadership there, while her brother is something pretty hanging off Ahmed Regius' arm. Just like you two pretty ladies," I added, kissing one, then the other, and seeing the jealous contempt on Raphael's face for a second before he turned to drink some wine. *That's it. Give me more of that ugly jealousy, Golden Boy, and I might cum again for you.*

"Come on, Ashton," Jen pleaded before nibbling on my ear and adding, "I want more. You tasted so good, hot and creamy." Fingers were stroking me once more under the water and I hummed for the girls. *I'm already stiff again, shit.*

"That seems to be the case," agreed Raphael. "Tomorrow, I will be registering roles for everyone; do you have a preference?"

"I know nothing of the game they've made for themselves." I stood, the water whooshing, slapping across the floor at Raphael's feet as the girls laughed in the wake of it. "Do with me what you will," I grabbed the back of Beau and Jen's necks to lead them to the edge facing Raphael before forcing them both to bend over the tub lip. "Which do you think I should punish first?"

"Pick me, Big Daddy," Beau pleaded, wiggling her ass.

Raphael arched a brow, his eyes looking at the women before a smile struck. "Tell me, Ashton, have you ever served under someone before?"

Jen pinched Beau's arm. "No, I was the one trying to make him stop talking," she confessed.

"I've been bossed around by my father plenty," I drawled, hands sliding down the backsides of Jen and Beau. Slowly, my fingers rubbed across their swollen valleys as I narrowed my gaze. "Why?"

"I will need several positions filled, such as advisor, and…" Raphael paused, eyes flashing up to meet my stare. "Would your father be capable of being my head butler and advisor? Could he manage to serve someone and let go of being clan chief so easily?"

Scoffing, I looked away as I groped an ass cheek on each woman before giving them both hard slaps, the sound a loud snap making them yelp. "He was the only one who laid it on the table that fighting would be more damaging than any other means." My fingers slipped between their blossoming pink folds, making both women gasp in unison as I played and thrust, slow and steady, enjoying how wet and hot they were. "Seeing as he's willing to kneel before Grandmama, he'd give you everything he can without question as long as it meant he could have a finger on the pulse and play mind games. He can be relentless." Biting a lip, I stroked more aggressively to gain whimpers and moans from them. "Pick one already, Raphael. My arms are getting tired," I demanded.

Sucking on a cheek, Raphael continued his conversation and ignored my attempt to get him involved. "As for your sister, I wish to keep her out and off the books. She seems well connected with the underworld and seems to take after your father for being able to handle things with her words, or lack thereof, as needed." Again, his eyes glided over me as my arms flexed with their efforts, and my cock rose once more. "As for you…"

"And as for me?" I slowed my efforts, tilting my hip forward to ride my cock between them, enjoying how his gaze fell upon it. *No interest in two panting, busty, beautifully plump women, but my cock plays peekaboo and you forget your words. I'm honored to be the gem of the evening in your sapphire gaze, my newfound Lord.*

"You, I have plans for." Clearing his throat, he looked away, his face growing red. "The one on my right. Take Jen first. After all, she did slow such an urgent discussion and confessed doing wrong." He winked at her.

"Not fair," pouted Beau, standing with her hands on her hips. "Ashton—"

Pulling Beau to me, I kissed her deeply as I pushed inside Jen. "You know you're next," I warned before turning my attention to the task at hand, grinding slowly as I turned my fierce gaze upon Raphael. "Any requests?"

"I want to see this legendary stamina," he chuckled, settling into his chair once more.

Gripping Jen's hips tight, I hammered into her. With each thrust, she yelped, her hands gripping the edge of the tub. I edged closer, eyes locked with Raphael as I peaked, pressing into her to release, the tingling of my orgasm waving over me. I paused and Raphael flicked his fingers.

"Again," he commanded. "But this time, I expect you to release onto her." He motioned for Beau to do something, the hand signal strange but practiced.

With a grunt, I stroked slowly, my cock taking a moment to regain its hardness. Leaning over Jen, so she stood leaning into me. I slid a hand over her hip and between her thighs to rub her jewel. She arched, screaming as she came. Again, I slid my cock into her swollen pussy and began to slam her hard and heavy. It was at this moment that I realized Beau had knelt in front of Jen, mouth open as she waited to receive my offering. *He wants to see me release, dirty boy.* The tightness in my balls and I pulled out, turning to Beau. I released, stroking as I kept

The Art of Watching

watching Raphael's face. He shifted in his chair, eyes on my hardened shaft as she took what I offered.

"Stick it in her mouth and let me see you release again." Raphael inhaled deeply, gulping his goblet dry.

Gripping Beau by her hair, I left her on her knees but turned her in such a way so that he could watch the silhouette of my cock slide across her tongue. Jen was panting, arm slung over the edge and face flushed as she rode out her orgasm still. I pushed deep until I bumped the back of Beau's throat and pulled free. Again and again, I repeated this agonizing act, slow and teasing Raphael, who watched with such intensity it gave me chills. The arousal this man brought me as he took in the act of me pleasuring others and myself brought on a new sensation, a desire to make him… *I want him to grow jealous, to want to bed with me and me alone.*

"Faster," Raphael commanded.

"No," I rebelled. *Fucking join me.*

"Everyone out," he demanded.

Fuck. There goes my fun or he's going to want me to bend over for him. I could dig that too right about now…

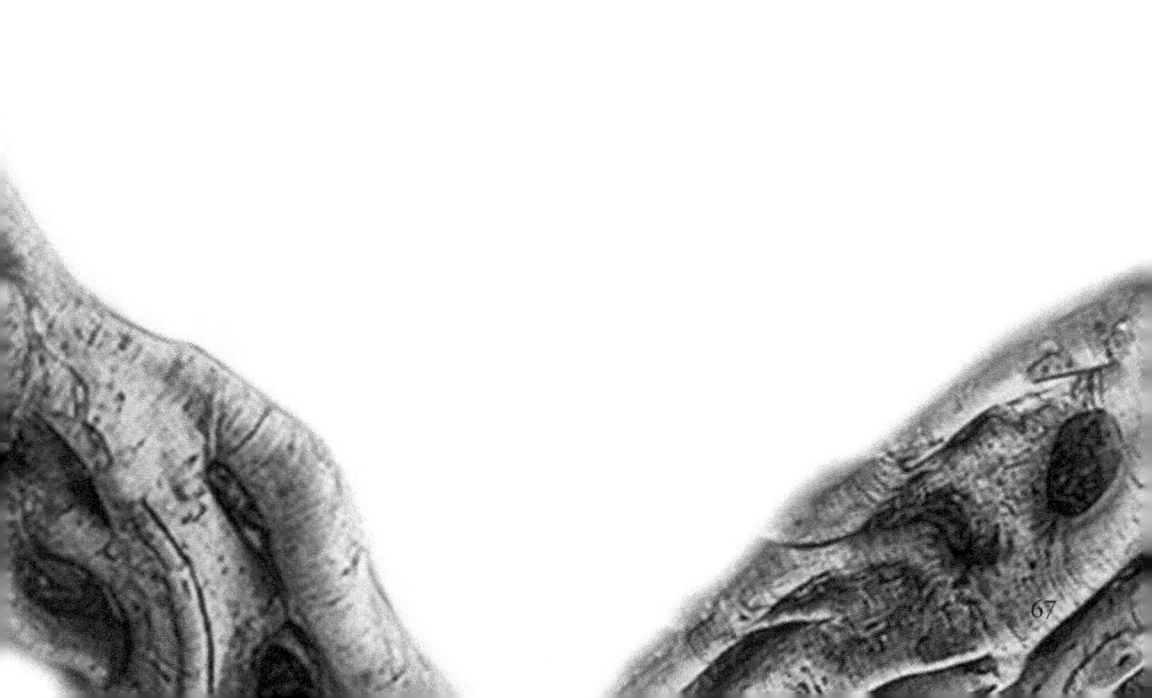

Chapter 14

Valet de Chambre

My heart fluttered as I stood alone in the tub, my reflection making me snort at the end of it. Beau was bickering at Jen with a jealous back glance. I gave her a wink before they were gone; the door thudding behind their wet naked bodies. Raphael huffed, glaring at me for a long time. I sank under the water, staying there in the muted world until my lungs stung as they begged for air once more. Bursting up, I inhaled deeply. Pulling my hair back, I scraped the water from my face before opening my eyes. Raphael still sat in place, unmoved.

"Are you not taking a bath?" I teased.

"I'm waiting on my new *Valet de Chambre* to finish fucking around and do his job." Raphael crossed his legs and sipped his drink with a smug expression.

"How facetious of you," I drawled, pulling myself back to my feet and leaving the bath.

I wrang the water from my hair and began to braid it. "How many knots do I need to carry in my new position, my lord?"

"Fifteen," he replied.

"Will they accept a daemon dubbed the honor of being a royal guard?" I began braiding slowly and counted as I went. *He's just aiming to stir flies on the shit pile.*

"I've had over twenty or so royal guards as a prince with the emperor's blood." I locked eyes with him before Raphael confessed, "And not a single one has lived a full year."

"Is that a challenge?" I arched a brow.

"Indeed, it is." There was a pained expression, almost one of guilt and mixed emotions.

What game do you have planned for me, my golden boy? You've caught my attention, my desire, and now you plan on wielding my wrath, it seems. Raphael remained silent as I dried myself off. *I have all night, and so does he,* I thought bitterly as I found myself doing quite the opposite of what I had come to the Scarlett House to do. Turning to face him, I took only a few steps toward him. Raphael threw up his hand, an annoyed expression on his face.

"Do you intend to do this naked?" he quipped.

"Why not?" I shrugged.

"Dress and do this matter right," he hissed. "I have a short timeframe to prepare you."

"Prepare me?" Snorting, I pulled on my pants and threw on my shirt. "There, clothed, my lord."

"And half undressed now," he scoffed. "Dress yourself properly. Again."

The flame of my temper grew a little as I turned, jaw muscles tight. I slowed down, tucking in my shirt, lacing it properly, and began to cinch my belt back in place. *You don't deserve what I had in mind for us,* I thought with much contempt. Muttering an apology to my beloved staff, I pulled on my boots before jumping back to my feet with a *ta-da*. His eyes judged me, bouncing to my toes and back to the top of my head.

"It's tolerable," Raphael winced as his bottle came up empty and unable to fill his glass.

Marching over to him, I stood, hands on hips, impatient. "Come on. If you wish me to bathe you, do it proper," I sneered. "Up with you, my lord. Let's get you out of those knickers," I chirped in my best Old Continent cockney accent.

"Don't do that ever again." Raphael glared as he stood. "You had your fun before we came down to this part."

Still, I get to have some fun with this, surely. Grinning, I licked a fang as I crouched to unbuckle his pants. The heat in my face and sudden gallop of my heart made me pause. I looked up, and relief washed over me to be out of Raphael's gaze. *I know I wanted to see him naked, but this isn't the romantic rendezvous or the man I thought I was dealing with.* Narrowing my eyes, I inhaled deeply and held it. *No, the prize is worthless without the proper victory lap. This is just spoiling the fun.* The pants unfastened, I pulled gently and averted my gaze, pulling the pants from his feet as he stepped away. *Not until I aim to take him.* Chest aching, I folded the pants and grew rigid in my actions.

"Come," Raphael commanded, and I jolted away from the table, eager like the horse pulling the plow across the field. "I wish to bathe in juniper tonight," he announced.

Quiet and avoiding his gaze, I moved like a phantom. Part of me seemed content to do this, while another part raged in silent protest. *What is it about this man that makes me willing to obey and serve in such a way? Is it the power of his presence or the way he stares at me? Or am I that desperate to swoon him so I can fuck him later?* Taking a jar of juniper, I began mixing other herbs with practiced intent. With a scoop each of rosemary and birch, I turned back to the bath. Rolling up my sleeve, I dipped the basket into the water and worked the herbs, paddling it to swirl across the whole depth.

"What else did you add?" Raphael sloshed around, but I didn't dare gaze upon him, too enthralled in my duty.

"Rosemary for circulations and cleansing, it works well with juniper to wash away illness," I announced.

"And the other?" Raphael came closer, reaching beside me for a fresh cloth before pushing away.

"Birchwood," I answered, my voice softer now. "For the wounds that don't heal or close far too slow." Looking up, our eyes met, and my breath hitched, making me jerk my arm out and turn away. "Think nothing of it." Clearing my throat, I moved to where he once sat, far from the edge of the tub. "What else does your Valet de Chambre need to attend to?"

Raphael blinked a few times, shaking off my words. "You have more power than an advisor or head butler, even above a viceroy. I want you to have access to me in the most private of spaces, more so than a Royal Guard." Raphael dunked under the water and came back up, leaning against the side of the tub, eyes closed. "It seems with Madeleine and Cruza teaming up, we will be facing agents of Arbre Tombré soon enough. I doubt they let him go."

"Tell me more about Fallen Arbor." I sat in the chair, propping my elbow on the table and leaning my chin in my palm. "I know they took control of the empire and most of the Old Continent. So, what kind of enemy are they?"

"Espionage, bribery, blackmail, spies, assassins, and, as you know, dark magic." Raphael rattled it out as if a list one takes to the market for shopping. "They prefer to point their enemies at one another until they maim themselves to no return. Essentially, they managed to goad the nobles into fighting one another and spilling long-kept secrets to gain favor for them. In the end, what you see here is all that's left of the players of their game."

"Ah, so you suspect Farrow has been consorting with them beforehand." My body grew heavy with sleep, the adrenaline from sex dwindling in the pungent aroma of herbs that started to bring a calm over me at last. *Maybe we should hit a tavern after and rest?*

"No, your father did. When you left in a mess today, your grandmother gave us news that she, too, has discovered this since the battle." Raphael inhaled deeply, holding onto the smells before blowing it out of his pursed lips. "Lillian is an interesting one."

"Leave my sister out of this and off your filthy tongue. She's annoying enough," I snarked, tired and annoyed my night had been derailed. *Owner of the Scarlett House and he doesn't even pleasure himself here. How dull…*

"Fine," he chuckled at the idea as he caressed the top of the water with a finger. "Ashton, I hope I haven't misplaced my trust in you."

"And here I was just thinking to myself how obnoxious the man who owns the pleasure house can be to his lowly servant." Closing my eyes, I yawned before adding, "It's not about trust, Golden Boy. We're past that after the journals, the apothecary, and even our spat in the council room. The Fates have tangled our strings and I doubt either of us has the patience to see it untangle anytime soon. If the Sacrificial Daughter really cut and tied us together for the rest of our days, we're royally fucked."

"Can't she cut it again?" Raphael seemed intrigued. "And I thought cutting the thread meant death?"

"No, not when she holds your strings. Her job is to mend where she can. After that, she hands it off to the Devoted Sister to protect it, and getting cut there, that's when your thread returns to the Mother of Life to give you a new fate. Once cut and tied, that's it, the Fates have started to weave you into one another's souls, they say. For better or worse, you're in for the long haul until death."

"Ashton, are you implying our meeting was an act of the gods themselves?" Raphael tilted his head forward, glaring at me as I peeked at him from one heavy-lidded eye. "Don't mistake me as religious. I don't believe any of it, but I don't know much about the Fates, so I'm intrigued every time I hear you speak of it. You're very religious compared to others I know."

"Of course, I am religious. It's complicated to express why, but deep down, I feel it. I suppose Philippe Farrow might be more of a zealot than me. Ha, but as for the gods bringing us together," a grin crested my lazed face, "Who else would find humor in tying the Anointed Child and the Fates' descendants together in such a twisted way? Perhaps your Arbre Tombré has called forth something too dark for the common man to face. Ah, a prophecy. We should seek out the Nameless Prophet to see if we're already written in his books."

"Nameless Prophet?" Raphael swam across, arms on the tub's edge as he rested his chin on his forearms. "I'm not familiar with this god."

"He's new, but the…" Another yawn took hold, leaving my jaw aching before I continued, "…but the followers don't show their faces. They tend to the sick and no one knows where they come from or where they go. In fact, it's rumored they no longer have names. Either way, they say he's announced a new beginning is coming, but first, blood must spill for a hundred years. Dark shit. Don't really like the idea he says the end of Grandemere is near."

"Dark indeed." Now Raphael stifled a yawn. "Come, dry me, and we can rest until we are ready to face the council once more."

Rubbing my eyes, I aided him in drying. Still, I couldn't bring myself to indulge in staring upon his world. *I don't want to spoil what should be claimed in pursuit of pleasures.* We were silent as we played the part of Lord and servant. Dressed now, Raphael took a seat, and I quickly pulled on his boots and laced them with haste. Standing, Raphael assessed my work and made nothing more than a satisfying hum before heading out the door. Unlike before, Raphael slipped through the back, and we exited into the back alleyway.

The sky showed a softer, deep blue, a sign the sun would be rising soon. Another yawn and I followed him, aimless and inattentive. *Where in the hell is he leading me? To the docks? Does he have a ship or even own a tavern and lodge down there? So annoying…* Raphael glanced over his shoulder, checking to see if I still followed and nodded. Rubbing his shoulder, he made an odd gesture before slowing his walk.

A man in a cloak squatted as if waiting, and I slowed, watching how his head turned to follow Raphael. He stood, the flash of a blade in the moonlight enough for me to lunge forward. Gripping his wrist tight, I forced his own blade to his neck. He was small and mousy. My body walled him in as his boots scraped the cobblestone, and I lifted him with my arms tight around him. Raphael turned around, throwing the hood back and gripped the man's jaw. He turned it left, then right, looking for something. *Does he know this man?*

"Does he smell odd? Like sulfur, or worse?" Raphael glanced at me.

Sniffing him, I shook my head. "No. Just been squatting outside sweating at best. Why?"

"Lemme go!" The man tried to yank my arm but found he couldn't make any change in how firmly I held him. "Fucking daemon cunt-sucker—"

Raphael punched the man in the gut before searching his pockets. He took coin, a paper, another knife, and odds-and-ends as he turned pockets inside out. Grabbing the satchel, he dumped it across the cobblestones, the man wheezing still where he lay crumpled. Kicking the items and smashing the jars, Raphael grabbed the man's other hand. He had it balled up tight, a ring on his finger. Raphael made a face and glanced at me.

"Listen, if you want to keep those fingers in working order," I growled deep, the wolf in me excited at the promise my lord enticed me to make, "I suggest you give my lord what he seeks."

Blood dripped from his nose and off his chin, hot against my arm as I gripped him up again. Once more, I pressed his own blade firmly on his neck. He opened his hand. A crack of a breaking finger sent him screaming as Raphael retrieved the ring. Walking to a torch, Raphael looked at the emblem and marched back, fuming. The man was sobbing as his crooked finger stuck out away from the back of his palm.

"Which Vendecci gave you this ring?" demanded Raphael.

"They didn't," he pleaded. "You'll never see me again. Just let me live another day. I beg you, show mercy—"

Valet de Chambre

CRACK. The man wailed for a moment before catching his breath.

"The ring," I snarled in his ear. "Who gave it to you to honor the contract?"

"Some white-haired daemon bitch," he sputtered, and I dropped him.

"Madeleine's already made her move." I kicked the man and he slammed into the wall, the force of it knocking him out cold. "I hope you're ready for a bloodbath, Golden Boy."

"She doesn't have a wolf," Raphael declared, gripping the front of my shirt and kissing me. "Now, let us go wage war against all who dare threaten what belongs to us and only us. Blood for blood."

What the hell was that? I pushed him against the other wall, searching his face. *He knew we were being tailed, but was that why he didn't… that he just watched?* I kissed him deeply, and he allowed it. *How long has he been holding back?*

Chapter 15

Down by the Bay

Raphael's tongue twisted with mine, moaning into my mouth. I tugged up on his shirt, hungry to do what he had denied me moments before. Gliding my hand under the shirt, his body soft and clean under my palm. He broke the kiss, grabbing my wrist to stop my ascension. His heart raced under my palm, and he was breathing rapidly. We froze there in the dark alley, adrenaline fueling us to chase one another.

"Don't," Raphael said at last. "We shouldn't."

I retreated and turned away, covering my mouth. *So close. If I force it, he'll cave, but would I really be satisfied when I can tell there's something more … aggressive if I take this slow.*

"Let's leave before he wakes up." Raphael tucked his shirt back in, and once more, my opportunity was denied. "We need rest and some place safe."

I followed him, my body alive with my arousal, pants tight, and the heat of my lust making my temper rise. *Why can't he just give in? He wants me. I want him. Why let me get so far, to shut me down so hard?* A shudder shook me as we came closer to the bay. At last, we were in the last row of businesses before the docks. Ships rocked and creaked with the waves, sails flapping in the sea breeze. Even this early in the morning, before the sunlight had crawled over the horizon, the sound of a squawking gull could be heard. Water sloshed and slapped against the canals and sea wall. There was not a moment without some sort of sound coming to one's ears in this place.

Raphael marched into the Red Waves Inn. Much like the Scarlett House, this tavern and inn never slept. Sailors came and went at all hours and the singing swallowed all sounds of the ocean and docks. Raphael tossed a few coins to the innkeeper, who tossed him a key without a word. Raphael didn't stop or look back to see if I was even still following him, and it irked me. *Either he sees me as a lost pup or secretly hopes I'm not heeling like a good wolf.* I gave chase up the stairs after him. By the third floor, the music had muted enough I could shout.

"Raphael!" I barked, and he froze at the far door. "Are we going to talk about it? I normally enjoy cat and mouse, but this is… is…" I bit my tongue, unable to find a word for the complicated emotions.

Raphael unlocked the door, pushing it wide open before glaring back at me. "I'm undeserving of your affection, even if it's just to satisfy some carnal desire for us both, Ashton."

"I don't give a fuck, Raphael." I marched down the hall until I thudded a palm on the door and stared him down, our noses nearly touching. "We're tangled, and I want something more from you. You want something more from me. What's so complicated about it?"

Raphael's eyes fell away, his cheeks flushed. "We're here to rest. I need more time to—"

With a finger, I forced his gaze back to me. "I'll wait, but I expect you to continue to watch and command me. To grow jealous until it drives us both mad. If I am to suffer for your indecision, so will you."

Anger fueling me, I marched in and flopped onto the closest bed. Raphael sighed, knocking his head against the door before slamming it, the locks drawn. We lay on separate beds in the darkness, both silent and angry at ourselves, each other, and the world. The heaviness returned to my body, and soon sleep took hold, lulling me off to my dreams filled with a mixture of lust and regret.

I woke, having slept deeply for the first time since I lost my mother. Rolling over, Raphael still slept, his breathing slow, where he curled like a cat. A halfhearted smile urged me to sit up and stretch. *Last night was a fucking mess. I can't believe Madeleine is going for blood out of the gate. She's power hungry after just a small taste. Devoted Sister, protect me in the battles ahead.* Raphael opened his eyes, his eyes bright blue in the sunlight. He watched me, silent and picking me apart. I leaned on my knees, huffing as I glared back. *We don't even know what to do with the desires running through us. Can we really get through this? And if Madeleine figures it out…* Dread came crushing down on me, and at the shift of my expression, Raphael sat up in alarm. *Of course, he noticed. We've been spending the last few days pining after one another and now I look…*

"What's with that expression?" Raphael visibly swallowed. "You look like your world ended for a moment."

"Because it can." I shrugged, reading his face and picking apart anything I could use or decode. "If Madeleine finds out that we even remotely find one another … desirable," I licked my lips and his ears grew red in reply, "she'll use that against us."

"Will she suspect it, given you're the Valet de Chambre and Royal Guard?" Raphael knitted his brow, fingers tapping his lips in thought.

"No, as long as Cruza thinks it's a lowly position or a garbage standing." I stood, stretching my body more, legs aching to get moving. "So, what will Cruza's thoughts and voice be on the matter?"

Raphael smirked, glancing up at me. "That I'm culling the herd by putting a target on your head."

"And what will it take to convince him this is true?" I popped my neck one way, then the other, the cracking noise louder than the words we exchanged.

"I will toss you to the dogs every chance I get." A scowl developed on his face.

Marching for the door, I looked back with a fanged grin. "Lucky for you, I'm a wolf."

As I marched down the stairs, I met a man halfway up. Across his neck was a line where a blade had cut the skin and he was holding a wrapped arm with two fingers in stints. His eyes were in exhausted sags as he glanced upward before locking onto my face. His breath hitched. Backing down the stairs, he paled, hands up. The whites of his eyes were bright as fear poured from him, my own steps matching his.

"Why fancy crossing paths with you here," I cooed as his back hit the wall and he found himself cornered. "I believe you should have gone another way, my friend. Left town even."

"L-L-L-Look, sir," he managed to stutter. "I'm not following. Trying to leave town is all." His whole body trembled as his eyes darted all around. "I was after the other lad, not you, you see."

"Going after a friend of mine is far more dangerous than targeting me. But you know what's worse than that?" He shook his head, piss trickling down a leg as I leaned into his ear, growling. "Trying to draw blood from my lord. You tell Madeleine he has a Royal Guard at his command and hand her this." Digging into my pocket, I placed a totem of the Devoted Sister into his good hand. "She should spare you and even pay you, but be sure to leave post haste, because the blood curse that will follow will send you to an early grave."

"I don't understand," he stammered, looking at the tiny statue of the goddess. "How is a daemon a Royal Guard?" He paled, as if his words brought the truth forward in his own mind. "The other man, he wasn't just a noble, was he?"

Again, I growled into his ear. "Attempting to kill someone of royal blood is punishable by death. Consider this you making amends and send our warning to Madeleine."

Stepping back, he sank to his knees and bowed at my boots. "Thank you! Thank you for showing me mercy. You are truly merciful men."

He crawled away before daring to stand and, by three steps down the stairs, fled. Snorting, I pumped a fist in annoyance. Thuds on the stairs behind me made me twist to find Raphael finally catching up. He paused, confused to see me standing there.

He looked to the wet spot on the floor, his forehead furrowed in thought before scoffing, "I didn't say as my Royal Guard to go terrorize anyone within the same floor as me—"

"It was the assassin from last night," I announced.

"To finish the job? How tenacious." Raphael tilted his head in worry.

"No, to hide and heal, but he picked poorly in choosing where to do so." I smirked and motioned for him to lead the way. "Where to next, my lord?"

Brushing past me, he snorted, "To the tailor to get proper attire for the new stations we hold."

"Ah, am I picking the tailor, or are you?"

Raphael paused at the top of the stairs, a smirk on his face. "You pick, I pay?"

"A man after my own heart," I teased.

Raphael continued down the stairs and out into the busy street. It was the last one before the cobblestones gave way to the creaking panels of wood that made up the docking zone. Pulleys and cranes were busy, swinging one way then the other in a rush to unload and load the ships. Shouts rang out and soon followed the familiar swoosh and snap of sails opening and catching the morning winds. Seagulls cried out like trumpets announcing the departure of some noble creature. I paused, staring at it all. *If I wanted, I could be on a ship and gone before they knew it. Change my life, make a name for myself among the sailors or as the Scarlett Isles Queen's concubine, having her take me in as part of her harem. Wasn't it always an option to just throw myself to the wind and sea, leave this all behind?*

Chapter 16

Looking the Part

A hand gripped my shoulder, and I nearly jumped out of my skin. Raphael frowned, following my gaze. Another flurry of shouts and another ship was setting sail behind the first.

"What's the matter?" he patted my shoulder, and I started to lead us far away from the bay and the promises it whispered.

"Nothing." Clearing my throat, I glanced at a street sign and took a turn. "I just find the ships and docks so fascinating," I lied. *I'm tired of being called a coward, anyway.*

"I came in that way," he announced, trailing behind me as he glanced at some merchant wares. "It was dreadful."

I slowed down, allowing him to catch up and pass me. "Tailor shop sign up ahead. Hodge's Haberdashery."

Raphael smiled and walked slower now. I stayed behind him, much like I had done leaving the Scarlett House. *Isn't that where servants walk? Behind their lords and ladies?* Scanning the people on the street, I saw no signs of anyone out of the ordinary, nor had Raphael signaled like the last time. *No threats, so then…* Instead, I took in how some of the longer-braided nobles went about their business or shopping. Each of them with a single servant, while others seem to have a flock behind

Looking the Part

them. *They look like a mother goose with goslings hot on their heels. Ridiculous. Why on earth would they need all those servants to simply do shopping or even errands?*

The bell over Hodge's Haberdashery brought my eyes forward, where a young boy dressed in his best gentlemanly attire opened the door for Raphael. "Come in, good sirs!"

Following Raphael inside, I nodded to the young human boy who seemed half my height. "Good morning, Little Hodges."

"Ah, Ashton!" Little Hodges grinned wide, freckles across his face; the boy seemed delighted to have me. "It's been a long while."

"Indeed, and how's your father?" Raphael watched me, intrigued by the exchange. "I hope he's on the mend."

"He is!" Rolling up his sleeves, Little Hodges motioned for Raphael and me to enter one of the curtained-off rooms. "The herbs you commissioned made a difference. How did you know it would work? The doctor we consulted had failed, you know, and not to insult you, Mister Ashton, you're not known to be a healer or a doctor of any kind."

I motioned for Raphael to stand on the platform, and he did so, listening as I answered, "I've read many books. When I read something so important as what herbs can be used for, I can't help but store it in here for later." I tapped my head and the boy laughed. "Glad he's on the mend. Hodges has always spoiled me, so today, I have brought a customer with deep pockets in order to spoil you."

"Ashton," admonished Raphael. "Do learn to be more tactful in your words."

"He's always been rather rude, sir." Little Hodges bowed his head, nervous, as he grabbed up the measuring tape and started to note in his pocketbook Raphael's stats. "What sort of attire are we looking for? Going to an event of some kind, sir? For work, perhaps? We have some new leathers from the ships yesterday and new styles that would be fitting for your build."

"This one knows his job well, unlike a certain *valet* I know." Raphael narrowed his eyes at me before I began flipping through a catalog of sketches. "What is your name, boy?"

"Hodges, sir." And with that, Little Hodges noted something in his book and kept going without ever meeting Raphael's gaze.

"Little Hodges," I corrected, pausing on a page for a moment.

"Little Hodges," Raphael started, annoyance in his voice as I whistled a tune, ignoring him. "I will entrust you to make the best choices so that I'm dressed in the latest fashions for high nobles."

"As you wish, sir." Little Hodges wrote something down and shuffled around to continue his work. "I'll pull some samples in a moment. I can make alterations to most for someone of your stature."

"No need to pull samples." I continued flipping through the catalog, never meeting the heated glare burning down on me from the platform. "I will be choosing his attire today. We will both be needing an order for altered clothes immediately, fitting *properly*." I snorted, enunciating it how Raphael had done to me. "After that, I wish to commission two more outfits for myself and several for my lord here so he can carry on his business *properly*." I wobbled my head, still unwilling to look up from the catalog.

Raphael remained silent.

"That's … a lot." Little Hodges knitted his brow. "It may take me and Father some time to complete them all, depending on the pattern."

"Indeed, it should keep you in business until he's fully back on his feet, correct?" Again, I flipped the pages and ignored the eyes on me.

"I can't wear them all at once anyhow," Raphael spoke up, startling Little Hodges.

I see Raphael has caught on to why I am here. Granted, he'll be pleased with the final product. Their stitching is top-notch. Sniffling back a tear, Little Hodges nodded and set out to do the job. After several minutes, Little Hodges had finished taking measurements of Raphael and started to pull out an everyday frock coat and fine undershirts. I waved them back, and Raphael's eyes narrowed. *You wanted us both to look the part, so be it.* Pulling Little Hodges closer, we walked through the curtain and abandoned Raphael, where he stood on the platform. On the other side, I pointed to a display that had an outfit I had noticed Cruza and Ahmed wearing the day before: the *habit à la française*.

The coin I pushed into his palm was enough to reassure Little Hodges we had brought enough to pay for it and everything I had listed. Returning through the curtain, Raphael gave me a disapproving glare as he recognized the pieces we carried in. The trending attire was comprised of many parts, much to Raphael's horror. After living as a hermit in the woods with nothing more than a jacket, shirt, and breeches for so long, the custom of returning to layers of embroidery and lace appalled him. This particular arrangement had three key elements: a blue coat with gold and silver threading in floral patterns, a grey patterned waistcoat with brown leaves and pheasants to decorate the pocket and edges, and lastly, breeches in the same style as the coat. As I suspected, it fit Raphael's build with only minor adjustments needed, then came the peacock-worthy additional bits.

"It's like putting a saddle and regale on a horse," I jested as I aided Little Hodges.

"I'm going to pretend I didn't hear you say you're saddling me up." Raphael scowled. "You sound as if you want to ride me out of the store."

Arching a brow, I leaned into his ear. "If you wish it of me, my lord, I will gladly do so."

Palming my face, Raphael pushed me back as he set to work out the various parts of the concoction. A pair of silk stockings, a jabot for his neck, a cotton shirt with decorative sleeves with lace, and the finishing element of a cravat in tandem with the jabot. When Little Hodges finished buzzing around Raphael with a thread and needle, adjusting the clothes to pull in or let out in such a way, I took in my handiwork. I sat watching on occasion as I noted on paper what else should be ordered. *He needs to look worthy of being an emperor. Yesterday, he came as their equal, and they dared challenge his very presence. Today, they will be reminded of who he is and where they shall kneel before him. Yes, blue and gold are striking on him.* Turning a page, I smirked. *This one in white would be perfect for events and balls.*

"Thank you, my lord," I muttered as I scribbled something on the paper.

A grunt escaped Raphael as Little Hodges tugged on the breeches trying to get the fitting just right. "What for, my deplorable valet?"

"I never knew how fun it could be to dress a man like a peacock until now." I chuckled, shutting the book at last. "My work here is done."

Raphael looked in the mirror at himself. "I suppose I can tolerate your tastes and entertain you further." A wicked smile crossed his face. "Hodges."

"Yes, sir?" Little Hodges stepped back, smiling with his own sense of pride.

"I wish to dress my *valet de chambre* in something more appropriate." Raphael's gaze glided over me, and he turned to Hodges. "I wish him to wear a white shirt, one he can easily move in as needed. A pointed vest, a cravat, a pocket watch to keep us on schedule, and black breeches with new boots."

"What color vest, sir?" Hodges's eyes had a shine to them.

"Burgundy or some deep red to match his eyes." Raphael nodded as if making up his mind, adding, "And a black cravat, or ascot of sorts."

"Absolutely," Little Hodges confirmed before turning to me. "Would you like to dress in the other—"

"Here's fine." And I began to strip naked. *Not like my lord hasn't seen what I have to offer just last night, no?*

Raphael sat, crossing a leg as he motioned for me to stand on the platform. "So uncouth, but the stage is your oyster, Ashton. Enjoy your new uniform."

"And you yours," I remarked, turning to face him with arms akimbo.

Raphael was unmoved, even annoyed, as he tugged at the lacey sleeves and jabot at his neck. Hodges exploded back into the curtain and brought his findings to Raphael. Holding each of the three shades of vests up, Raphael chose one, and Hodges began handing me each component. With each item, his nimble fingers worked away and tugged my outfit here and there. On occasion, the cold metal of a needle and the brief warmth of his touch directed me where and how to move.

For someone so young, he's mastered his father's craft with uncanny efficiency. I guess the days of digging my fingers in the dirt and shoveling shit are behind me. Granted, I didn't mind the burn of my muscles. Something about losing yourself to hard labor that can't be found anywhere else. Now, I'm taking a dive into the viper's den. Not that I haven't lived the life as a council brat, but this isn't a community. None of these men have each other in mind, only their own greed and need. Here's hoping I don't take down everyone with me. Can you really put clothes on a wolf and claim it tamed? Even consider it a man?

Chapter 17

Taking a Seat

Unlike the day before, the guards opened the gate to the Tower without a word, and their mannerisms were more appropriate. Our new clothes had earned us mixed reactions on the walk there. Sneers and smiles were evenly matched among the street's foot traffic. *Honestly, Raphael got the smiles, and I got the sneers. Is it because I'm a daemon serving a human? Does this burgundy vest really make it more noticeable I'm a daemon? Raphael did that on purpose. Dick.* I narrowed my eyes at Raphael as we walked through the castle's front doors. The servants lowered their heads, acknowledging us in a new way, matching of our station. *Well, at least looking the part has helped ease the awkward abrasiveness we faced yesterday.* Once more, we were led up the stairs and straight into the council room, where Regius and Forestier stood talking with one another.

Henri stood, excited to see us once more. "Lord Raphael, it's good to see you have indeed returned."

"Where's Cruza?" I drawled, unwilling to talk formally.

"He's on his way." Viceroy Forestier approached with Viceroy Regius at his side. "He and the twins are always late these days."

"Shouldn't Philippe be by your side?" I arched a brow at Ahmed Regius, and Raphael elbowed me in punishment. "Look, I'm here with you when I'd rather be elsewhere." *Scarlett House... don't worry Beau, I know you get—*

Taking a Seat

Regius laughed, patting my shoulder. "I'm jealous, your majesty! You found quite the lively one."

"Too lively," scoffed Raphael. "Forgive his informal mannerisms. He's still learning." He shook their hands and, lastly, Henri's. "That being said, it is alarming, Viceroy Regius, to think your advisor prefers to be with another Lord instead of you."

Ahmed scratched his jaw, nodding. "Yes, it's something I've mentioned a few times. Cruza insisted I should allow the twins time to adjust before driving a wedge between them."

I choked, clearing my throat before speaking my mind. "Philippe is older than I am by a long shot. He could do with some separation from his sister. They never really got along since she tends to bully him into things for as long as I've walked this world."

"Oh? Is this true?" Ahmed smiled, turning his question to Henri.

"Ashton, don't you think that's rather crude to expose someone's private affairs?" Henri hissed, face red with rage.

He thinks I'm insulting all of daemonis, but what we need is to split the twins so they can't coordinate anymore. Foolish old man can't see beyond the fly on his nose.

"I've even heard rumors," announced Winston Forestier. "Certainly, it would look ill back home if an advisor of another house spent more time with another Lord."

"It would," agreed Raphael. "Always looked bad even back home, did it not?"

"Enough." Ahmed Regius threw up his hands in defeat. "I will take your advice, monsieur?"

"Ashton Le Denys Thompson." I bowed, smiling at my victory. "Forgive me that I'm such a blunt individual."

"He's always been that way," Henri huffed before clapping my shoulder and prompted for me to stand. "But I can't deny the truth in his words. It would be in everyone's interest if we establish proper boundaries outside this council room."

"Agreed." Winston nodded, nudging his glasses up his nose. "We should be able to bring to the table different schools of thought, not canoodle with one another outside of here."

"Aw, Winston." Raphael frowned, leaning an arm over the short round man who was nearly half his height. "Don't tell me I can't come over for wine and dinner anymore."

"You can come over anytime, your majesty." Winston rushed the words, alarm in his voice.

A great roar of laughter left us all. Henri shook my hand, firm and strong. *He's acknowledging me and accepting me as part of the council in his own way. Perhaps he sees what we're aiming to do. We can't have the Vendecci and Farrow families running Grandemere without checks and balances in place.* The doors opened, and we turned to watch Cruza Vendecci and Madeleine enter. Their facial expressions betrayed much. Cruza faltered in his gait as confusion and surprise hit him at Raphael's presence before shooting a heated glare at Madeleine. As for Madeleine,

83

who walked behind Cruza in a lacy black dress like a queen in mourning, the rage as she met my gaze made her eyes glow. *I got you good today, Fanged Lady.*

Regaining his composure, Viceroy Vendecci gestured, and the other viceroys went to their seats without a word, *obedient cowards*. I looked across the table; no new chair or place had been added to accommodate Raphael joining despite the display of power from the day before. *What misled confidence allowed this farce? I'm going to eat them alive over this one. Insolence will come with a well-met consequence, as Father says.*

"Don't worry, my lord." I couldn't cage the wild grin on my face as my voice boomed off the acoustics of the room. *After all, this is a place built so a single voice could be heard loud and clear.* "There's a seat over there for you." With a hand on the small of his back, I rushed Raphael to Viceroy Vendecci's own throne, the only overly embellished seat in the entire room. "Here, this one is worthy of your station." I pulled it out, and Raphael winked before spinning about and taking his seat.

"Oh!" Raphael exclaimed, now seated across the length of the table, staring down Cruza, who still stood just inside the doors. "It seems we don't have a chair for you, Viceroy Vendecci. How unseemly that must be for you." Raphael snapped his fingers, a regal ambiance exuding from him that made my heart flutter. "Guards. Bring a chair in from the sitting room at once."

"You're mistaken, scoundrel—" Cruza raised a hand and silenced Madeleine before she could get words out.

"My apologies, your majesty." The anger flushed across Cruza's face now. "But we need to first agree to add you as part of this council before—"

"We decided yesterday, did we not?" Ahmed Regius's smile faded. "It was agreed we would gain much from having him join, and at last, have access to the Thompson clan, per Henri's wonderful information. Did you forget?"

Cruza opened his mouth, but the guard banged through the door, lugging an equally embellished chair for him to use opposite Raphael. They sat at the stone circle with the Fates watching as a silent war of rage-filled thoughts and angry glares were cast among the four Cardinal Lords of Grandemere. *Never have I seen such resentment and hate at this table in all my decades. May the Fates find a means to end this. How can Grandemere prosper with everyone at odds and bloodlust on their minds? Where is the concern of addressing the people's needs? Has this room and council lost all meaning the moment these invading Lords took over? How vile.*

"There, we're all settled," announced Raphael. "Let's go ahead and decide on a matter that irks me the most. Our uneven stations at this table will be most destructive to the meaning of what this room has been designed to do. With me above you all, and—"

"Forgive me," interjected Viceroy Regius. "I would like to propose something on this matter." Raphael motioned for him to go on while Philippe had a look of confusion on his face and glanced at Madeleine, who looked as if she was growing ill. "We should appoint one of us as Speaker of the House, or this may get rather … savage."

Taking a Seat

"Normally, the people appoint it but considering the…" Winston cleared his throat before saying, "…method in which we took power, this may be unwise."

"I will be the Speaker of the House," declared Cruza. "I was here the longest."

Henri whispered to Winston, who glanced at Raphael and nodded. "If that's the method of choosing, I'm afraid there are plenty of records here in Captiva City to prove his majesty Lord Raphael has been here for over a year or so."

Cruza's face bloomed red once more. "Perhaps I was too hasty in my decision," he backpedaled. "Perhaps we should give this more thought. As for other matters, I think we meet too often. Let it be that we meet once a month."

"A week," amended Raphael. "There's too much to resolve to drag it one month, but certainly every day is too obnoxious, as we have estates and households to manage along with territory."

There was a rumbling of agreement on this and nods.

"Very well, a week," relented Cruza before Madeleine whispered in his ear.

"I think it best you should fight for the position, or perhaps the speaker leads for a year or season," cooed Madeleine into her master's ear.

"That's a death sentence," Cruza hissed back, covering his mouth in case someone could read his lips. "They would never agree to it. Winston's too old and out of shape, and Ahmed would never lower himself to such a trivial task. And as much as it stings my pride, Raphael didn't survive this long because he doesn't know how to win a fight."

"But sire, there are others who can fight for you, could they not?" She spun her web as his brow rose high in interest.

How bold of them to do this here and now, I thought. *She's planning to sacrifice daemons to this game of power. Fucking cunt.* Temper rising, my eyes glowed as I clenched my fists. *If I could, I would slay her here and now, spilling her blood before the Fates and in the name of the Devoted Sister. The Farrow clan has sworn on the name of the Mother of Life, and here she tosses her family's legacy and promise to the side for her own blood-driven desire. Hateful, vile bitch.*

Raphael tugged my sleeve, and I leaned to his lips as I watched them conspire on the other side of the room. "Can you hear them?" he whispered so softly I could barely hear him, his lips tickling against my ear.

"Can't you?" I whispered back in confusion, but he smiled smugly at the response.

This time, his hand cupped my jaw, his lips again tickling and hot as he replied, "I don't have the ears of a wolf like you."

Looking at Madeleine, she hadn't noticed me listening as she poured her poisoned words into Viceroy Vendecci. "Master, with the Le Denys gone, there are no warriors left among the daemonis except our house. The Thompsons are librarians at best, and the Pomeroys are carpenters. Both also favor digging in the dirt and playing farmer. But we, the Farrow clan, we have mastered many skills and have the majority of the weapon-smiths and armorers. They will not be able to compete, no matter how often said battle should happen."

"What a wondrous idea, my Fanged Lady." Cruza smiled with a sparkle in his eyes.

Shifting, I returned the favor to Raphael, my lips against his ear as if a lover as I whispered, "They intend to make everyone fight for the position of Speaker and use servants."

Raphael took on a grim expression. "We'll talk on this matter in private, then."

"*As you wish, my lord.*" I stood straight as Cruza rose to his feet.

"Next week, I want us each to come with a proposal of how and what we intend to be the deciding factor for Speaker and divide out our duties. Until then, I wish to gift the remaining territories to his majesty as an offering of peace." Cruza bowed, a wicked tone to his voice. "The immediate connecting property has been claimed, as you know, so it seems fitting we gift you Farmlis Woods between the sister lakes, Willow Waters and Sullen Lake. Does anyone disagree?"

Ahmed spoke up, pushing Philippe off him. "I agree. Besides, is that not where the Thompson clan now resides?"

"It is," answered Raphael. "If I may, I'd like to include all land north of the sister lakes as mine. Seeing as the House Forestier has all property between Sullen Lake and Thirsty Crossings to the east, followed by House Regius has all land west down to Terahime, and lastly, House Vendecci claims all land south of Captiva City, which means you own the most ports and harbors for trade it seems. Quite profitable for you, I imagine. Congratulations for holding the majority of the ports, Viceroy Vendecci."

My breath hitched. *In a single statement, he was able to pointedly make them aware he knows their borders while addressing the fact that someone has already made a greedy sum for themselves.* Heated glares came down on Cruza, and he shifted in his chair. His knuckles grew white as his grip on the chair tightened. *He's pissed to be called out and there's nothing he can refute in this.* Licking a fang, I fought the ill-mannered thoughts trying to creep forward. *My heart won't stay still and I'm ready to kiss this man. Seeing this side of Raphael is … exhilarating. Keep the belt buckled, Ashton,* I warned myself as chills of yearning took hold. *Keep your pants on. As you know, this is not the time, and there may never be a time with Mad Madeleine as your rival.*

Chapter 18

Cutting Threads

Ahmed slapped his hand on the table, turning heads in Raphael's direction. "Does that include the Perines Mountains? You are being rather sweeping with saying everything north, Raphael."

"Who would want that," scoffed Winston. "I agree to it. It's a savage and cold land. If you want it, your majesty, I vote in favor of you claiming it."

"How about that's where my line is drawn, the base of the Perines Mountains," offered Raphael. "But I vote that the mountains are unclaimable and neutral land."

Cruza snorted, adding, "According to records here, no one has ever made it back from those mountains alive. We'll freeze to death before even knowing if we can make any use of it."

"Then it's agreed the mountains will be no-man's-land?" Ahmed cast his stare across the whole room.

Cruza leaned back, gesturing with a finger for Madeleine to come closer to whisper, "Is there any value in those lands?"

"No, it's true. No one has entered north of the tiny village of Winter's Perch and returned. They say it never stops snowing there, and the chill is so deep, it cuts to the bone," Madeleine answered.

"I agree to this as well." Cruza waved her off once again. "So, there we have it. The territories divvied out properly for today. Welcome to the council, Viceroy Raphael Traibon."

"Ah, one last matter before we part ways for a week to finish the Speaker of the House matter." Raphael drummed his fingers on the stone table, his gaze on the statues between them before it fell upon Cruza. "Are we all equal Houses here, or shall I remind everyone per empire ruling who begets who?"

Everyone shifted uncomfortably, looking at one another, waiting for the other to boldly say what Raphael and I knew. *They wanted him to be lesser, if not at all, part of this new system of fuckery they've replaced my father and his council with. What a complete shitshow.* Philippe moved to whisper to Ahmed, and Madeleine's pointed stare failed to slice her brother back. *Ah, there is a divide that needs more distance. Otherwise, she wouldn't fret every time he does his job.*

"May I relay what Henri has suggested and I agree upon?" Winston spoke up, his voice trembling slightly as he placed the blame on Henri for what words he desired to say. "We should take a page from the former ruling body and be equal houses." He held his breath as Henri rolled his eyes.

Nodding, Ahmed agreed. "That is the very same matter Philippe and I were just speaking about. I think this will be a sign of putting the past discrepancies of the empire behind us and starting something new and more valuable as the last standing Houses of the old empire."

Madeleine's heated glare at her brother made him wince as she lipped in ancient daemonis, *traitre—traitor.*

Raphael weighed this in his mind a moment, Cruza leaning forward, hoping he'd disagree. "Yes, let's put the past transgressions behind us." His blue gaze cut into Cruza, who scowled in reply. "I expect us to show true to this. No more need for formal speech as 'your majesty' and such, no?" Seeing the nods in agreement, Raphael added, "Well, let's make sure all these chairs match next week, and I hope I'm still considered an honored guest, and yesterday's offer for me to stay the night here before returning home is still on the table?"

"Absolutely! You have a long way to go, so of course, you are welcome to stay the night here in the castle." Winston seemed to be the only one in celebration over the matter.

"Do join us for dinner tonight, Raphael." Cruza stood. "Let us adjourn, and I look forward to the proposal next week, gentlemen."

"One last matter," interrupted Ahmed. "Before we go, I'd like to address a matter that has been an issue for me for some time." He motioned to Philippe. "This man here is my servant, not yours, Cruza." Madeleine opened her mouth, but Cruza silenced her with a raised hand. "As of today, he will be joining my household along with those who fall under him."

Red-faced, Cruza slammed his palms on the table. "House Vendecci has signed the proper paperwork to claim the Farrow clan is theirs!"

Cutting Threads

"Correction," Winston cleared his throat and spoke loudly. "You signed an agreement with Madeleine Farrow. She and Philippe are on equal standing from one another, according to Henri and the records that were well written and kept. The moment we executed their mother, the former clan chief, the Farrow clan was marked to be split evenly between them."

"Is this true?" Cruza spun to face Madeleine.

Her face wrenched, and she relented. "The clan was indeed divided between us."

Philippe dodged his sister's sneer, and at last spoke up. "I shall make arrangements tomorrow—"

"Now," demanded Ahmed with a heated glare.

"Henri, bring the documents immediately. It seems today we will be signing two servitude agreements." Winston huffed a sigh of relief.

We shook this enough to pry power away from Vendecci and Farrow households. Granted, we didn't do it alone. We just had to give them an opportunity and a nudge to speak up. What childlike men they are! Snorting, I looked down at Raphael, who held an unyielding expression. *I can't tell if he's indifferent, being stoic, or really good at being straight-faced. He did the same thing at the Scarlett House. He's going to drive me mad before I ever unravel the secrets behind his desires. He toys with me so boldly at times*—I shook my head, flustered over the way my mind kept slipping back to chasing my cock over the game of cat and mouse at hand. *Cinch the belt.*

Henri returned with two scrolls, rolling them open as two other servants came with four quills. Winston motioned for Raphael, Ahmed, Philippe, and me to come closer. On one, the names *Traibon* and *Thompson* were written. As I read the document, I winced at the level in which everything my clan laid claim to would fall into the possession of House Traibon. *Do I really trust this man not to take advantage of such power? Could any man not exploit such an arrangement in their favor, eventually?* I read on while Ahmed and Philippe had signed and left the council room in hushed whispers. Cruza and Madeleine lingered, a greedy need to see if this was indeed happening. *Why not? The top clan and House are joining forces. It's a dangerous transaction between Raphael and ... Germaine?*

"Let me show you, since it may be confusing, since we aren't using ink for this." Raphael took my hand, turning it palm up as he jabbed the point of the quill into my flesh. "Not even a flinch. You impress me, my wolf." I furrowed my brow as Raphael pointed to a line. "Here. Sign your full name, Ashton Le Denys Traibon, on this line here."

Without hesitation, I did so, marveling at how he had managed to work this out. Signing my name in my blood meant nothing. *The document calls for the clan chief. I'm not clan chief until my father passes, so this is null and void because the law of the land says I can't promise something that's not mine, even if it might eventually be mine. This contract would have to be dated after that event transpires. He knew that the moment he chose me to be here in lieu of my father. Not only did he dodge my father's execution, but we're allies in verbal standing, and this document is as good as paper for my ass. This man! A wolf in sheep's clothing, ha!* Raphael pierced his own palm and signed beside my own name. His handwriting was gorgeous, worthy of an art form with the curls and swashes he added.

"Thank you, gentlemen." Henri and Winston gathered everything up and left with it all to be locked in the record vault.

"Then it's done." Cruza turned, following Madeleine out the door, adding, "See you both tonight for dinner, then."

With that, Raphael glanced up at the Fates before marching out, and I followed like a well-trained dog. A servant stood waiting for us in the receiving room and led us through the castle. Soon we found ourselves in a familiar room, and I fought the urge to reveal I knew the castle's layout, let alone that where every bed chamber was located was etched to memory. Nights of sneaking into bedrooms and chasing foolish desire came rushing into mind while my eyes were gliding over Raphael's backside. *Before everything went to shit for him, I wonder if he did the same back in the Old Continent? He was the emperor's son. Who did he choose to bed with, or has he always been the sort to watch?* A shudder rocked my shoulders. *I'm just jealous I didn't think of purchasing the Scarlett House. The Fates can attest I certainly have spent enough to buy it tenfold. Who knew you could buy the place…*

Chapter 19

The Marriage of Desire and Despair

The servant stopped in front of a door and my heart caught in my throat. *This was the room I had always stayed in. I mean, this is my room. Did they do this intentionally?* They opened the door, and nothing had changed in the layout and presentation. *Of course not,* I reasoned. *Most of these rooms were fitting of a king. These petty men would enjoy such luxurious displays of wealth. Granted, it was to show how well-off Grandemere was and not one man's own vanity.* I slid my gaze to Raphael as I followed him in. The door shut, and I took a step back to lock it in our wake. *I wonder. Will I be able to break that wall down tonight in a place I dominated so many others?*

Raphael spun, arching a brow as he followed me with his gaze as I marched through the room. Twisting a carved statue of the Devoted Sister, something clicked elsewhere in the room. His eyes widened, and I motioned for him to remain quiet. Tugging on a bookshelf, it swung open. Raphael leaned to see what it held. Tugging another switch, I turned toward the next sound. A smirk crossed my face as Raphael's eyes chased me around the room. *I have his full attention.* The bookshelf had hidden and kept safe an assortment of toys and oils. *Nothing out of order since my last sexual conquest during my last gathering.* Next, I tapped my foot on a wood panel beside the head of the bed, and it opened as well. Inside was an empty, hidden corridor, and I sighed with relief.

"Okay, it's safe to speak." I grabbed the lantern, lighting it to kneel just inside. "The sand is all intact here, so no one's come through here or has discovered the hidden corridors since I last used them."

"And of that?" Raphael pointed, tapping his lips as he continued to be more enthralled with my lustful stash.

Shutting the wooden panel, I drawled, "Untouched, much to my disappointment."

I aimed to close it, but Raphael slapped a hand on my chest before I could walk across the room. "Leave it open. I wish to pry." He marched forward, picking up various bottles and inspecting them, smiling on occasion as a look of recognition crossed his face. "You really have a way of giving in to lust, don't you, my wolf? This isn't a cheap collection. You have all the high-end novelties here at your disposal."

Turning back, I sat the lantern back on its table and flopped into the chair. "Am I wrong to assume that contract is no good since I'm not *Germaine?*"

"It's worthless," he announced. "You now owe Henri a favor since we were both certain Winston can't tell one daemon from another. Such a clueless twat."

"Now, what of this 'even' and 'equals' non-sense?" I sat with my legs gaped open and completely in my element once more. "Wouldn't it be more advantageous to use your emperor's blood to be at least Speaker of the House?"

"There was no point in fighting on the matter. I need them to want to support me, Winston and Ahmed, in order to overpower Cruza." Raphael bent over to reach for something on a lower shelf. "This single decision opened more doors than closed. It's not like I could do anything as a prince of a now-dead empire."

Licking a fang, I tilted my head to enjoy how the coat's tails split to give me a peek of his ass. "Madeleine may have put a nail in that coffin today."

"How so?" Raphael stood, and I snapped my eyes onto the back of his shoulders, unable to see what he had in his hands.

"She wants Cruza and the others to use their new daemon slaves to fight. Winner gets the seat of Speaker of the House." I leaned, curious about which of the toys he held.

"Doesn't that put her and her clan in harm's way?" Raphael glared over his shoulder at my words, and I sighed.

"I told you. That one wants blood just for the fun of watching someone die," I sneered.

"Good job on splitting her and her brother apart." Raphael rummaged through the shelves again. "You went in bold, and it worked. Though it took till the end for Ahmed to act on it."

"Philippe has spent decades for a chance to do so." I shifted in my chair, the visual of Raphael playing with all my sexual toys and oils causing my cock to rise. "But that means she's going to take revenge on us and him for it. He'll be lucky to live long enough to see her take Cruza's seat."

"Not if I can stop it," Raphael declared in an instant, squatting now where I knew my favorites lay within wooden chests. "I take it you don't believe in the

The Marriage of Desire and Despair

Old Continent's current trend on the matter of self-pollution, by the looks of your collection here."

"What?" Another shift as the front of my breeches grew sufferably tight. "Exactly what in the Fates is self-pollution?"

Raphael laughed, opening each box to see what they hid. "Let's just say you are polluted beyond saving by their accounts. I imagine when you have no one within reach, you are well-equipped to find relief by your own means." Raphael picked something out of one chest and turned back to me. "I'm not familiar with this one." In his fingers was a ring too large for a finger to wear, black and sparkling even in the low light from the hearth. "Is this carved out of some sort of stone or gem?"

Closing my eyes, I bargained with myself. *Do I act on the throbbing in my loins or answer him in a more sterile manner? What's a man to do when his latest obsession is pawing at his prized toys? The very same ones I wish to use on and with him? In the bedchamber, where I only fuck my favorites before sneaking them out the back corridor—*The heat of his breath on my neck and the nudge of a knee against my crotch and hardening cock brought my eyes open in alarm.

"Tell me." Raphael's lips at my ear sent chills across me. "It's for this prized possession of yours, no?" His hand rode the underbelly of my erection through the fabric. "If I commanded it of you, would you wear it for—"

So bold! I gripped his wrist and pulled it away, fighting the instincts urging me to take my prey while it seemed willing. "Keep this up, and I will not be able to hold myself from acting upon you. Say the word, and I will take you under me this minute, Raphael."

There was no smile as he searched my face before pulling away. "Hold this." He placed the cock ring in my hand and circled back to explore my sexual treasures. "What stone is that?"

Fuck, I ruined it. Huffing, my body buzzed with the weight of my arousal. "Black tourmaline. It's a gemstone." *I'm so turned on right now. Shit.*

"Hmm, isn't that a powerful gem for rituals?" He didn't look back as he plucked another item from my box. "Surely you picked it on purpose."

"Indeed, I requested all of those items to be made with certain crystals and stones." I spun the cock ring on my thumb a few times, admiring the deep dark polish and carvings of wolves chasing a buck inlaid into the sides before placing it on the table. *I'm too hard to play with this now.* "This one is for shielding against all sources of physical and ethereal negativity so one can focus or center themselves." Caving, I unbuckled my pants quietly and loosened my breeches to give myself relief. "You'll also find a dildo of Shiva Lingam for powerful sexual energy and positive masculinity, a carnelian plug to increase sexual energy and inspire sexual encounters, and lastly…" I began to stroke myself, flustered that I had grown too hard to indulge in wearing my favorite cock ring.

"It seems my wolf comes with his own collar." Raphael turned to face me, his back to me as I pleasured myself. "And the stones on this one?"

"Citrine." I bit my lip to stifle a moan as I edged closer, pulling my shirt over in hopes I could release and become flaccid long enough to place the item my lord had brought me onto my shaft. "To help one ask what they want more boldly and for more enriching pleasure." Toes curling, I peaked, biting my tongue as he rummaged through my toys more aggressively.

"It seems your spirituality even finds its way into your bed chamber," he jested, reaching in for another item. "And this other cock ring? It's quite beautiful. What stone is this piece?"

"Tiger's eye." My shirt soiled as my sexual tension finally fled me, relief and exhilaration filling me. "That one is special." I steadied my breath; my dirty secret aimed to stay that way. *I see why he enjoys watching so much, but how can he not touch himself?* "That one is for self-confidence and self-worth. It's meant to ward off threats to one's sex life and…" I slipped the black tourmaline cock ring on, the coolness of the stone quenching the fire for only a breath. "…to increase one's chance at a threesome." Raphael turned to me, standing as his eyes picked me apart with his indifferent expression written on his face.

His eyes fell from my gaze, my shirt disheveled, belt unbuckled, and legs still sprawled wide. Raphael's watchful eyes circled back, following my shoulder and down until my arm disappeared under my shirt, where I still gripped my cock. He sucked on his cheek as his eyes lingered there. Without a word, he turned back to the shelf of erotic treasures. *Fuck me.* I could hear him placing items back in before the lid closed. He slid it back in place, stood, closed the bookshelf, and paused there for a long while. *Please, let's fuck and get this out of our system already, Golden Boy.* Raphael's hand held something, and I shifted, cock growing hard with the ring constricting me.

"I'm keeping this one." Lifting his fingers over a shoulder, he held up the Tiger's eye cock ring without glancing back. "Perhaps I may find a use for it."

He's fucking with me again! I stood, closing the gap between us as my temper soared. *Give in already!* Twisting him around, I pushed him against the bookshelf. I held the wrist of the hand in which he held my cock ring prisoner in a tight fist over his head. Raphael didn't push back. Not a sign of struggle, as he completely submitted to me. We searched each other's eyes for a moment, each wanting the other to show, *what exactly? I can't tell if I'm more pissed off or more turned on. What do… fuck it.* I kissed him. Lips pressed firmly against one another. His other hand gripped my shirt to pull me closer. The parting of his mouth as his silken tongue explored my mouth made me moan. My hands descended until they fumbled with his belt and breeches. Loosened enough, tongues wrestling and rubbing against one another. My hand followed his torso down until my fingers met their target.

Raphael moaned as I gripped his cock, stroking and rolling my thumb over the tip. Slick with precum, rigid and firm, I broke our kiss to drop to my knees. Jerking his pants off his hips, I hungrily pulled him between my lips until I could go no farther. Raphael moaned, his gaze upon me as I pushed off him. Glancing up to meet those blue gemstones, I began sucking and kissing the underbelly of his cock. My lips teased him, descending to his sack before licking my way back to the tip. There, I circled his crown and repeated the motion. His cock jumped in reply as the heat of my breath washed over it. Raphael's fingers caressed my hair, fighting the urge to grip me and force me to take him back between my lips.

My hands wrapped around him, snaking under his shirt to glide over the taut muscles in his lower back, licking up his shaft once more. He moaned, hips tilting as I rode my tongue over his length. My fingers followed the divot of his spine down as I gripped both ass cheeks. I took him in once more, bobbing in and out, tongue wiggling until I felt the familiar stiffness of his back. His cock was hard, and I pushed myself onto it, the tip pressing into the back of my throat. Another moan, one of relief and release, as heat filled my mouth, and I swallowed. Sucking, I pulled another wave and took him in, swallowing again.

The muscles in his body loosened, and I let go, rocking back on my heels before sprawling on the floor, flat on my back. The taste of him was still on my tongue as I stroked myself. My own tightness, the tingle and rise of my orgasm as the cock ring pressed around me as it kept me from peaking. *Fucking asshole.* The ecstasy of it made my breath hitch. *It's so…* My eyes watched as he laid his gaze upon me, sliding to the floor, back still firm against the bookshelf. We both breathed heavily in silence for a long while. *He wasn't aiming to do anything.* A smug expression filled me. *But to hear him moan… next time, it'll be when I'm hilt deep in him.* Calming, it took a long while before I could pull the cock ring off and meet his gaze again.

"Feel better?" I offered.

"Indeed." Raphael tucked himself away. "And you?"

"Could have been much better," I retorted. "We should have done this much last night, no?" Swallowing, I waited for the reply that took eons to come. *Why the hesitation after allowing me to play with you so eagerly?*

"Perhaps I'll entertain this much between us." Raphael's face flushed, and he picked himself up off the floor. "A bath is in order. Prepare me one immediately."

Is he upset? Or was this his first time having a man on his cock? I wonder… what exactly unnerved you about the ease and quickness of our actions? So much pining that I'm going to tire of it soon enough.

Chapter 20

A Broken Creature

The bath proved painfully boring. Raphael made me stand outside the room as he "tended to himself," as he phrased it. *I imagine we're jerking off in there one more time. What a waste.* Another set of clothes was brought over from Hodges Haberdashery in time for me to dress Raphael for the dinner. Fixing my own cravat, I paused to take this new version of myself in once more. *How dashing I look, as if I rolled off a boat from the Old Continent. Obnoxious.* Scoffing, I turned to where he waited at the door and bounced his eyes over me.

"Did I do it *properly* this time, my lord?" I smirked as Raphael turned away, ears red.

"Yes. It seems there's hope for you after all." As I pulled the door open, a maid was startled on the other side.

"Forgive me, my lord." She bowed her head. "Dinner is ready if you wish to join still."

"Absolutely. Lead the way, my dear," Raphael cooed in a sugary voice.

A pang in my chest made me blink. *What's the matter with me? Did I just get jealous over him not talking to me like that? The Fates must jest!* We wove our way back down to the first floor and soon entered the grand banquet hall. At one end of the table, sat Viceroy Vendecci with Madeleine on his right. Much like in the council room, Viceroy Regius and Viceroy Forestier sat across from one another,

A Broken Creature

each accompanied by their own daemon advisors. Raphael paused, looking at the empty chairs between each viceroy and at the open spot at the end of the table opposite Viceroy Vendecci.

"Ah! Viceroy Forestier, do you mind if I sit beside you? It seems so obnoxious to sit far off at the end of the table when I can enjoy food and wine with you and Ahmed here." Raphael earned a heated glare from Cruza.

"Yes!" Ahmed threw out his hands. "Come sit! If not there, here with me and Philippe!"

"Wonderful." Raphael turned to me, motioning. "You sit beside Viceroy Regius, and I'll be here across the table, no?"

"As you wish, my lord." I narrowed my eyes as I leaned on his shoulder to whisper, "It's because you don't want to walk a mile to have a seat."

"Yes, yes," Raphael gloated. "Thank you for reminding me!" He boasted, putting on airs as if I had whispered some important reminder. "Let's drink and be merry!"

Walking around, I chose the path that would take me by Viceroy Vendecci and Madeleine. Raphael took a seat beside Winston, leaning an arm over Viceroy Forestier as they began to banter. Glaring down at Cruza, my eyes caught the glow building in Madeleine's eyes. *She's pissed. We're breaking everything, ruining her plans to pull these men under her control. How far will she go to wrench back her power, I wonder?* I smirked, breaking away and rounding the end of the table. A scoff escaped the viceroy as I did so, but as I passed Madeleine, she gripped my hand. Nails dug into my flesh, drawing blood, and I met her gaze, unmoved. *Oh, it seems someone got my message finally. I wonder, will you respond to the totem I sent?*

"What game do you play at, little Thompson?" she hissed. "Do not meddle in my affairs any further."

"Game?" I blinked, brow rising in surprise. "Madeleine, I'm no politician, as you know." I motioned to Raphael, who was waiting for his wine to finish pouring. "I'm a servant to an invader now in order to secure my own survival and feed my coffers for the flesh. Much like you."

Madeleine's nails dug deeper as she tugged me closer, snarling at me. "You've done enough damage with your wild schemes. Back down."

"That reminds me, Madeleine." Now my eyes glowed, reflecting off the lavish gems on her necklace as I snarled, "Did you happen to find my trinket of the Devoted Sister?" Madeleine cringed before letting go of her grip and putting the statue in my hand. "I see, so is that your final decision? You do know what a returned totem in blood means, right?"

"Indeed." Madeleine's eyes seemed feral and violent. "Consider this my reply, and I will agree to it as the Devoted Sister intended."

Walking away, I glanced down. The Devoted Sister totem was broken in half and covered in blood; my nose tingled in recognition of hers and my presence. *She wants a war. Such an ill omen for someone to break a spiritual totem. Did she try to deactivate the curse, I wonder? Dammit, this means she's willing to trample on the gods themselves. Keep that up, Fanged Lady, and we'll both fall under their gaze and be put through a hell like no other. Ah, and to think there are not many of these totems left from the old days.* Pushing it into my pockets, I made my way to where Ahmed and Philippe sat. Glancing back at Raphael, he arched a brow. *Fuck. My sour mood is written on my face. This is between me and him... stay out of it, Golden Boy.*

"Where would you prefer me to sit, Viceroy Regius?" I bowed my head to try to hide the scowl.

"Sit here on the other side of Philippe. Surely you two have much to catch up on!" Ahmed stood, reaching across the table. "Raphael, try this wine. I assure you it's sharp and dry upon one's tongue but has a buzz like no other!"

"Yes! Let me try all the wines of Grandemere!" Raphael shouted, downing the glass in order to make room for the next option. "Fill my goblet, Ahmed!"

As I sat down next to Philippe, he didn't spare me even a glance. He took a sip of his wine as he drummed his fingers on the table. I motioned for the bottle of wine, and when he ignored me, I stood and reached over him and his plate. Philippe shoved back, looking at me like I was a wild man, and I retreated with the bottle. Smiling, I hummed to myself as I topped off my glass and clunked the bottle between us. *I wonder. Does he know his sister agreed to a blood curse with a Thompson? Should I bother to tell the only other man more religious than myself?* Raising my glass, I gave cheers to him, and he rolled his eyes, sucking on a cheek as he looked away once more. *Na, he's in a sour mood. Let's not press my luck. He nearly freed me of my head in Winter's Perch over a flower that was plucked by many others before me.*

"You've always been ... uncivilized," Philippe retorted at last.

"He speaks," I jested, taking a large gulp of wine. "And here I thought you were still mad at me, Philippe."

"What was the meaning of today?" Philippe inquired as Ahmed leaned over the table once more to play some strange drinking game with Raphael.

"You're welcome," I replied, earning a side glance of disapproval. "Come on, Philippe." I threw an arm over him, finishing my wine and pouring more into it. "You're older than I by a long shot, yet you let that bloodthirsty-witch-of-a-sister continue to torture you after she offered your mother's head on a platter to the man she now serves, well, plays on her puppet strings for the fun of destroying our home. Tell me I'm wrong."

Philippe inhaled deeply and said nothing. He took another gulp of his wine as he stared off once more, his thoughts and emotions guarded under his stoic demeanor.

He always falls silent when he doesn't want to reveal he's wrong or in agreement with matters involving Madeleine. Must suck to have a shit sister like that. Lillian, whatever thing you are doing in this moment, know that I adore you more every day! Don't change, you shady wild woman!

A Broken Creature

"Listen, we can't let these assholes ruin the place we love, right?" I refilled his glass now before setting the bottle down. "And we both know she'd burn it to the ground to hear everyone wail in pain as they died under her thumb."

Philippe sighed, a loud and annoyed sound, as he took a larger gulp of wine.

"So, I will do what no one is willing to do," I announced, clinking our glasses together before downing the whole cup.

Philippe tapped his fingers on the stem of his glass before asking, "And what is this thing you are willing to do?"

"Accept the blood curse and plan on fighting your sister. We all know she has wanted one with a Thompson for so long. How could she resist when I offer it for her willingly?" Philippe glanced at me but shot it away. "You know what I mean, right?" I refilled my glass. "It's no secret about the animals and that girl she killed. Far as we know, she's simply better at hiding it nowadays. The Fanged Lady is a hell of a title for someone who feigns innocence."

"You jest," Philippe deflected, grabbing the bottle from my hand to fill his glass.

"It saddens me she first sent an assassin for me and my lord." Philippe choked on his wine. "She keeps secrets from even you." I clinked our glasses again at my small victory. "Here's to taking down the daemon that might end us all. May her better half live long and prosper." I pulled off Philippe, finishing another glass as the heat of alcohol burned through me.

"You're mad," Philippe admonished, downing his glass.

"Perhaps I am." I shrugged, emptying the last of the bottle between both our cups. "But what better match for Mad Madeleine?"

"Stop it," he growled. A servant came by, taking the empty bottle and replacing it with another, and he waited for her to leave before adding, "She doesn't even know you didn't battle that day."

The wind in my sails left me, and I sat in silence. *If she doesn't know that, then where the hell was she during it all? Everyone knows. Surely the Fanged Lady is aware of my cowardice, no?* I reached for the bottle, and Philippe gripped my arm. *Why stop me? If I want to drink my sorrows away, I have every right to do so!* Glaring at him, I tilted my hand in silent warning, but he didn't retreat. Instead, Philippe grabbed up the bottle and took a swig of it before handing it to me. *What was that just now?*

"To those we lost that day," Philippe offered.

"To those who went to the Mother of Life, may our threads cross paths once more." I drew a long draw before my lips popped off the bottle.

Another wave of servants came, bringing the first course. We ate and drank; the backhanded conversation quickly turned into sharing stories of youth and folly. From chasing lustful endeavors to sharing embellished old man stories of a time something amazing happened. We laughed and poured one another more wine across the table. There were even stories of the Old Continent, and the time a horse was set loose in the castle only for my mother to tame it when no one else wanted to try anymore. All the while, Cruza Vendecci and Madeleine sat silent, staring at the drunk soiree unfolding in a knot at the middle of the long table. Before long, they were gone, desserts were eaten, and all that remained were foolhardy men alive with alcohol.

"Forgive me!" Raphael wobbled to his feet and took an unsteady bow. "It is time for me to retire to my bedchambers," he slurred. "Come, Ashton!" He flung his arms out. "Carry me off!"

Laughing, I jogged around the table until we hugged one another. "Carry as a man in need of a shoulder? Or a damsel in distress?" Another roar of laughter erupted from the table. "Damsel, it is!" And I swooped Raphael off his feet.

"Good night, good gents!" Raphael slurred from within my arms. "May you find your own knight to swoop you off!"

The laughter dulled as I made my way through the castle with Raphael in my arms. My heart raced, the wine making me unable to put armor around it or tame it. Raphael nuzzled his head into me, and I sighed. *What a mess we are. Letting our guard down in front of our enemies was dangerous.* I shook my head as a servant opened the bedchamber door for me, and I carried him to the bed. *I fear undressing you would invoke unwanted play on my part.* Abandoning him there, I turned to the chair from before, flopped into it, and dozed off. *I'm a fucking coward…*

Chapter 21

Back to Calm Waters

With headaches and mouths full of cotton, we opted to pay a carriage to take us back to the farm. We sat across from one another, nursing our hangovers in joined misery. Sunlight shot through a crack in the curtain, and I pulled it closed, cursing it under my breath. Peeking at Raphael, he looked horribly grim as he stared out of focus. *It would have been worse if I had... why does he look like his world ended?*

"What troubles you now?" I asked at last, wincing as my head throbbed at the sound of my own booming voice.

"I'm sorry to have put you in danger," Raphael replied, leaning on his knees and pressing his forehead against clasped hands. "What have I done?"

I snorted, reassuring him, "It was not your decision. Trust me, when we see Father, he'll have more for us to do. All our work was for fun, but he'll put us to work the moment we get into calm waters at home."

"Ha, home." He glanced up at me, grimacing from his own headache. "I wish I knew what that word meant."

Daring to look out the window, I squinted at the passing trees. "My home is your home."

Smirking, Raphael quipped, "You say that in hopes I reply, *my whorehouse is your whorehouse.*"

"Perhaps." I arched a brow and added, "I don't think I can forgive you for ruining my fun with Beau and Jen the other night."

"And what of our night?" he pried, and my stomach knotted.

"I should be asking you that." I met his gaze, at last, my expression fierce, and he flinched. "I haven't hidden my intentions or wavered back and forth on how I feel, or at least, what I want. I'd fuck you any time, just utter the words. Even hungover and in this shit carriage, I'll make it happen." I lowered my voice and leaned forward to threaten him, "What of your intentions, Golden Boy?"

Raphael shook his head, glancing away. "I don't know anymore."

I scoffed, ridiculing him. "You came to my home with such confidence. One night with me, and you're as useless as a glass hammer."

"That's not it," he shot back. "It's just… I thought I was undeserving, and you've made me rethink it all. Three years of my world empty, and… you make me want to fill it until it spills over."

I leaned back in my seat as the carriage bounced on the rough country road. "Then we fill it slowly but stop hesitating when it comes to me. I'm impatient, but I find pining annoying," I announced. "You're my lord, and I'm allowed as your Valet de Chambre to service you in any capacity when we are playing those roles. If that's not romantic enough for you, then when we tire of it, we should make a trip."

Raphael furrowed his brow. "A trip to where?"

"To the hermit's shack?" I shrugged, crossing my arms. "Or my home off the beaten path."

"You have a place outside of the farm and castle?" He gave a baffled expression.

"One that only you know about," I confessed. "But it's a day away from the farm and not much. When my mother died, I disappeared for a while, and well, I built it to burn off the rage and calm down again."

"I see." Raphael inhaled deeply, his eyes wandering all around the carriage before declaring. "Fine. But I must aim that we can't do… we can't be…" The words were as painful for him to say as they were for me to hear. "We can't be official. It must stay a secret."

"Not until it's safe. If we overcome this before getting ourselves killed, I expect more of whatever develops between us." I went back to staring out the window, my headache gone, replaced with heartache. *Is it ok to acknowledge our feelings to one another in such a way that it feels like a business transaction?* "Madeleine has declared war with me, and it's not going to be pretty. She fights dirty."

"You seem so sure of this." I pulled the broken totem from my pocket, and he rolled the broken pieces in his fingers. "Ah, so that's what she gave you at dinner last night."

"Let's see what my father has in store for us for plan and information on the situation as a whole. I'm sure while we played Lord and servant, they were out gathering allies and news."

Raphael nodded, and we fell back into silence once more.

Back to Calm Waters

When the carriage came to a stop, we both woke from our unexpected naps. The sun was setting by the time we made it to the road in front of my father's farm. He was in the field sowing seed with a few of the other clan members when I helped Raphael from the carriage. I tossed a bag of coin to the man, and he circled back for Captiva City. *I wonder if he'll spend a night in Tavern Way. It can't be wise to travel at night with the wolves so rampant as of late. They always seem bolder in spring, still driven by winter's hunger, I imagine.*

"Ashton! Raphael!" My father waved at us from the field. "I'll be inside in just a moment!"

Waving a hand, we entered the house, and Raphael took a seat. His stare was far off as he lost himself to the fire in thoughts I couldn't predict. *What sort of twisted fate has the Sacrificial Daughter given me by tying our strings together as she has done? He may not believe, but deep down, I know something ground-shaking is unfolding between us, and all of Grandemere may have to pay the price. How could the Devoted Sister let such ill-fated threads make it past her sword and shield, hmm?*

The door opened, and my father walked in wet from washing the sweat from himself at the spout. "Forgive my presence today." Father's eyes fell on me. "My, you look rather handsome in that vest. Matches your eyes." He grinned, the glare that told me he could see through Raphael and me in regard to our infatuation over one another, at the very least. "Do you need to rest before I divulge the information we've uncovered?"

Raphael shook his head, pressing, "Please tell us what the next step in our plan is."

"R-right." Germaine sat and motioned for me to pour him a cup of water. "The Assassin's Guild is gathering information, though it's proving dangerous. House Vendecci is indeed getting some kind of support from the Old Continent still. Goods are being smuggled to them along ports in Amethyst Harbor, but what exactly this may be is still not known. I know Grandmama wants to speak with you both when you return to Captiva City."

"I can arrange that." Nodding, Raphael met my father's gaze. "We wedged doubts between Cruza Vendecci and the others. Farrow clan has officially been fully pulled apart. Philippe is under contract with House Regius now. The territory we mapped out has been awarded, but the best I could do for the Perines Mountains was get it declared as no-man's-land, which brings me to my first question. Why was it so important to secure the north and mountains, especially if no one returns from there?"

My father smiled, gulping the whole glass of water down and handing it back to me for another. "It's one of the Thompson's biggest secrets. I suppose I owe you some transparency on this one." Leaning forward, Germaine tapped the table as he spoke. "You see, there are a few things that need to be off-limits or protected. First is the old Temple of the Fates. No one knows it's out there and still stands on the northern point of the Forest of Wayward Souls, or whatever is left of it after the Great Culling when they locked away the world's magic to protect mankind.

The other is that there's an ancient city in those mountains, and there are folks who live there. We suspect it belonged to the Fates and gods themselves long ago before they abandoned it, and it was rediscovered. Unlike the rest of the range covered in ice and snow, the city there is within a pocket of warmth thanks to hot springs from underground."

"That place actually exists. I thought those were just some old bedtime stories." I placed the cup in front of him, marveling over the information.

Gulping it down, Father sighed. "Your mother and I have visited both. As clan chief, I must travel and check on it every so often and make historical notes in the records we house here in the vault. It's our duty to protect our past and relics. These two detailed are among those precious legacies we Thompsons only keep."

"So, the other clans are unaware these things exist?" Raphael shook his head, processing the information. "Why keep them secret from other daemons?"

"Dark magic," answered my father with ease. "They say these are places rooted in magic or in connection to the gods, which means if someone wanted to undo what the Fates have done, you'd need to do it there at the temple or even in the ancient city of Prevera. Well, that's just what I suspect from what I have researched."

"Are we sure Madeleine knows nothing of these places?" Nausea waved over me as my imagination cooked up nightmare fuel to last me all of eternity. "The Fanged Lady surely would destroy the world for just a taste of it."

"Positive." Father stood, pointing to one of the three doors. "You boys get some rest. Lillian just returned and is taking up a bed in there, and the other one is mine, and I'm not sharing."

Father walked out, and we froze, exchanging worried expressions. *After what I said in the carriage, would he even feel okay sleeping in a single bed with me? Should I express that I'm honestly too fucking tired for...* At last, I shook my head, walked over, and pushed open the door. Inside there were two beds on opposite sides, and I could breathe again. *Damn you, Old Man. I completely forgot that during planting and harvesting, we set up two beds to a room, besides yours. Fuck me. Since when do I panic about sharing a bed or sleeping on the fucking floor?*

My temper rose, and I turned to Raphael. "There are two beds. Let's rest."

Raphael pulled to his feet, a look of relief across his face as well. *This awkwardness had better go away after some sleep, or we're going to get caught when we go back in a few days. I fucking hate pining.*

Chapter 22

Sowing the Seeds

The sun beat down on my bare back as I cut rows into the field. It was the last one to plant, and Raphael was still asleep when I snuck out. My arms burned with my efforts as I drudged the soil, churning the dirt to break the hardened top layer and leave a trench for seeds in my wake. Sweat trickled down my forehead, dripping off my brow as I leaned into the rhythm. Following behind me were some farmhands, both snickering and whispering as one dropped seed and the other kicked the dirt over and splashed water to start the germination process. My thoughts were muted as I lost myself to the repetition of it. Thud, scrape, push, chop, pull, a giggle, whisper, rummage for seed, slap, and slosh. I let it fill me until it's all I knew and lost my connection to time and the world completely.

"You could use the wheel hoe to speed this along. Hell, even hook a horse to the plow." My father had come back out of the cabin after taking a nap for himself after his morning efforts.

"I prefer this method." I didn't break from my drumbeat, breathing slowly and enjoying the smell of freshly broken soil.

"I can't lie. You might be able to beat the rest of us if we raced you using the wheel." Father swapped buckets with one of the girls, giving her a full bucket of water to keep pace. "When do you need to go back to Captiva City?"

"Depends." A grunt escaped me as the hoe caught a root, and I chopped it up. "Should we see Grandmama before the next meeting?"

"I imagine so." Father scratched a cheek and squinted his eyes up at the sky. "She seemed pretty angry."

"Yeah, well, she can stand in line." I made it to the end of the row, turning to keep going as I started working down the next row, passing them. Thud, scrape. "There's not a person in Grandemere who isn't pissed off at me at this point."

"She was mad at both of you," Father added, arching a brow at me.

"Raphael has a line, too, but we knew that." I hit a rock, the handle jolted and vibrated, threatening to numb my arms. "What we're doing is going to only piss more off before it gets better, but we knew that, too." Reaching down, I picked up the rock and threw it into the woods, and crows cawed in reply to the intrusive falling stone. "I deserve to be hated after what I did that day."

"That's your opinion." Father watched as the crows circled and started to settle back into the trees. "You don't see what I see in what happened that day."

"Spare me your theories today, Old Man," I drawled, growing frustrated with the conversation. *I came out here to not think about that shit. Just let me work. Fuck.*

"I'd like to hear his take," interjected Raphael.

I flinched, pausing to lean on the hoe and give him a disapproving scowl. "Don't encourage this."

"See, at least someone wants to hear me out." My father had a mischievous smirk on his face as he advised, "I think my son was brave that day."

"Here he goes again." I rolled my eyes, my temper spurring me back to cutting the ground.

"How many men have you seen go to the battlefield and voice their stance and walk away with their head intact?" Father pointed out.

"Well, I doubt a mother, even if she were the commanding officer, would be the one to free him of his head or ego," Raphael reasoned, the bitterness in his voice reminding me that he, too, knew the pain I carried deep within so similar to his own. "Saving one's skin comes with the cost of losing ten others in its wake, does it not, Germaine?" Raphael's words stung to hear, my own shame and guilt crushing me. "I could have died and saved entire families from being slaughtered." My stomach knotted at his words. "My death could have stopped even this—"

CLANG! The hoe slammed down, connecting with another rock. The metal end was dented and rendered useless. Breaking the handle over my knee, I seethed, meeting Raphael's gaze. His indifferent expression only added to the wrath boiling at my center. My father's lips moved, but his words were mute. I was too far gone. The girls yelped, backing away as I gritted my teeth, hands white-knuckled on the broken halves of the tool as my emotions ran away from me.

I threw the broken hoe across the field. "Fuck this!" I roared.

Marching away, I didn't look back as I aimed for the woods. A wall of cool air hit me as I entered the shade of the trees, but I didn't slow down. I could hear the throb of the pressure my rage brought pumping through my veins. My fangs

Sowing the Seeds

elongated, which only added to my torment of how much like *her* I was. *But not enough like her to join her on a battlefield!* I admonished myself, a shoulder connecting with a tree. The scrape drew blood but vanished as I smudged the blood and bark off my shoulder. *Fucking Le Denys and their Devoted Sister blood ties.* I weaved through the trees, and the forest grew more dense and darker. The crows overhead shouted at me, demanding I leave their territory.

The murmuring of water started to fill the air, and I finally slowed my gait. I remembered to breathe again, my jaw aching with how intensely had I gritted my teeth. The trees began to thin, and soon I could see the river just a few feet up ahead. The land fell steeply there before it met the flowing water. Farther up, a large boulder sat wedged between the trees and river, sunlight making it glow in comparison. Reaching it, I climbed on top and sat down, trying my best to calm down. My thoughts were garbled, a combination of self-hatred for my own actions and heartache to know the man I desired carried this same wretched curse of guilt on his shoulders. *Fuck the pining; we're both broken.* Laying down, the granite burnt into me, and I closed my eyes, trying to slow down my inner turmoil.

Hours passed, the sun gliding overhead until the night sky banished the light completely. A waning crescent moon rose, but its light was dismal. A low growl from the bushes beside the boulder made me sit up. Turning, I rolled slowly to face what I already knew in an instant. *Wolves.* Three sets of amber eyes cornered me on the boulder; the raging river behind me was too swift without risking drowning before it slowed closer to the Willow Waters farther south. I rose to my feet gradually as one leaped up onto the edge of my cursed rock island. The black wolf lowered its head, eyes deadlocked on its prey. *Boy, did you pick the wrong guy to fuck with tonight.* It snarled, and a second wolf, grey in color, jumped up alongside the first. With a hand out, I snarled and growled back. *Back down!* They barked and snapped, slobber and foam building and dripping. My heart thudded loud and fast, adrenaline pumping.

I blinked a few times to allow my eyes to adjust to the dark better. I reached down to my side. *Fuck, I don't even have my pocketknife on me. No shirt. This is going to fucking hurt when they attack.* Stepping back, I took a quick glance into the river just to confirm what I feared was inevitable. *Yeah, not happening. The water is up and swift. If the spring showers hadn't started, I might have had a chance of just being cold and cranky by the time I made it down a mile or so.* A wolf stepped closer, and finally, the last one joined the first two, a mottled black and brown-furred monster bigger than the first two. *He's the alpha. He'll wait for these two assholes to wear me out first, but maybe I can…* Now a wall of fangs and fur stood between me and the only path of escape. *Fuck.* They were large, full-grown, and nothing like I'd ever seen before. Each pushed close to my own weight and more than half my height. *I think they're bigger than Little Hodges. Shit.*

I shouted, throwing out my arms, and they snapped and barked, taking a step back, weary of my actions. "Fuck off!" I roared, growling back.

The alpha chattered its teeth, and the grey wolf lunged forward. I sidled to avoid the toothy maw, only to push myself too close to the first wolf in an attempt to not fall into the rapids. Teeth sank into my flesh, skin popping as it broke and gave way, the smell of blood blossoming in the air. The black wolf's head shook, ripping and tearing at my leg. I dropped to my knee, and the grey wolf leaped onto me. Raising an arm, I managed to block its aim for my neck. Now a second limb was held captive in rows of teeth as I heard my blood slap across the granite under me. *Fuck, this hurts!* Rage filled me; I set loose a battle cry in reply to my pain. Reaching down with my free arm, I wrapped it around the massive neck of the black wolf gnawing at my leg. The wolf panicked, trying to back out, but it was too late. Meeting the gaze of the alpha, I squeezed until, at last, it squealed and yelped before the inevitable snap of its neck cracked under my strength.

Recognizing the risk, the alpha yelped and leaped off the boulder. In an instant, the grey wolf released and was gone in the shadows of the forest. Scruffing the neck of the dead black wolf, I looked at it closer before huffing and dropping it. The tension left me, and my body trembled in the wake of life and death. Curling in a ball on the boulder, elbows to knees, I cried out once more. Pain and fear filled me, and in some sick twisted manner, it took me back to that day. *Why does my soul hurt more than my body is even capable of achieving?!*

The granite was black with my blood, like a wet carpet. Wounds burned, unable to heal as efficiently as the scrape had done on my march here. This was fear, not the rage that goaded the ability I had inherited from my grandfather, the gift the Devoted Sister had given to the Le Denys clan that skipped a generation and was only inheritable by males. *Inheritable by me. I was the next to carry it, and I've done nothing with it.*

"I'm cursed," I muttered before unfolding myself.

I checked my arm and leg; the wounds were deep but tolerable. *Some rest, and they should start to mend.* Looking down at the large carcass, I stood pondering what to do. *I don't want to go back to the farm. And I can't let this go to waste.* Reaching down, I lugged the massive corpse across my shoulders and worked my way back the boulder. My bad leg collapsed, and I slid down the side of the boulder onto my ass. *Fuck! My back's scraped up. I'm a fucking mess.* I looked to the sky; the constellations twinkled brightly overhead. *I suppose I can go there and get some much-needed isolation again.* Standing back up, I recentered the wolf on my shoulders and followed the river north. After a while, a bridge barely wide enough for a horse to use came into view, and relief washed over me. *I guess it isn't that horribly far.*

Crossing it, the water rapids and white caps glowed in the moonlight underfoot. The rocks here were sharper, more jagged, while the water ran swifter than where I had started. On the other side, the wilderness devoured the footpath. This is where one entered the true wilds of Grandemere. This forest took on a more ancient sensation. The trunks were wider, the trees reaching higher and blocking out the sky completely under their many branches. They called it the Forest of

Sowing the Seeds

Wayward Souls because so many went in and died lost, with no means to navigate through its never-ending acreage. *I suppose this is a fitting home for a derelict like myself...*

Chapter 23

Home of the Wayward Soul

By the time I had found the cabin, the sky had shifted to red and orange overhead. Reaching the side of the house, I dropped the carcass and leaned against the wall. I was covered head to toe with blood, sweat, dirt, and now fur. *I've never felt so disgusting...* Stumbling over to the well, I pumped the handle several times before the gurgle of water started to groan out of the pipe. *Come on, you damned thing. Don't be clogged again.* Water began to trickle, and at last, it rushed forward, smacking the trough. I ducked my head under and started to scrub my face and arm. The wounds had stopped bleeding, but the gashes on my forearm and lower leg looked gruesome. *These are going to scar and stick around for a while.*

Snorting, I pumped the handle a few more times and rinsed the wounds in my leg. *So much for these breeches. I'll have to buy new ones.* Something white and yellow protruded from a portion of my arm, and I yanked it from my flesh. *Definitely not giving this fang back.*

I ripped the shreds of fabric off, rinsing them before using them as bandages. Needing more, I puffed out my cheeks. *Fuck it. What does it matter? They aren't wearable like this.* Shimmying off the breeches, the only clothing I had on. I began to rip the fabric into bandaging. *Never going to work the field in only my pants ever again. No boots, no shirt, no knife. Fucking out here with my sack swinging in the breeze and not a person to bend over for me,* I thought bitterly. Lugging my leg into the trough, I pumped the handle and scrubbed the wounds that riddled my calf and shin. *I'm going to walk with a limp if this doesn't heal right.* Frowning, I glowered at the wolf carcass as I wrapped up my leg. *You and your fucking buddies thought you had easy pickings. Don't you worry, darling. I'm going to make you... make you...*

I licked a fang as my mind ran through a catalog of options, many of the images from Hodges Haberdashery still fresh in my mind. *Oh, I have options for days, but I need to get this healing now if I'm going to get back in time.* While taking a step forward, the wounds stung, and I muttered curses. *By the Devoted Sister, next time, toss me a blade if you want to see me fight. And you, Sacrificial Daughter! Making a naked man think he's dead is fucked up. May the Mother of Life punish you both!* Limping, I grabbed the wolf and dragged it over to where I had set up a dressing rack. With the wolf straddled and hung, I hobbled to the cabin and inside searched for the skinning knife and leather working kit I had left behind.

Upon finding it, I eyed a pair of worn-out pants tossed over a chair. My eyes rolled back as I tried to remember. *Did I wash those before I left? When did I wear...? Nope. I definitely tossed them there because they were dirty, grabbed the only other pair and went to the farm for work and...* Inhaling deeply, I walked out of the cabin. *I'll be tanning this hide in the nude. At least I won't have to scrub clothes clean after this.*

The day grew hot as I worked to skin the wolf and began taking off slabs of meat for food. Satisfied I had what I needed, I rolled the meat in the hide and sat it inside. Grabbing what was left of the carcass, I limped off until the cabin disappeared and a cliffside within the depths appeared. Tossing it down and away, I wished the crows a good meal and returned. Rummaging through barrels in the cabin, I found the sack of salt and started the next step, salting the meat. I left it on a burlap sack on a table.

Outside, I had built a table for the sole purpose of tanning or stabilizing hide. With a scraping tool, I worked the meat and fat off the hide. *I struggled to do this the first few times when taught back on the farm years ago.* After isolating in the forest, it was as natural as working the land for crops. I rubbed salt into the hide, into every crevice and seam I could find, until the flesh side of the fur had salt rubbed into every part of it. Rolling it up, I limped over to the curing rack slung between two trees. It tilted the hide so the fluid could run off in the drying and stabilizing process. Again, I did another round of rinsing myself and checking on the wounds. After pulling and rinsing the bandages, I inhaled deeply for the next move. *These wounds are too gapped and open, considering everything... I really hate thinking this, but fuck me!* I howled as I pressed salt in the worst of the wounds on my leg and arm. The salt made them sting and burn. It took everything I had to fight the urge to rinse it, *but this will keep infections at bay and speed up healing.* Breathing slowly, I rode it out, my teeth aching with how much I fought not to scream out a second time. *Salt. The does-it-all mineral of survival.*

The Champion's Lord

I looked at the sky. It was bright now, and I assumed noon had peaked, although the trees blocked the sky. My leg and arm were throbbing; I turned back to the cabin. *Fuck this. I'm tired.* Slamming the door shut, I locked it and pulled up the cover from the bed, shaking the dust from it. I was happy to see not much had settled on my bed. Laying down, I pulled the cover over me, and the world fell dark.

A howl brought me to my feet. My leg gave a sharp pain, and I let myself flop back onto the bed instead of forcing the matter. *Those assholes tracked me home. Shit.* Heart racing, I darted around, looking for the short blade I knew lay among the organized chaos of my home. At last, my hand found the hilt between two barrels, and I pulled it out. Pushing myself against the door, I listened through it. *Should have put windows on this damned thing but got lazy.* Grabbing the lock, I froze. I retreated from my intent and backed away to sit on the chair, eyes still focused on the door. *No, I'm injured and naked. They shouldn't be able to get in.* Another howl, this one closer than the last. *It's the alpha from before. I'm sure they tracked me all the way here. After all, I'm prey and I was lugging their buddy on my shoulders.* A shudder shook my shoulders, and I leaned back with the sword in my hands across my thighs.

I woke to the chirping of birds outside, still sitting in the chair and gripping my blade. Rubbing my eyes with the bottom of a palm, I examined my leg and arm to assess how my healing was going. *Still red, not yet completely closed.* I was happy to see healing was in order. Looking over at the salted meat, I turned my attention to starting a fire in the wood stove. *It cost a small fortune and took a draft horse to drag it all the way out to the cabin as heavy as it was. Granted, it beat the pitiful attempt I made at a chimney.* A smile crested my face. *The top of the damn thing crumbled twice, much as my life has.* Opening the percussion fire kit, I cut a few strands of twine and unraveled it to make tinder. Making a nest, I tucked a piece of char cloth into the nest of fibers. With my flint and steel striker, I cast sparks until the char cloth caught the embers, glowing red. I blew on it, and it lit the tinder on fire I tossed it in, and it latched onto the dry logs.

The warmth of the fire forced me to retreat to the chair, where I dared to lift the pants to my nose. The fabric was stiff from the salts of my sweat from ages ago and crackled as I attempted to unfold them. *Nope, needs washing!* Grabbing the short blade, I cracked the cabin door. There were no signs of anything more than small prey animals and birds. Crows scattered from the outside table where they had been indulging in pecking at the scraps from the previous day's work. I grabbed the bucket by the door and, with my leg still aching, limped back to the water pump. First, I rinsed and filled the bucket before starting the arduous task of rinsing the pants free of the dried sweat. Flinging the pants over a low-hanging branch, I hobbled with the bucket back inside. I eventually found my poorly placed pot and began the process of boiling the water.

Back outside I went, unrolling the fur to shake off the wet salt. With another layer rubbed into it, I once more rolled and returned it to the rack before pissing and retreating to the cabin. *I missed this solitude. Strange, the idea of nothing to fret over, no one to defend or offend, just me and myself.* The water boiled, and I began slicing the meat into cubes, dropping them into the boiling water. Once content with the amount, I went back outside, only circling back to grab the short blade. *Naked and wolves, yeah let's not do that again.* With a basket, I went in search of wild carrots and mushrooms to add to the stew. Returning with a decent amount, I rinsed them and checked the pants. *Still wet. Dammit.* Back into the cabin I hobbled, chopping and adding the final elements. Soon the smell filled the cabin, and my stomach rumbled in anticipation. I pulled the pot off, grabbed a ladle, and sat at the table eating and slurping until I had my fill. Belly full, I was back under the covers and asleep in a matter of minutes.

Awwooooo! The howl shook my lungs. Outside, I could hear the pattering of feet and the panting from the wolves. I lay there, frozen, as my heart nearly fled from my chest. Reaching over, I held onto my short blade while my forearm lay across my head. *Son of a bitch. Are the Fates testing me?* Another howl, this time on the other side of the wall where I lay. Anger filled me. *Fine, you want a fight, I'll bring a fight. Now I've got a damn sword, assholes!* I threw the cover off and marched to the door, flinging it open. The new moon blanketed the world in a dark abyss made of night. Amber eyes approached. Snarling, I yanked the sheath from my short sword and stood ready to fight. The wolf growled, and I matched it with my own. *Go on! Fight me!*

The mottled black and brown alpha stepped into view, our eyes locking. Unlike before, he didn't snap or bark. Pacing behind him was the grey wolf, its lips curling and the missing fang noticeable. Every muscle in my body drew tight, I took several steps forward, and he matched me until we were only an arm's length apart. My wrath fumed from me, the wounds healing more rapidly as I glared down at the wolf, reigning dominant over him. His head rose, and he howled into the night. Strangely, I found myself joining him until my voice gave out. I realized I stood naked in the night, alone. *Fuck. Am I having fever dreams, or did I eat the wrong shrooms?* As I panted, the tension cut loose, and I glared at the wolf tracks in the ground. *Shit, he was here. Did he just acknowledge me as a fellow alpha?*

Chapter 24

A New Phase

I lingered for another day, my focus on stabilizing the wolf hide before I left the cabin. Fully healed, I went about repairing and organizing my chaos, clearing my head. My last night there, I could hear my fellow alpha howling in the distance, and I smiled to myself. *Few can say a wolf met them as equals. Does this mean I'm indeed a predator of my own making?* Checking the hide as the first rays of morning light cut through the trees, I was happy to see I had managed to stabilize the hide at last. *Now, to get this to Hodges so he can pickle and finish the process. It should make a fine coat, even for a man of my size.* Smirking, I rolled it up and tied it with twine. Pulling on the clean pants, I started for the farm.

The birds chirped and fluttered overhead as I weaved my way back the way I had come. It didn't take too long before I heard the rush of the river and soon spotted the red bridge a little south of where I was. When I had finally broken completely from the trees at the start of the footpath, I froze. A man leaned over the bridge's railing, staring off to where the water ran south. I blinked a few times, and my eyes caught the golden braid laid over his shoulder.

"Raphael?" I asked, surprised.

Raphael spun around in alarm. "Ashton."

I opened my mouth, wanting to know when he had come, how long he had waited there for me. *He actually came here for me. You pining son-of-a-bitch.*

A New Phase

Closing my mouth, I found myself annoyed at how well he tamed his emotions on his face despite his actions screaming quite the opposite. *Not an inkling of relief, surprise,* but longing on his face. I picked apart those sapphire eyes as we stared one another down, unmoving, tension taut between us. *Part of me wants to kiss him, the other part wants to fucking throat-punch him.* I scratched my bare chest, adjusting the wolf's fur on my shoulder. His eyes took all of me in, and he, at last, smiled in that half-hearted way he was best known for.

"Are you ready to leave?" Raphael asked, motioning to the other side of the bridge.

"I need to stop by the farm for a change of clothes." I brushed past him, my tone clear at how displeased I was. *Not going to give you any attention, Golden Boy.*

Raphael's steps fell close behind me, the heat of his body and the scent of him so close as I neared the far end before he let the words loose from those locked lips of his. "I was worried," he confessed at long last.

"You shouldn't worry over me," I snapped back, stopping at the last plank of the bridge.

"Sorry for what I said." He shifted, the bridge creaking under his weight. "I know…" He struggled with his thoughts and emotions as much as I did. "I know you feel that way, too, don't you?"

My stomach knotted, but I turned to face those blue gemstones. "I do," I confessed. "And I don't like knowing you know the way it feels."

Raphael scoffed, looking away as he sucked on a cheek. "You're impossible."

"I prefer to be that way." I leaned to catch his gaze, and he gave way to it. "But don't expect me to give chase to you anymore. I told you that those emotions were no longer yours to have. Regret and—"

"—guilt. Those belong only to you." He finished my words before changing subjects. "What's that?" Raphael nodded to the fur on my shoulder.

"None of your business." I turned away, leaving the bridge as dirt met my bare feet.

"Of course, excuse me for prying," he drawled. "I did bring horses."

I paused, the two horses appearing as the path turned. "Oh no," I muttered. "You did not bring that vile thing with you."

"Your father insisted these were the best horses in the stable, and we were free to have them to help us travel—" I shot him a fiery glare, and he snapped his lips closed.

"That one," I pointed to the chestnut-colored Percheron. "That's Feran. He bites and eats my shit. And that one," I pointed to the dappled grey mare. "I'm too heavy to ride her. So what horse am I riding?"

"Feran?" he winced. "Your father said the horse is, and I quote, 'much like you and definitely *madly in love* with you.'"

"No, he's not." I puffed out my cheeks, looking back at Feran, who curled his lips and pawed at the ground as if saying, *come at me, bitch.* "Have you ever seen a horse greet a man in such a way?!"

Raphael laughed and stifled it, clearing his throat before saying, "Honestly, Ashton. Are you scared of him?"

"No, but we definitely don't *love* one another." Feran whinnied in agreement, head bobbing. "Being *mad*, that, on the other hand, is of some truth."

Caving, I approached Feran, who snorted at my approach. He reached out to bite me, and I pushed his head away, wide-eyed. *I can kiss my damn fingers and toes goodbye.* I gave him the death glare, Feran turned around and complied. Strapping the leather onto the saddle, I pulled myself up. He didn't even shuffle his footing. I turned to Raphael, and he got onto the mare, Ginnie, who danced on her feet before leading the way. Clicking, I squeezed my legs, and instead of following them, Feran reached back and bit my leg.

"Fucking cocksucker," I roared.

With that, he lurched forward before I could react and trotted to catch up with Raphael and Ginnie. I scowled, and Raphael furrowed his brow and encouraged Ginnie to speed things along. On horseback, the farm was only an hour or so away at a good trot. Abandoning Feran, I marched into the farmhouse and rummaged through my chest of things from under a bed. My father sat unflinching at the dinner table as he watched me do so. I pulled a shirt on and dressed more properly. Father sipped his tea, watching as I did my best to ignore him completely. Searching under the bed, I huffed, looking for my boots before turning back to tuck in my shirt and button the burgundy vest on, pocket watch still in place. *There, I look like a pretty boy valet again.*

"Your boots are in here," Germaine offered, before letting out a long sigh. "I imagine you went home for a few days."

"What does it matter?" I glanced around before spotting them under the dinner table. "I'll replace the hoe."

"You always do when you break anything." Father sat the cup down as he watched me sit and pull my boots on. "Do you want to talk about it?"

"No." Something in my boot made me pause before I pulled it back off and shook it out.

A potato hit the table and rolled between us, and he smiled before remarking, "That's where that went."

Looking to the ceiling, I held in a breath before groaning. "You're trying to slow me down."

"Well, my son won't do so on his own, so I'm having to get creative," he explained. "Your mother would want better for you."

Slipping on the boot, I stomped on the floor to pop my heel in place. "Every mother wants better for their child, no matter how horrible of a person they turn out to be. Look at Madeleine Farrow."

"Ashton," he warned. "We are talking about you and your guilt."

Checking my other boot, I pulled out a foot-shaped turnip and gave him a baffled look. "Really?"

"Your guilt," he pressed, dodging the turnip I threw at him.

A New Phase

"It's mine, and you can't have it," I declared, pulling on the boot and standing once more to stomp my heel in place. "Now, I'm off to save Grandemere even if it kills me."

"Ashton, you're smarter and stronger than you know," he called after me as I reached the door.

Looking over my shoulder, I sighed before nodding. "I know. I'm counting on it."

I know what he's trying to do. It's not that I don't want to hear his words. I was back on the saddle, and we set off down the road toward Captiva City without further delay. *He needs to know I fear the idea of having his death or even Lillian's staining my hands. This time I will stare my enemies down and howl. After all, that's what the other wolves taught me to do. I am a wolf at heart and this man at my side isn't afraid to encourage me to embrace it.*

Chapter 25
Grandmama's Insight

The ride on Feran proved more comfortable than the carriage ride. *Never taking a carriage again. Well, not while hungover.* Captiva City blossomed on the horizon, and we broke into a gallop to finish the last stretch. Feran's hooves thudded, the horse heavy, his muscles stretching under me. Ginnie whinnied and began to slow down, steam rolling from her nostrils as she panted. I pulled the reins; Feran snorted as he slowed and turned back to the exhausted mare, bobbing his head and high-stepping over his insignificant victory. *Dammit, this horse is an asshole to even his own kind!*

"I think she's too old for this shit," chuckled Raphael. "And I must agree, my back and loins are going to suffer much after that ride."

"Where to first? I know Grandmama wished to speak with us." I circled around and came up even with him. "And at the least, the apothecary can provide something to ease that, or herbs, for the bath tonight."

Nodding, he patted Ginnie's neck as her breathing slowed. "Let's go straight there, then to Hodge's? I can't have my valet in patchwork pants. Perhaps we should add some clothes for your little excursions back home in the wilds." A grin crested his face as he signaled Ginnie into a trot.

"Why does that amuse you so?" I sneered, unamused by the grin and sparkle in Raphael's eyes. "I almost became wolf food a few days ago."

Grandmama's Insight

"Oh? I thought that was none of my business," he quipped, not even looking back at me.

I opened my mouth to fuss but shut my mouth in contempt. *Damn my temper and emotions. I'm still all over the place, and my father's little chat is still riding on my nerves.* The gates were upon us now; the guards looking at us as I followed Raphael past the line. *Father and I always waited our turn, though I guess things have changed in this matter too.* Raphael flashed a ring and the trinket, gesturing to me as I furrowed my brow at the sour glares looking at us from the line that was as far back as the first fork in the road. *This is embarrassing. These people are going to lynch me the moment they find me inside.*

"Go on. You're good to go, Viceroy." The guard's words pulled my attention forward, and I followed Raphael through the gates.

We worked our way through the crowded streets. The Scarlett House girls and guys waved at us as we passed by, including Beau and Jen. *I have unfinished business with those two,* I thought bitterly, shifting in the saddle. Following the street to the right, it wasn't long before we were in front of the apothecary shop. My legs ached from being in the saddle for so long as I led Feran to the hitching post. Tying him up, Feran reached out and nipped the back of my elbow.

"Fucking quit it, Feran!" I roared.

Everyone in the street paused, staring at me before rushing and giggling about their business. Raphael had already gone inside, and I huffed in annoyance. *I'm going to eat that horse one day.* Catching up to where Raphael waited in the shelves, we followed the path back to the dead end once more. Looking at one another, I motioned for him to knock. The door swung open; a masked assassin peered at us with maroon eyes. *A daemon. They must be all daemon from Le Denys clan or stragglers from all over.* They nodded and let us in, and we walked down the long corridors once more. I hadn't paid attention, but Raphael led the way without hesitation. *I was out of sorts last time, but can I really keep my shit together when she starts up with me again?*

Before long, we were back at Grandmama's office and were guided in by one of several masked sentinels. This time, she was pulling books from the shelf behind her desk. Maps and letters were scattered across it. I leaned over, my eyes taking them in. *This one is in the Old Tongue, that one is Ancient Daemonis, and this one is Ogrean? Hmm, this is talking about Arbre Tombré, but I don't understand*—A pointed finger pressed into my forehead, the nail digging into my flesh as it pushed me back.

"Stop prying, boy," warned Grandmama with a fiery gaze. "Granted, one look and you've memorized it. You get that from your father's blood." She sounded annoyed as she sat gathering the documents and stacking books on top to block my view. "Good, you're both here."

"Father said you wished to speak with us both, so—" The snarl on her face halted my words.

"You," she hissed at Raphael. "You didn't say anything about the *Arbre Tombré* being hot on your heels."

Raphael huffed, taking a seat and crossing his legs. "Who else would be so daring as to chase a runaway to another continent? They did kill my family and destroyed the empire."

"That's not what I am speaking about." Grandmama slammed a book open from the stack and pointed. "There are records here from the docks showing they were the ones who had been kidnapping daemon children before you showed. You know something, don't you? You came here to see for yourself, no?"

My stomach twisted. *The missing person's reports peaked at one point before it went silent. Then a few years later, the invaders came and*—my heart leaped to my throat. *Could it be related to the journals? Did Father tell her our findings? The dark magic and—no, that's why we're here. She aims to pry it from us since she knows he won't say a word to her on the matter. But what does she aim to do once she knows? Chase down the missing children in the Old Continent?* My heart raced, my mind filtering through all I had seen, piecing it together. *I know he mentioned something about them that first night. Did Father ask him? Did I walk out before hearing it all that night, or has Raphael dodged this matter? What do my bloodline and his have in common? And what does Fallen Arbor have to do with it?*

"I didn't take part in it." Raphael relented, his gaze meeting hers. "It did come to my father, the emperor's, attention, when I was much younger. A young boy had escaped *Fallen Arbor* and was brought to him by the Ogrean Warlord, Sebastian l'Ifrit. Come to find out, he's the only known *disparate,* half-breed of his kind."

"Human and daemonis?" I joined in the conversation, intrigued by this.

"No, but at first glance, easily mistaken. He was ill, running fevers for weeks at the time. His memories were wiped when he recovered after nearly dying a few times." Raphael furrowed his brow as he tried to recall it all, pausing in thought. "They didn't know what to do with him."

"Was he even part daemon?" Grandmama's temper had faded for the time being; she, too, pondered over the details.

"Yes, I think that's what Winston Forestier was confident of since when the child got angry, his eyes would glow maroon." Raphael heaved a sigh, frustrated. "Forgive me. I was very young myself and trying to recall the details is a bit difficult."

"So, how long ago was this?" I pressed. "Ten, twenty years back? How old are you?" I fretted, realizing I had failed to acknowledge as a human, Raphael would be far younger than myself, despite us looking of the same age.

Raphael scoffed, smiling at the panic written on my face. "Almost thirty," he answered, amused. "And I think I was barely eight or so. So yes, over twenty years. And how old are you, Ashton?"

"Old enough to be your ancestor," I muttered under my breath. "So, if he wasn't human and daemon, something that hasn't been established despite so many attempts, which means he's the only known case of a daemon and ogre offspring."

Grandmama's Insight

"Exactly," Raphael confirmed. "Though the two races were never in a scenario to cross paths. It's already known that humans with either race are sterile in all cases."

"Wait, why is he the only known case? Surely there have been ogre and daemon couplings in the past." Grandmama started to flip through another book. "Surely, he's not the first."

"In all the records I've come across, it's too risky for any ogre to chance to lie with human or daemon," I answered with confidence. "You see, ogres mate for life. Something in their anatomy or built into the psyche is this drive that they couple with only one, and that's it."

"Right, right," Raphael interjected. "I remember later, Warlord Sebastian saying that once an ogre imprints on their mate, they can only reach heaven with that single person for the rest of their days." Raphael laughed, rubbing his forehead. "As a child, I had no earthly idea what that meant, but looking back, I imagine it comes down to the idea they don't ovulate or release unless with that person. I've seen Ogrean Scarlett men and women, but their endurance and never…" His words halted as his face turned red and met my jealous glower. "So, yes. The child," he redirected, clearing his throat and shifting in his chair, "means a daemon came to the Old Continent and whether by choice or forced to do so, an ogre chose to imprint with them. In short, he's the first *disparate* of his kind. Until now it was only ogres and humans that could breed, and even then, it's rare if it happens at all."

"Why would Fallen Arbor be fascinated with such a child?" Grandmama arched a brow.

"That is the most bothersome part about it, no?" Raphael thought for a long while before adding, "I believe he was sent to a monastery where they could keep him safe and tend to his fevers. They said his bloodlines were at war, and perhaps that was a sign that something sinister had unfolded. Whether it was a forceful imprint or an attempt at dark magic on the child, I can't even confirm if he survived."

Should I reveal they want the guardian bloodline? Or the idea they believe Raphael's own has some ties to magic? Glancing at Raphael, he gave me a confused expression. *Or was I the only one who understood the journals? That someone with Fallen Arbor is looking into blood magic with the aid of the dark gods to subjugate those who carry blessings of the gods? Would he even believe me seeing how he denounces all faiths, even the one from his own family?*

Chapter 26

Blood Ties to the Gods

Shifting, I rolled up my sleeve, loosened my cravat, and leaned forward. I realized the reason my father had said nothing to her or Raphael. *Surely the old geezer figured this much out. He's as good as me at translating all the old languages.* Clearing my throat, I glanced at Raphael and Grandmama but winced. Their eyes fell to my arm, and I followed them to see the white lines of the scars left by the wolf attack. My stomach knotted as I jerked to meet the wrath of Grandmama. *Shit, she's going to think I went looking for trouble after the way I acted last time!*

"And what is that?" Her eyes glowed as she drummed her fingers. "It takes a lot to leave a scar like that on a daemon like yourself."

"It just happened a few days ago," I defended, holding it up. "It's still healing."

"How bad was the wolf attack?" Raphael questioned, alarmed now that he was closer and could see how maimed the flesh had been.

"I'm here, aren't I?" I offered them, realizing I was cornered on the matter. *Are we really going to discuss this here and now?*

"How could you let a wolf tear into you like that?" admonished Grandmama, sounding disappointed at the wounds.

"I was practically naked with no weapon!" Rolling up my pants, I shared the more gruesome one on my leg. "And there were three of the bastards!"

Blood Ties to the Gods

Grandmama leaned over the desk, staring for a long while before her eyes met mine. "Why are you running off to the wilds naked to fight wolves? Do you have a death wish? What's wrong with your head?"

Raphael remained silent, his eyes chasing the white lines of scars across my arm and leg, undecided which he thought was the more terrifying patchwork.

"Grandmama," I pleaded, pushing down my sleeve and pants to hide it all away once more. "I didn't do it on purpose."

"Ha!" Grandmama leaned back in her chair and slapped her desk, making Raphael and me jolt in our chairs. "He who let my guards nearly stab you to death here in my office only a week or so ago?"

Snorting, I gave her a sharp answer. "Let's just say, Grandemere reminded me that despite how much I wish to be dead, I'm very willing to fight wolves naked to keep breathing for another day." Crossing my arms, I put the focus back on task. "Fallen Arbor has been working with the dark gods. I imagine blood magic is involved, and they are perverting the nature of things forcibly."

"Ha!" exclaimed Grandmama with a wave of her hand. "The Fates sealed magic away long ago."

"Yes, so I've heard," Raphael replied, shaking his head as he refocused his own thoughts. "But why else aim to crossbreed races? Not that I think magic is possible either, but what is there to gain from a half-breed between ogre and daemon?"

"Soul weapons," I offered. *Father, you left it up to me to decide to say something. You want to give me a chance to feel I can redeem myself, and after the last few days, I know I'm willing to take this chance even if I have to fight my way through it.* "We know that ogres have had magic despite what the Fates said about taking magic away. A means of creating living, breathing weapons using their own souls, and yet, no other record of humans nor daemon seems to have duplicated or come close to doing this. Whether that was seen as sacrilegious or just impossible in past attempts, no one knows. I imagine they are trying to create these same weapons using daemons and humans now with the aid of a dark god or using an altered ritual."

"But magic breaks souls, doesn't it?" Grandmama wasn't completely clueless on the matter, and it goaded me to keep going, to dive deeper now.

"Exactly." Nodding, I pressed on. "You see, that's why the Fates locked magic away. It didn't cut or tangle threads. Magic burnt them, harmed the very god deemed to hold and care for the life threads, and worse, could set fire to any threads attached. With that in mind, when the Fates locked away magic, it's written their hands were burned and scarred from their efforts to save who they could. In the wake of it, three clans were gifted the tears of blood from each Fate, and they alone would carry just enough magic to protect mankind, er well, daemonis in the newer books." Clearing my throat, I shifted as I voiced the speculations my mind had circled back to and had ignored until this moment. "You see, the Mother of Life left a little magic to the Farrows, the Sacrificial Daughter left something for the Thompsons, and lastly, the Devoted Sister left her own magic with Le Denys."

"What magic is that?" Raphael pried, curious now as he leaned forward in his chair, legs uncrossing with the weight of his curiosity. "You speak as if you have some sort of evidence of it."

"It's long forgotten," answered Grandmama. "Well, we can speculate on some of it, but as far as how to use it, what it was, and the exact terms of said contracts made in the beginning, were never written down or passed on. But the families all have strange quirks passed down the bloodlines that are rather unusual."

My eyes darted around in thought as I added, "And what is written simply states we'll know when the time comes."

"How dubious," scoffed Raphael. "Sounds like the rubbish from The Church."

"I can say this much, the strength of Le Denys and temper, even the healing, has a link to it." Licking a fang, I voiced more of my beliefs, reassuring them both I was well aware of what the signs were, having to study them for my own. "Same goes for the ability to retain knowledge with ease for the Thompsons, and let's not forget, the Farrows have a dirty secret of bloodlust that might have connections as well. It's seemingly obscure, but it's consistent and strange at best."

Grandmama took in my words, her face paling before she built upon my information with, "It skips generations, though. For Le Denys, it's every other generation for the males to have swift healing. For the Farrows, in every other generation, for the females to be born with a sort of madness about them and a strange obsession with blood."

"And the Thompsons?" asked Raphael.

"That's the oddball," I answered. "We are all born with this trait, no matter male or female. Though we have a tendency to self-sacrifice…" I halted my words, redirecting with alarm, "And what of the Anointed Child? Didn't you say you have ties there?"

"A fable at best," dismissed Raphael. "A story made up by my ancestors wishing to prove the emperor is one with a god or of god's blood. None of the men or women in those fields of saplings showed an inkling of talent. Not unless it's to have horrendous luck as a trait."

"Are you sure?" I pressed. "Surely there is something interesting enough for Fallen Arbor to power through all your relatives and still come chasing you to Grandemere."

"I am certain, but they deal with the unknown, even if it's not plausible in my own opinion, no?" Raphael made a disgusted face. "Honestly, I don't believe in the gods or magic. What gods would allow the sins I've seen to unfold over the greed of men? How could they not intervene and stop all of this… this…"

Grandmama raised her hand and spoke sternly. "It is not the gods' job to clean up after what we have allowed bad men to do and achieve. We must clean up our own mess as the children of this world."

Raphael's face twisted, Grandmama's words striking a nerve and forcing him to look away.

Blood Ties to the Gods

"Regardless, we're in over our heads on the matter." I stood and began to pace the floor. "If they find a way to use magic, we're done for."

"The gods would intervene if that happened," reassured Grandmama, contradicting herself.

"No, they wouldn't," spat Raphael, still not meeting anyone's gaze. "We children must clean up our own mess, even if it does us harm … as I recall."

She scowled, her eyes glowing with rage. "So, what plan do you have? I'm sure your father has thought of some clever scheme or elaborate plan on this?"

"I don't know," I confessed, stealing a glance at her. "The first thing I'm focused on is the situation with our … current council." I gestured with my hand as I spoke. "We managed to divide the twins, but my concern is Madeleine and Viceroy Vendecci's aim to make us fight for Speaker of the House."

"He wouldn't dare, not with me being more fit and experienced in battle than all of them combined." Raphael arched a brow as he twisted to watch me pace.

I scoffed. "He made that clear to her, too, and she was quick to offer the rest of us as replacements for his shortcomings. She told him it would be the servants, the slaves, pitched as champions to represent the houses in battle. Do our clans proud, or some other grand vision just so she can watch us bleed before her."

"Madeleine's lost her mind. She's willing to throw anyone in the way of a blade." Grandmama drummed her fingers, covering her mouth in deep thought.

"We already knew that long before the invaders came." Halting, I met Raphael's worried expression. "What do you think?"

"I'll do everything I can to dissuade them from this. It's the same process they started in the empire before everything went to shit. Seems foolish to even chase such a method seeing what damage it did in the Old Continent." Raphael looked off for a moment before snapping his eyes back to me. "We can't let them do this again. Worse, it's no longer members of their household like before, and they will be more likely to agree to it."

"Then we will aim to convince them of another way." Looking at Grandmama, I pressed, "Are you still mad at us?"

She jolted from her thoughts and sighed, speaking softer than before, "Yes, but for far different reasons. I was scared this man had misled you and your father, but it seems he's been more than willing to share knowledge. If you can't convince them to not start battling for power, who will be taking the role of champion for House Traibon?"

"It doesn't matter," interrupted Raphael, rising to his feet. "I will not let anyone come to harm in my name, especially those I promised to protect." Raphael marched for the door, signaling he was done talking. "We must get going, but we will return and compare our findings often, Lady?"

She smiled, her gaze gliding over to me for a fleeting moment before she answered, "Call me Madame Cabernet."

Rolling my eyes, I followed him out the door muttering, "Of course you'd name yourself after your favorite wine. Why not?"

The Champion's Lord

I followed Raphael out of the assassin's hideout and through the apothecary shop. He remained silent and tight-lipped, not even exchanging a glance with me. We rode our horses to Hodge's Haberdashery, where he commissioned a few items and was back out the door. I stood there, baffled by the speed with which he went about his business, holding my wolf fur in my arms. Fighting the urge to rush back out of the store after him, I shook my head and refocused on the equally confused Little Hodges.

"Your father?" I inquired.

"Walking about on his own now." Little Hodges nodded, taking the fur from me. "Stitching a commission for you and Lord Raphael personally, since he says he owes you both that much."

"Good. That means you can keep more business pouring in here." I helped him unravel the skin, and he gasped. "Gorgeous, no?" I arched a brow, a sense of pride building.

"Sir Ashton!" Little Hodges looked up at me and marveled, "This wolf is twice my size, sir! How did you come upon a fur that…" He flipped it and searched it before finishing, "…has no arrow or blade wound? Not even marks of a fight or scavenger!"

Leaning closer to him, I gave a fanged grin. "I killed it with my bare hands, naked."

His face fell flat as he drawled, "You shouldn't tell such embellished stories, sir. It's not very gentleman-like."

I shrugged, tickled at the reaction. "I'll remember that bit of advice, Little Hodges. Can you tan this for me?"

"Yes, in fact, on the house," he added. "But what on earth are you going to do with this? It's even big enough to wrap around you and make a full-bodied coat."

My eyes widened. *That's it!* "A coat for my lord. Is that doable? Put it on my tab, though. It's a gift, after all." Rummaging in my pockets, I sprinkled all the wolf's teeth across the counter. "Maybe fashion the fangs or teeth into it somehow?"

Hodges grabbed them up, excited by the trinkets. "Yes, of course." Looking up, he asked, "Are you all right if the price is higher than expected? I wish to go shopping for jewels and things to incorporate alongside these."

Pondering it, I grinned. "Only if it's Tiger's eyes or, perhaps, citrine. Yes, boldness to express…" My face heated, and I shook that night out of my thoughts, remembering the treasure of mine he kept.

"Absolutely." Little Hodges scribbled in his notebook and smiled widely. "And I already have his measurements, so this will please my father. We will both work on this; it'll be the first fur coat I've ever done." He winced at his words, a distraught expression on his face as he hurriedly added, "That is, if that's alright with you?"

Reaching over, I ruffled his hair. "Very well. I look forward to the first of many masterpieces you make, Little Hodges."

Walking out, Raphael sat on his saddle, waiting for me. Again, that indifferent expression irked me, and my temper flared. *That's fine. He can give me that mask*

126

anytime, but I'm starting to piece together who and what he is under the skin. Broken as I am, bitter to the core, and soon he'll be bent over the table for me, and me alone.

Chapter 27
Master of my Lord

With our horses in the castle stable, we made our way to my bedroom within the Tower. Once more, the maid led us, and I barely held back the smirk on my face as Raphael's face flushed in front of the door. *I don't mind this, but I do wonder. It seems rather strange to be visiting officials and given the same room again and again. Normally, it's never the same one twice.* Grabbing her arm, I held her there until Raphael entered and, at last, pushed for an answer.

"Is this our designated room moving forward?" I whispered.

"Y-yes." I let go, seeing how she trembled.

"And who chose it for us?" This answer mattered the most.

"I believe the head butler did," she offered, uncertain.

"And who is that? Did they not change the head butler when the new council came into power?" I searched her face, hoping that some hint of information or emotion would reveal more than the words she had to offer me.

"They did, but, but…" She swallowed, bowing and backing away. "I'll send the head butler over. Perhaps they may be best to—"

"No need." Sighing, I waved a hand in dismissal. "I was just curious." *Perhaps someone on the staff was promoted to that position. It's not like it was a grand secret that this was always to be my bedroom when I stayed here before.*

"V-very well," she stuttered before rushing off.

"What was that about?" Raphael arched a brow, leaning on the door frame, arms crossed.

"I was curious who assigned the rooms." I brushed past him and flopped into my chair.

Closing the door in my wake, Raphael walked over to the statue that doubled as a lever to my treasures. "And why would that matter? Do you not like this room anymore?" He shot me a heated glare, and I sat up, intrigued by this new expression.

Are we upset to think I would want a different room, far from my secret stash of pleasures? "Well, if she had said Cruza or Madeleine insisted, I'd be a little wary of assassins," I offered, enjoying how his fingers caressed the statue as if tempted to open the shelf. *I dare you. Just twist it. You know you want to, Golden Boy.*

Ripping his face from me, Raphael replied, "I see. So, who was it?"

"The head butler, but practically all the staff know I prefer this room and decorated it myself." On that note, Raphael's eyes swiveled about as if seeing the room for the first time.

"I suppose I can tolerate your tastes." Narrowing my eyes at him, he broke away from the statue to shed his coat. "I wish to bathe; dinner will start shortly."

I rose to my feet with a grunt and marched to where a tassel hung next to the door. Pulling it, I rang the servant's bell and waited. After a while, someone knocked at the door, and I relayed to ready the bath. Raphael stood at the vanity, glaring himself down in the mirror. *Deep, dark thoughts are on his mind tonight. Is it about what we discussed with Grandmama? Or are they thoughts of me? Preferably the last.* Approaching from behind, he didn't react as my arms came around to relieve him of his cravat and jabot. Blue gemstones locked on me as I unlaced the top of his shirt before my arms descended. I pressed my body behind him, and he stood, leaning into me for a fleeting second before righting himself. *As I thought… those are dark desires of his daemon wolf.* Biting my lip, I stifled the urge to smirk.

My hands worked slowly, the mirror showing me the wondrous actions of my teasing. Raphael watched, straight-faced as he had done in the Scarlett House. I unbuckled his belt, pulled it away, and placed it on the vanity. Now I unfastened his breeches, and he held his breath as if he had forgotten how to breathe for a few heartbeats. With his pants loose on his hips, I tugged his shirt free with agonizing patience, slow as I did so, teasing those watchful eyes. Our gazes locked in the mirror with one another as I started in the center front and swung behind and back around. The last portion, I slowed further, pulling the last piece of fabric from the front slowly until his eyes closed and his heart fluttered in my ears. *Oh, this is too easy.*

I wonder, how far will you let me go this time? Slipping under his shirt, I splayed my fingers to roll across his ribs and push his arms up as I lifted his shirt up and off. I dropped it to the floor as his arms dropped. No signs of him resisting, no signs of him engaging. *Just watching, but I know you're getting hard, Golden Boy.* Inhaling deeply at his neck, I took in his scent. Chills rolled over me, the moments we had here only a week ago rushing forward. Again, my arms wrapped around him as I pulled him against me, my cock tight in my own pants as I grinded against him. My palms were on his hot body, sliding off his chest, following the pointed muscles until I paused there between his navel and opened pants. *Are we not going to intervene?*

Caressing the skin there with the tips of my fingers, teasing him about where I contemplated taking this moment. *At what point did you close your eyes? I'm waiting, my lord.* In the mirror, his eyes opened again, the thrill of his gaze spurring me to press my hardened length against him. *I want to fuck you.* Raphael knew this and didn't reply or refuse me as I played with him. My own heartbeat thudded in my ears, the rush of lust rising now as my fingers crawled down, down, down. Fingertips slick across the hardened cap of his cock, and his body stiffened as, again, I rode the underbelly of his own hardened length down, down, down. I cupped his sack, and he grunted. My lips kissed his neck, a shudder striking his body as I massaged him. Another moan and I glanced in the mirror; his eyes watched as I worked him over. *Oh, we want this to go further now. Were we thinking about all those things I said in the carriage when I went missing? Do we wish for our valet to service all our needs at long last? Hmm?*

Drawing my tongue across the top of his shoulder to his ear, I, at last, whispered, "What else do you want to watch me do to you, my lord?"

Inhaling deeply, Raphael let his exhale go slowly from his lips as my fingers released his sack and glided up his shaft before he, at last, insisted, "As I've told you before, I love to watch."

Again, I pushed my own cock against him before gripping his shaft firmly—
KNOCK-KNOCK-KNOCK!

I rested my forehead on his shoulder. "The bath," I reminded him.

Leaning forward on the vanity, Raphael was breathless. A look of wonder and pained frustration on his face made me grin. *Yes, I was intending to edge you closer before leaving you high-strung, but this works as well.* Another round of knocking. *The staff is as timely as ever. I'll have to remember that.* I retreated my hand and started for the door.

"Wait," Raphael huffed and dropped his eyes to the tent in my pants.

With a smirk, I yank on my shirt, untucking it to cover the offending visitor. "Gone," I announced and answered the door. "I imagine the bath is ready?" The maid blushed as I leaned on the door.

"Y-yes, Lord—I mean, Monsieur Ashton." She stammered, and I recognized her from one of many nights of pleasure before the invaders were even a whisper on the breeze.

"No worries," I cooed and leaned in closer. "Do you think you can do me a favor tonight? Like before?"

Now her face shifted to a darker shade of red as she nodded.

Master of my Lord

"Retrieve two women from the Scarlett House for me for some fun later this evening." I smiled sweetly and licked my lips. "Beau and Jen, to be exact. And if you're off duty by then, you may join us as well, like last time." I gave her a wink.

She bowed deeply, her breath hitching before stammering, "Y-y-y-yes. I am f-f-f-flattered you would r-r-remember me."

"Is the bath ready?" Raphael approached, his pants fastened and shirt on to cover what mess I had started.

A shame, have some pride in such a glorious hard cock, Raphael. I arched a brow and announced, "Why yes, my lord. Shall I accompany you?"

A palm hit my face as he pushed me back into the room. "No, you're misbehaving this evening." Hooking an arm with the blushing maid, Raphael met my gaze with a smug expression and reached for the door. "Instead, I'll have her address *all my needs*." He smiled, winking as the door slammed.

How could he spoil our fun so easily? I paced, finding myself annoyed and flustered. *Why so much jealousy? Are we not both loose and wild men in our own right? How come...* I caught myself in the mirror and bit my lip. *That scoundrel,* I thought enraged. *He's spoiled me! All I can think is...* Covering my mouth, I hesitated before confessing, *At least let me watch you as I have allowed you to watch me. I want to...*

CHAPTER 28

Apples, Apricots, and Assholes

By the time Raphael returned, he had been dressed fully by the maids, and I had dressed myself. *Look at us denying one another any fun,* I thought to myself and chuckled. *Wait until tonight, I'll get you tonight. Golden Boy.* We entered the grand banquet hall and once more found Viceroy Regius, Viceroy Forestier, Henri, and Philippe in attendance. Glancing at both table ends, I found them empty, and relief filled me. *One less person to perform for tonight. At least we're in good company for the meal.* Again, I decided to take my seat beside Philippe, who seemed disinterested and annoyed all in one expression.

"Where's Viceroy Vendecci?" remarked Raphael pouring himself wine.

"Coming tomorrow, it seems." Ahmed Regius flicked his eyebrows. "When the cat's away, the mice play, hmm?"

"Indeed," agreed Winston Forestier. "He and that woman damper any good spirits."

"I wouldn't talk too outwardly ill of them," warned Henri Pomeroy. "If anyone is likely to act out over such commentary, it's those two."

Everyone chuckled over it, all but Philippe.

"Why the sour face?" I whispered, topping off his wine. "Did your sister's twisted knickers get your own balls in a bunch as well?"

"You're an asshole," Philippe declared and took a gulp of his drink.

Apples, Apricots, and Assholes

"Come now," I soothed, filling my own glass. "You may be right on that point, but why not enjoy yourself?"

"Because of what she will force upon us all." Philippe huffed and met my gaze, a rare moment for him with anyone. "Will you be willing to fight and put your life on the line to protect your world as you know it, Little Thompson?" Now he threw an arm over me, a new side of Philippe blossoming before me, and it unnerved my confidence. "You have tossed my shackles to the wayside, a wolf has freed another wolf, but now we will have to fight one another for the position of alpha, no?"

I scoffed, clinking my glass on his. "I just learned a new lesson on this matter. It seems there's nothing wrong with more than one alpha in a territory as long as you stay clear of each other's intended prey." With my thoughts back on that rock, my arm and leg throbbed with the sharp pain of the memories so fresh and vivid. "And you know, if you find yourself in need against bigger prey, I'll gladly assist. We'd make a good-looking pack of wolves, don't you think?"

Philippe pulled away, snorting as he focused on the meal being laid in front of us. "Let's eat and drink to that alliance, then."

"Indeed." I smirked, satisfied with how it ended. *He's in better spirits, after all.*

Viceroy Forestier rose to his feet, glass high, as he motioned for Henri to stand. "Please enjoy tonight's meal, a sampling of the Pomeroy clan's recent harvest. Many of the dishes before you come from his very own orchards of apples and apricots."

"Eat and be merry," added Henri before they sat down.

"And to assholes!" I roared, raising my glass as I locked eyes with Raphael. *"Especially the ones I aim to fill!"*

A roar of laughter resounded through the room. The night went on with meats sweetened with the fruit and dessert, trumping it even more so. Filling up with wine, I found a far less drunk Raphael at the end of the courses than the last time. Part of me was sad about it. *No damsel to carry off tonight, it seems.* Instead, riding the heat of my buzz, I grinned ear to ear as we made our way back to the room. *I have you, Golden Boy!* Slinging an arm over Raphael's shoulders, I carried an unopened bottle of wine in hand, eager to return to the room and play with what I knew awaited us. *If they haven't shown, then I shall get us started!*

Leaning into his ear, I whispered, "I want you to watch me again."

Raphael groaned in a disapproving tone before concluding, "I will never again allow you to undress me. You make a terrible valet de chambre."

"Lies." I scoffed and giggled. "I make a wonderful one. Men have wished for a valet to service them as I am willing to do at a moment's notice."

"Is this how you imagined servitude would work?" Raphael looked aghast at my information on the subject.

"Well, it's how it's worked for me in the past," I offered.

Raphael paused in front of the door, gripping the back of my vest to tug me back. "Next time, I expect you to ask permission."

Oh, temper, temper. I licked a fang as I looked him up and down before leaning close into his ear and replying, "I ask permission from no one to hunt my prey as I please, including you."

"You're drunk," he drawled, giving me a nasty side glance before palming my face.

"You wish." I pulled his hand off, his wrist hot in my hand, before I let go of it.

Flinging the door wide, I came in with arms outstretched and roaring, "Ladies! Your stallion has—" A blade came swinging at me, and I rolled away, the tip slicing my vest and barely drawing blood in a shallow cut across my chest. "Asshole!"

A quick scan of the room and I found three masked men in tricorn hats. Looking back to the door, Raphael gripped his side but found his blade missing. *His rapier!* I kicked the door closed and dove to the side, heading for the vanity. *Before he called me over!* There I saw it, Raphael's blade leaning against the side. Grabbing it, I yanked it from its sheath, only to find the thinnest blade I had ever witnessed. *This is an overgrown sewing needle at best! Fuck! Rapiers, I read about fencing, what was it*—Ducking under a swing, I managed to jog to a better spot to see all three more clearly. Images from books brought over from the Old Continent flashed in my mind. *It's a rapier of sorts, and it's for stabbing...* I shifted my position and lunged forward, the blade catching on the man's metal chest plate. He paused, looking down at the bowed blade before knocking it to the side with his dagger.

"Fuck," I muttered and rushed forward to kick him dead center, sending him flying back.

Now I was at the foot of the bed with the other two men chuckling. One had a hatchet, while the other gripped two stiletto daggers. They came at me. I deflected the hatchet with the scabbard and used the leverage to half-turn and dodge the first stiletto. Blocking with the rapier, I hissed. *Deflection. They are not like my short blade!* The other stiletto punctured through, the high-pitched pain letting me know he had indeed hit a kidney.

"I got him. He's a dead man with a hole in his kidney!" He remarked, pulling the blade free.

I winced as pain worse than my fight with the wolves rolled through me. "Asshole…" I managed to croak as I dropped to a knee, sweat pouring over me.

"He's a fucking daemon!" The dagger man pulled himself to his feet, wheezing. "Gave me cracked ribs, but it takes a lot more than that to take his kind down, you cur. Attack! Kill him dead!"

The hatchet man ran forth, raising it high. I stabbed the rapier forth, mimicking what the stiletto man had done to me, now aware of the lethal and painful means it brought. The hatchet fell from his hand, and he stumbled back, letting the blade pull out. He gasped, gripping his wound and staring at his companions in alarm.

The stiletto assassin came forward, and I managed to use the rapier to deflect his attack, sliding on my knee. Dropping the scabbard, I snatched up the hatchet and threw it with all my strength. It cut through the metal, thudding with a sickening sound. The strange air and gurgling meant I had hit a lung and possibly

𝒜pples, 𝒜pricots, and 𝒜ssholes

his heart. Yanking a stiletto from him as he started to slump to his knees, blood pouring from his mouth; I aimed for my last target.

Adrenaline numbed my pain. My blood was hot and thumping fast. The world seemed to slow down as I deflected the dagger with the stiletto before drawing the rapier across his throat like a bow on a violin. Blood sprayed, hot and thick, across my face and body. He gurgled, and I shoved him to the floor, turning back to the other two. The only one still alive was the hatchet man, writhing in pain. I marched to him, my temper feeding me. *They'll pay for daring to enter my room, my territory, and...*

A hand grabbed my wrist. I spun the stiletto high and ready, but I met Raphael's scowl. He jerked the rapier from my hand, and I dropped the stiletto and turned back to the last breathing assassin.

"I was going to finish him. He's a dead man," I grunted as the searing pain started to come back from my own stab to the kidney.

Raphael approached the man and knelt down. He was groaning, pale, and dying slowly now. Shoving off his hat and mask revealed nothing. Looking at the other two bodies, he glanced up at me as I winced. Blood oozed between my fingers where I held the puncture wound. *I'm so mad, yet this seems to not be getting better.*

Sucking on his cheek, Raphael sighed and looked back to the man, and started searching him. The man tried to keep him from a pocket and Raphael's temper flared now. He dug a thumb into the man's wound. My own stomach knotted, our pain the same. The man howled, arching where he lay. Raphael twisted his finger; his efforts made the man pass out, and he pulled free what he was after.

"You could have questioned him." I looked at the chair, then at the blood soaking me, and chose to sit on the floor instead. *I love that chair. They will toss it out if I bleed all over it.*

"Says the man who was going to finish him off." Raphael unraveled the slip of paper. "He's with Fallen Arbor, anyhow."

Furrowing my brow, I looked at them. "They suck at fighting."

"And so do you." Raphael eyed me on the floor before adding, "You were the first one to be wounded, twice before landing a killing strike."

"Teach me, then." I forced myself back to my feet and stepped over a body to twist the statue.

"Now is not the time to pleasure yourself." Raphael aimed to stop me as he placed a palm on my chest.

Chuckling, I pulled his hand down. That wound healed though the line of blood struck his palm. "I need to check the passage."

Blinking, Raphael retreated and turned to hit the next lever before shutting the shelf. "I see. That is a valid matter. Did someone let them in, or did they know of this place's hidden secret?" He took my arm over his shoulders, giving me some reprieve as we made our way over the other body and to the panel. "Who else knows of it?"

135

"Whores galore." I smiled, kicking the bottom to unlatch it completely, and it opened. "Joking aside," I winced, the pain seeming to worsen. *A hit to the kidney sucks.* "Only the Thompson family knows of these." The door swung open, and inside, the sand still lay undisturbed. "Good, that means not every secret is theirs. We have a chance." Looking at the bedroom door, I added, "Do you think more are coming?"

"No." Raphael pulled the secret door closed in time for a maid to step inside and scream.

The room wobbled and spun as the pain ate away at me. A cold sweat formed, and I managed to curtly answer the questions the incomers had for me. It wasn't long before Viceroy Regius, Viceroy Forestier, Henri, and Philippe were bursting through the doors. Guards were lugging the bodies out and searching the castle grounds for more. Ahmed and Winston were chatting it up with Raphael over the night's events. *I can't follow the conversation. I need to sit down.* None of it could be processed. *Shit, this hurts.* Words spoken to me bounced off like leaves falling in autumn as I sat back on the floor. *Oh, I feel weak.* The pain in my kidney grew; the wound was still bleeding. *What the hell did they do to me? Was there poison on the blade? Fuck. Do they know...* Philippe left Ahmed's side and squatted next to me. *It's like the one Mother died from. That seems fair...*

"When I said if you were ready to fight, Little Thompson, this is not what I intended." Philippe pulled his blade and cut my shirt and vest away. "You're too pale for such little damage. They had poison on the blades, didn't they? You're lucky you were able to take them down after getting hit with it. The Devoted Sister's blessing is indeed worthy of its reputation, but…"

"I know," I panted, wincing. "It hurts. Burns, and I can't seem to focus. The wolf attack was much better," I jested, trying to lighten the dire state I knew I was in.

"Shit. What blade was it?" Philippe stood in alarm, the weapons still scattered on the floor. "Ah, this!" He plucked one of the stilettos off the ground.

A flurry of disapproving curses rang out as Philippe burst through the small council. He hovered the blade in the flames of the fireplace before the room filled with a sweet aroma. I scoffed, smelling it, recognizing it. *That's the one. Yup, I'm fucked.* I heard Henri's shouting, but the words were lost on me as I fought my eyes from rolling back. Philippe and Raphael were under each arm, and time passed strangely. I blinked, and we were on the first floor, my feet dragging the carpet. It hurt to move, it stung to breathe, and it burned through my veins like a fever, though I felt horribly cold. Another blink, and we were in front of the Scarlett House, Jen and Beau each carrying a leg to speed me through. My eyes stopped showing me the world. More shouts, jars breaking. My clothes were cut from me, and with a great whoosh, I found myself underwater before it all fell dark.

Of course, those Fallen Arbor bastards know about the hyper-reaction daemons have to The Beautiful Death. After all, that's what killed Mother in a matter of minutes after her first wound. A fitting death for me. Did your heart race away from you like mine? Did your body refuse to move until it no longer allowed you to feel?

Apples, Apricots, and Assholes

Did the great weight of your existence press down on your chest and burn in searing pain as mine does now?

CHAPTER 29

Fever Dreams

I couldn't tell how long I'd been knocked out when the first hints of life came back to me. I was still breathing. My strength and energy had been completely wiped out. Never in my life had it seemed so hard to draw breath, but the herbs filling the air seemed to ease my attempts as I worked to pull in more and more, desperate to fill my lungs. The sound of water sloshing and the heat of it wiping my face. The room was silent; not even the sounds of the outside world seemed to make it to my ears. *My head is pounding. The Beautiful Death is a horrendous plant, and there's nothing beautiful about what it does to anyone, but it's amplified in daemons to the point … I should be dead.*

Cracking my eyes open, I saw Raphael from under his chin—the way his collarbone carried his neck, the pronounced apple of his throat, and the sharp chin and jawline. I beamed. *He has me in his arms. This isn't how I imagined this finally happening, but I'll take it,* I humored myself. My limbs were heavy and unwilling to move for me just yet. I drew in another deep inhale; the herbs seeming to ease the effects with each breath. My side throbbed where the poison had entered my body. Raphael shifted, and I became aware that we were both sitting in a tub, he was naked under me as he hooked his arms to pull me up once more. *How could I sleep through this?!*

Fever Dreams

"By the Divine Father, you're as heavy as a dead horse," Raphael muttered as he struggled to pull me onto his torso.

Oh, so we do have a religious streak when it suits us, no? I grinned like a fool, looking up at him, Raphael unaware I was awake. Managing to move a little, I pressed my heel against the bottom and pushed into him. The motion was faster than he had been ready for, and I knocked the air from him as I slammed into him. Raphael flustered. *Aw, he's upset because I wasn't gentle. Doesn't he know I like it rough by now?*

The cloth fell from his hand, tickling the top of my own. Fingers twitching, I pushed through the last throngs of the paralysis; the poison cutting loose at last. Slowly, carefully, I pulled the cloth away from his; panicked, he searched, tapping around under the water. The room was dark, save for a low burning lantern somewhere beyond my world inside the tub. *He's shit at seeing in the dark,* I mused as I relocated the cloth to cover my cock. Licking a fang, I let my hand float back to where it had been in time for him to pat the top of it.

Another huff as Raphael froze there and muttered, "I think my luck mocks me." He was hesitant before he patted near the wound, gentle as he searched my torso for signs of the lost cloth. "I have no intentions of patting a sick man down," he continued murmuring to no one but himself as his hand now patted down my hip. "But knowing Ashton, he'll never let me hear the end of it if he finds out." He now patted my thigh, working around to the inside, my cock rising. "What ill-will you gods have…"

Gripping his wrist in my impatience, I placed his hand on the cloth and my cock, purring up at him, "It's here."

Eyes wide, those blue gemstones found my playful gaze. "Ashton!"

"Last I checked," I grinned sheepishly.

Raphael rushed to his feet, and water slapped across the floor. I found myself dropped under the water's surface. Gripping the side of the tub, I crawled back out of the water, sputtering. I choked for a moment, my body aching and painful to move after being so stiff. My strength was only a fraction of what it once had been before. Raphael had fled the bath. He stood with his back to me as the water ran off his body. Gasping, I managed to calm my fit of choking, but he seemed too afraid to turn back.

"Sorry," I sputtered at last. "I woke just now."

"I see," Raphael mumbled before turning to face me. "How do you feel?"

"Dreadful, but in good spirits." I managed a smirk as I settled more comfortably on the edge of the tub. "I couldn't have asked for a more beautiful view upon returning to the land of the living."

The expression on his face shifted, rage filling him. "Why didn't you say something sooner?! We should have prioritized your health first, and maybe, maybe, I…"

Heaving a sigh, I tried to stand, but my legs wobbled, and I settled back in place, agitated. "Honestly, I didn't realize it until Philippe started, and I was in and out of it long before they showed."

"They didn't think you'd make it." Raphael covered his face, confessing, "I didn't think you would make it."

"I didn't realize you would miss me so easily," I grunted, pressing on my side to discover the wound still open. "Dammit, this still hurts."

"Ashton, you almost died." Raphael closed the gap, cupping my face with both hands. "How could you want to die for me like that?"

I searched his face. His body trembled with fear and rage that reflected on his face. "I'm a selfish twat."

Raphael frowned.

"You knew that," I reasoned, wincing as I pressed on the wound that seemed to be festering. "If you don't mind, I'm trying to take care of this…"

Raphael let go of my face, and I shifted so I could use both hands to press and squeeze out the rancid infection. "Ugh, this fucking hurts. It's got to drain. Water with juniper was a good start, but it needs to be expelled." I tried to sit up, but I couldn't get a proper assessment. "Fuck, help me sit on the edge and bring some light over."

Reluctantly, Raphael stepped back into the bath and helped me sit on the edge. The way his muscles flexed to lift me while my legs trembled and struggled to hold my weight made my heart flutter. *Fucking half dead, and I still want to think with my cock, ha!* Raphael muttered under his breath about the dead weight before aiming to retrieve the lantern.

I turned my attention downward. The first slice was healed and barely a mark, but the poisoned puncture wound was red and purple, and black and white puss oozed out, thick as tree sap. *Ugh, this is vile.* Pressing firmly, I felt something pop loose, the infection sacs breaking loose. The more pressure I applied, the more I could press out as I screamed through the pain that brought tears to my eyes. The heat of the pain made my joints ache in its wake. Another push and squeeze, so much pouring out, my stomach twisted as the rancid smell managed to push through the juniper. I heaved and shook it off. *This all has to come out if I'm going to live through it. Fucking had to hit the kidney, didn't he?!*

Raphael gripped my arm, his face paling. "Don't. If it hurts this much—"

Panting from my efforts, I swallowed. "I need a cloth to wipe it. It's all got to come out if I'm to have a chance."

Placing the lantern down, Raphael turned the regulator to coax a larger flame. I winced. It looked far more sickening, the smell putrid, and cutting past the herbs that filled the air. Raphael had a fresh cloth, and he dipped it in the water before wiping away the tangled mess of puss and blood clots. It was evident it had been eating away at my flesh deep inside, attempting to poison my blood. Another hard push on the swollen, feverish mound, hard from the amount. It festered so quickly that it seemed like dark magic. Another sensation of popping under the flesh as another sack of infection gave way. Pain erupted, and I wailed, squeezing it as Raphael wiped it away, helping pull out the threads of rotten blood and flesh from my body.

Fever Dreams

One more round of the torture, and at last, I could breathe. *Relief.* At last, with each agonizing push, a sense of relief was developing. The pressure and heat receded until, after what felt like ages, fresh blood poured from the gaping wound. The small puncture wound had decayed and eaten away until a cavernous hole big enough for a broom handle to fit remained in its place.

"Fuck. I'll face the wolves naked again." I scoffed. *I pray this was the worst of it!*

Raphael dropped the rag into the water and began to laugh.

"What's so funny?" I reprimanded him.

"I've only known you barely a few weeks, and in that time, you have had the sourest luck in battle." Now I couldn't help but smile at the idea of it. "And the only fool who would pick up a weapon he's never used in practice and attempt to fight with it."

Heaving a sigh, I nodded. "Yeah, I read a book once, and well, it took a moment to remember it's not for armor nor shielding. I must say, I don't care for your choice in swords. Stabbing and clever deflections is not my forte and does not come naturally to me. I prefer to press through as a bull would in most cases."

"I've noticed." His gaze fell to the wound that dribbled blood and seemed to be nothing more than red with irritation. "We should work on your battle training. Now that Fallen Arbor is aware and willing to come out into the open, it's only going to get worse."

"Yes, indeed." Scooping up the cloth from the bath, I wiped the wound clean again. "I'll need a bandage for this and some ointment with juniper and…" I thought a moment, trying to make a decision before settling on a choice. "White lily."

Raphael blinked. "White lily? I've never heard of using that before on a wound."

"It's not as well known." I peered down at the wound before giving him a half-hearted smile. "It encourages the wound to heal faster, but more importantly," I winced as it throbbed, "I want it for the way it can ease pain. The apothecary should have some bulbs on hand and can make an ointment or concoction with it."

"Very well." Raphael broke away, his glowing naked form bringing a smirk to my face before another thought crossed my mind.

How long was I out? Was there not a council meeting to decide… "What of the meeting?" My stomach lurched as he reached the door.

Looking over his shoulder, Raphael gave a grim expression. "I missed it, and with it, the right to vote against it. We rejoin in a month. Everything has changed." Opening the door, he whistled sharp and loud. "Let us go home and discuss it there."

My gut sank. *It was intended for us to be dead or miss that meeting. Madeleine and Cruza are working with Fallen Arbor. They weren't there, so they could feign innocence, but I know very well that hired men don't need a leash held by their master to do their work. Fuck. What did they do that we have to face now? No, it doesn't matter. I'll be the one to take them down, especially after this transgression.*

CHAPTER 30

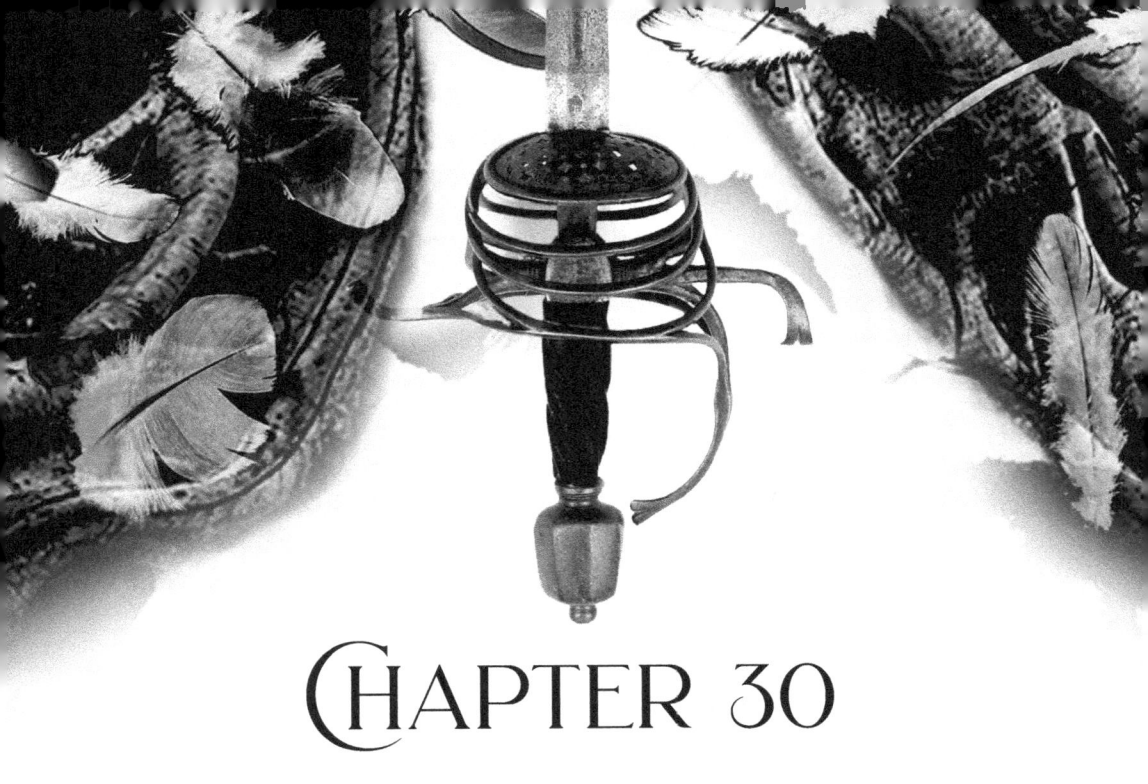

Healing and Helplessness

The carriage ride seemed shorter than last time. I slept through most of it, waking often to my head on Raphael's shoulder. A few times, I thought to pull away, but the wound kept me still. Each bump in the road made me wince and grunt in discomfort. *So weak.* Feran and Ginnie had been tied to follow behind, and when we pulled up to the farmhouse, the grim expressions on Lillian's and Father's faces said it all. *Raphael must have sent word about my injuries. They all thought me dead.*

Wincing, the wound still tender, Lillian rushed me, knocking the air from my lungs. I bit my tongue, ignoring the pain burning through me as she clung to me. Her tears were hot as they soaked my shirt, where her face pressed into my torso. For the second time, I was reminded that my elder sister was so much smaller and more fragile than I allowed myself to accept. Fingers clutched balls of my shirt as she sobbed. *She shed these same tears when they arrived with Mother's body.*

"I was so scared," Lillian choked, hugging me tighter as I tensed with the pain.

My lips parted, but I had no words. *What would I say to her? That for a moment, I thought it fitting to die our mother's death, hot on her heels, to see the Mother of Life? To be woven back into this world as someone new? No, she wouldn't want to hear that from me. It would be the words of my own despair speaking ill of the goodwill that the Fates have brought us.*

Healing and Helplessness

"I thought him dead myself." Raphael walked past me and fell to his knees before my father. "Punish me how you see fit. I nearly cost you your son and…" He shook with his dread.

My father's face wrenched, seeing Raphael kneel on the ground, waiting for his words, his anguish, his judgment. I met Father's gaze and saw wrath for a fleeting moment. *Sure, I've seen him flustered and mad, but that expression, even for the few seconds it crossed his face, is a first.* Father walked around Raphael, leaving him there in the dirt. Lillian pulled away, sniffling as she left me to stand alone against Father's warpath as he marched to me. Silence gripped me, and I swallowed, unsure what to expect. His gaze searched my face before he lifted my shirt. The bandages were bloodied already from the carriage ride. Dropping it, he looked off for a moment, thoughts reeling now as the clockwork of his mind ticked and toked through calculated decisions.

"You both may rest here tonight." Father turned away from me. "But you must go home with Ashton in the morning." He gripped Raphael's shoulder. "Wait there, and I will have someone prepare your horses for tomorrow."

"But I wanted to discuss—" Raphael started, but my father's glower made him shut his mouth.

"You both are not welcome here at this time." Father's words stung, and Lillian looked at me, heartbroken.

"Father, reconsider," Lillian pleaded, and he shook her off his sleeve.

"It's okay, Lilly," I spoke softly. "Come, Raphael, let's get these bandages changed and some rest."

I marched for the cabin, understanding what it was Father was doing. *He's so angry he doesn't know what to do with it. It's not all aimed at me, but mostly at the enemies and my carelessness. Despite it, he fears I may not be safe if I stay here… he's aiming to shield me yet again.* Scoffing, I winced, climbing up the measly two steps before pushing inside. *What an amazing father you are. Do you know no limits to what you are willing to do for your family and children? I wonder. If you had to eat the Beautiful Death for one of us, would you do so willingly and without hesitation?*

Making it to the bed, I sat and pulled off my shirt. The bandages were done for, and the smell of the infection was building up once more. Raphael came in carrying a bucket of water and cloths. He circled back to retrieve more items. Unwrapping slowly, I came down to the last few lengths, hissing as I pulled them from the tender wound, ripping away the last piece. It had fused to the healing flesh, and I grunted in annoyance. Raphael was back with hot water, along with the satchel that had my ointment and bandages. It took a while for us to work the infection out, using hot water to thin and warm it to ease the process of pushing it from my body. The ointment was working, the pain numbed, and the wound's coloration and healing started to fight back the infection with astonishing speed. He helped me wrap my torso back up and offered my shirt. Shaking my head, I lay down, exhausted from it all.

I startled awake, morning upon me and feeling as if I had slept for days. The bandage seemed clean, so I pulled my shirt back on and pushed out of the room. My father paused where he ate at the table. *Should I say something?* I searched his eyes before I turned and marched out the door. Feran bobbed his head, nipping at Raphael as he checked the saddle straps and packed a few more things onto him. Lillian was beside Raphael, helping and chattering with him. She noticed me coming down the steps, wincing, and came rushing to my side.

"I don't need your help." I smacked her hand away, irritated over the slow healing and crippled ego more so. "Besides, Raphael struggles to move me, so I don't see you doing much better than that."

"Well, I intend to ride with you both to the bridge. I was explaining to Raphael that it's not safe for the horses to go in on account of predators." I thought about her words as she rambled on, furrowing my brow. "In the satchel, I packed some tools, food, books, and … Raphael asked for a few things, but I don't think you two should be—"

"It's not for you to worry about." I shot her a disapproving glare. "You and Father be careful. When the time comes, we'll be coming back this way anyhow."

"I worry for you, Brother." She pouted, and I patted her head.

"As the eldest sister should," I replied, and winked at her. "Are we ready, Raphael?"

"Yes, I think so." Raphael shoved Feran's nose to ward off another bite. "I think this one likes the taste of blood, though."

I laughed, then winced. "He's got a taste for shirts as well. We can eat him later if he's too much of an asshole. Let's go."

Pulling myself onto the saddle shot pain through me to the point a cold sweat covered me. I held in the scream, holding my throbbing side. *Fallen Arbor has made an enemy of me, and I will make them feel my wrath for the rest of my days for it.* The pain dissipated and I could breathe again.

I nudged Feran, and off we went, working our way through the woods. It took all my focus to stay awake, my body hungry to rest more and heal properly. Behind me, Lillian and Raphael continued chatting, but their planning was lost in my ears. My own thoughts wrestled with what I wanted to do before I returned to Captiva City and the atrocities that had been voted in favor of Madeleine and Cruza's dark desires for blood and power. *A letter. I should send a letter out by way of a raven.* The red paint of the bridge caught my eye, and Feran stopped at the edge.

Unsaddling, another grumble of complaint over the pain escaped me. I started to pull the satchels and items off Feran, but Raphael was upon me like a fretting mother. He shoved lighter items in my arms as he gave me a death glare. *So hard to find such brilliant blue blossoms threatening.* I snorted and slapped the things over my shoulder. Lillian stayed on her own horse, taking Ginnie's reins as she waited for Feran's. Raphael groaned under the weight he took upon himself, and I arched a brow. He motioned for me to cross the bridge as he handed Feran off to

Healing and Helplessness

Lillian, who watched with a bittersweet expression. I leaned on the railing as we started our long walk, but the bridge shook. Turning back, Feran curled his lips at us, and Lillian was trying to pull him back.

"Let him come." I waved a hand, and she dropped his reins.

"But, Ashton, it's not safe," she pleaded. "If something happens to him—"

"I know you hold Mother's horse dear." I leaned, so I could meet her gaze. "But he's his own creature and always has been."

"Did you want to ride him home?" offered Raphael.

"Gods no." I snorted and pointed at Feran, who bobbed his head. "And you! It's on you if you get eaten by wolves."

"Should I hold his reins?" Asked Raphael, shifting the heavy items on his back.

"No, he'll just be a dick about it." Adjusting my own items, I glanced at the ornery beast behind us. "Don't depend on him to carry shit, either. He's bound to find it hilarious to scatter it through the whole forest because he can."

"Why would someone want a horse like that?" marveled Raphael, concerned by the nipping and nudging from the Percheron at his back.

I started to walk again, getting to the end of the bridge as the horse's weight made it creak behind us. "Mother said it reminded her of me so much; she wanted it even more." I spoke in a hushed tone without looking back at him.

Raphael chuckled a little, confessing, "I see. I suppose that's why I didn't back down when he nipped at me."

"Are you saying you'd let me bite you if I tried?" I furrowed my brow at the idea.

"You know," Raphael thought a moment before answering, "I think so. Without complaint, even if it was something you wished to do to me."

I paused in my steps and looked at him, and his face flushed. "You have some strange fetishes, Raphael. Perhaps we're both not right in the head."

After a minute, we smiled and shook our heads over the idea of it all. With that, I turned back to weaving through the woods. The pain grew with each step, and I felt the energy leave me. By the time I spotted my home, I couldn't move any farther, even when Feran nuzzled and bit my shoulder. I dropped everything and leaned on a tree. Raphael said something, and I shook my head, refusing whatever he had implied without even hearing his words.

Dammit. I need to get stronger. Being this weak is breaking me, and I can't stand it. Is this how Grandpa felt after Father defeated him? It's a mixture of shame, broken pride, and a horrendous weight of hopelessness. Granted, I came here to heal... but can I really recover from this?

Chapter 31

A Place to Breathe

This time I woke in my bed surrounded by the log walls I had built with my own two hands. Outside was the familiar crack and thud of someone chopping wood. I listened for a long while, afraid to move as I lay in complete reprieve of all the pain that had haunted me on my way here. Again, I looked around and frowned. *Fucking windows, you lazy ass. Next time, at least make one.* The wood stove crackled, a stew on the burner filling the air. My stomach grumbled, and I heaved myself up. The pain had receded immensely, and when I pulled the covers off, the bandage was gone. The ointment had been applied, but now the once angry wound had, at last, begun to close, and relief washed over me. *By the Fates, I'm past the worst of it.*

Standing, I had managed not to wobble, and my heart raced at the small victory. Eager to eat, I pulled the stew off and to the table. Ladling the potatoes, meat, carrots, and more to my mouth, I ate and ate. I couldn't fill the emptiness at my core as I slurped and inhaled the meal. The door opened, and Raphael caught me as a potato fell from the ladle and back to the pot. He smiled, the reprieve I had felt written on his face as he leaned on the doorway.

"Eat," Raphael demanded. "The wound has mended quickly the last two days."

"Days." I managed to say, mouth full, before swallowing and adding, "How long did I sleep?"

"At least a good four days, I'm not sure." Raphael stepped inside and pulled a loaf of bread out, breaking it in half and offering me my portion. "I couldn't wake you, but Philippe had said sleep was the best medicine for it if you managed to live that night."

"Ah, Philippe. I should fashion something in gratitude because he knew what was happening before I did." I dunked the bread in the stew, stuffing my face until my cheeks were full like a chipmunk.

"Already taken care of." Raphael reached for the shirt on the back of the chair to wipe the sweat from his face. "I'm impressed with the place. Did you really build this on your own?"

"The walls and roof. Granted, I cheated and brought in a lot of the other." I ladled the soup, hunting for a chunk of meat. "Rabbit?"

"Yeah, I caught a few. This forest is quite bountiful," Raphael remarked, chewing on a chunk of his bread.

"No one comes here," I explained. "It's hard to find your way with the sky blocked."

"And you?" Raphael arched a brow, dipping his bread in the pot.

"You can still see some sunlight, which, as you know, rises in the east and sets in the west." I scooped up another chunk of meat as my stomach grumbled, demanding more.

"But surely that's ambiguous because there are places here that get so dark, I thought night fell upon me." Raphael grabbed the ladle from me and ate the chunk of meat I had dug out.

"Yes, about that." I narrowed my eyes, leaning on an elbow to gnaw on my bread a moment. "There are other ways here to know which way is which."

"Is there?" Now I watched as he scooped up broth to sip.

"The moss likes the darker side of the trees, facing north." He knitted his brow and dropped the ladle into the pot. "And the branches like to grow on the south side where they tend to get more sunlight." Snatching the ladle, I scooped a potato up and enjoyed how it warmed my belly. "If you happen upon a sunny patch, note that the green grows on the south portion of the hole, and the top, despite some sun, is bare in comparison because it's darker for far longer."

"Interesting. I'll have to pay closer attention." Finishing the last bit of bread, Raphael headed for the open door again. "I just wish you were this clever about other things in your life."

"Hey!" I choked on my meal and looked back, but he had gone.

Rather pissed at me for almost dying, I see. What horrible humor the Fates have for pairing me with such a sour creature as my caretaker. Leaning in the chair, I looked at the wound and was happy with the result. *Ugh, yet I smell horrendous.* Heading for the door, I shut it behind me and found Raphael stacking firewood on the side of the cabin. I joined him, though he kept snatching pieces from me until it became a game. My smile only added to his frustration as I continued on like that until he stood with his hands on his hips. *Out here, I have all the time in the world to do as I please.*

"What are you doing?" Raphael demanded.

"Helping." I shrugged.

"Why?" Raphael snatched another log before I could lean for it. "You need rest."

"I've had enough." I swooped in and grabbed one before he could beat me to it and earned a scoff from him. "What we need is to bathe. We," I gestured with a finger, "smell horrendous."

We placed the last logs on the pile before Raphael dared to ask, "Have you a tub, or do we plan on a whore's bath with buckets and rags?" He gave a sour expression to the water pump.

Leaning into his ear, I jested, "Something so much better than that, my lord."

"I see we are high-spirited again." Raphael smirked to himself; it fell away when he saw I had caught a glimpse of it. "Let me guess. The river?"

"No," I answered as I started to walk into the woods with him close behind me. "Didn't I just promise something wonderful?"

"A spring of sorts?" Raphael's curiosity was growing as the cabin disappeared from view. "How the hell do you know your way so easily?"

Looking back, I smirked and kept going. After a ways, a great roar filled the air, and Raphael's eyes widened. *Yes, something that only you and I know exists here in the forest so many fear. A place where the world doesn't exist, where breathing is enough, and there's much to be admired despite the dangers.* I pressed forward, and the trees opened to let light cast down on a thin waterfall that sparkled in the rays like sand from an hourglass. Below it, steam and mist rose from the hot spring, a magical sight to behold. Raphael stepped out, staring up in wonder.

"Yes, a spring of sorts." I nudged him with an arm and started to shed my pants.

The water was every bit as hot as a fresh bath in the Scarlett House as I stepped across the slippery rocks. My wound stung for a moment, but the ease the warmth brought my aching body was worth the minor inconvenience. Pushing out, the spring was deep at its center, and I swam to the side where the waterfall fell from the cliff overhead. The water cooled from the spring above by the time it splashed down into the other, making for a refreshing experience of hot and cold. It slammed down on me, and I worked to undo my braid, eager for it to beat the dirt, grime, blood, and herbs off. *I want to be clean again. Start over even.* My toes finally found the highest point in the rocks, and I stood under the shower it provided. Arms out, eyes closed, I let it wash over me as I stood hip-deep in the hot waters.

A yelp and loud splash erupted from the other side, and I grinned. *Should I have warned him the rocks are slippery? Na, totally worth it.* Satisfied it had drummed everything from me, I dove off the rock and back into the depths in the center. Raphael had perched on the shallow rocks, wiping water from his eyes and face as I came up for air and joined him. His eyes marveled over the waterfall; *he's never seen anything like it either.* I smiled, leaning back on my arms as my body felt light and floated in the spring.

"It's amazing, Ashton." Raphael, at last, peered down at me. "Why'd you ever leave this place?"

A Place to Breathe

I frowned, my heart racing at his words. "It was hard to leave," I confessed. "Especially after my mother died."

"You had come out here before building the cabin?" He began to undo his own braid.

"I had a little camp set up. Much of what you see near the cabin has been here longer." I lifted a leg until my toes peeked out of the surface before dropping it again. "But I find I get the same troublesome thoughts every time that drive me to rush back into the chaos on the other side of that damned bridge."

"Family?" Raphael guessed.

I huffed, staring off at the waterfall as it filled the air with its drumming. My chest swelled with the word I couldn't let go of that lingered in my mind. *There's one emotion that always brought me back, the one thing I crave, I have lost, and desire even in this moment.* I sat up and glowered down at my reflection. *Can I really accept that this is the one singular star in my world that I navigate by? Will he think me reckless? Or a fool when I let this secret out?* My temper flared; anger pointed at myself as my eyes glowed at the idea of it all. *Everyone asks what is it that lingers on my mind, and I've always known the answer.* It was horrendously simple and yet, immature by far. *I've always known the answer,* I repeated to myself with sickening confidence. Clenching my jaw, I closed my eyes, fighting the rage I held for myself on this simplest of questions. *Everyone has far deeper resolves and mine, mine is lacking by comparison.*

"Love?" Raphael's voice rumbled low in my ear, a hand gliding up my inner thigh.

I opened my eyes and searched his heavy-lidded gaze, heart racing. "Just that. Simply only that."

His lips pressed against mine, and I pulled him closer, starving for the affection I had been denied. *This will break us, but here, we can simply breathe. To be nothing other than lovers where no eyes or ears eagerly wait to use our love against one another. Two wayward souls hoping to mend one another. The Sacrificial Daughter might actually know what she did when she tied our threads together.*

Chapter 32

What Drives Us

Wrapping my arms around him, I deepened the kiss, hungry to taste him on my tongue. Raphael straddled my thighs, our rising cocks rubbing against one another, making me moan. His tongue lashed out, drawing lines into my own, summoning it to slither between his lips. I suckled on the silken offender before abandoning his lips to kiss and nuzzle at his neck. Raising my knees, a hand gripping his ass, I slid him forward so our hardened shafts pressed between us. Raphael groaned as I worked my way down to kiss his collarbone, his hands clawing at my back and shoulders. I licked and sucked down to his nipple, the tip of my tongue circling the pink flesh. Raphael's heart thudded faster and louder. The heat of his body hotter than the spring that embraced us.

"We shouldn't," Raphael breathed.

"I don't care," I growled into his ear, and his cock jumped. "Save your sorrows for someone who cares."

I let my hand glide down his torso until I gripped both our cocks, frotting as he peered down at me. My other hand slid between his ass cheeks, pressing against the back door. *I want to take him. I've wanted to take him for so long now, and he knows it.* Raphael leaned back, the motion allowing my finger to slip inside him, and he moaned. *And he's been wanting me to take him, too.* My arousal filled me, tingling across my body as I fought to go slow. I shifted on the rocks, wanting to get a better motion to frot and thrust, our hardened shafts sliding and rubbing against one another enthralling. The flushed look on Raphael's face as he moaned drove me to do more, edging me closer. My breath hitched, and I peaked, muttering curses under my breath. *I'll peak a thousand times before I'm through with him.* Moaning, I watched as I came, and his cock jolted in reply, *so aroused by me—* Raphael's hand gripped my throat, snapping my eyes up to him.

"Don't stop," he commanded. "Don't look away from me."

I gave a fanged grin, and he squeezed my throat, his aggression goading me to throw caution to the wind. Two fingers entered him, probing and stretching him in anticipation of what would inevitably come. Raphael's eyes rolled back as he moaned. Frotting fast and steady, my cum adding to the slickness as we filled one another's desires at long last in those shallow waters. The weight of him on my thighs excited me; his legs trembled as he edged. *Cum for me,* I hungrily thought. My cock was still hard as his began to stiffen further, his balls tensing. *Now release, show me that face again when—*Raphael panted and moaned as he released. My grip slid over our cocks and teased the tips as the heat of his cum shot from him.

Again, his fingers tightened on my throat as I growled and groaned. *I want more.* Grabbing his hips, I pulled him forward and past my dick. His knees splashed down on either side of my hips as he assisted with my aim, the tip of my cock pressing against his passage, covered in our cum, slick and hard. *I wonder if this is his first. Or perhaps it's been a while?* I tilted my hips, and the crown of my cock entered the tight heat of his body. Raphael's breath hitched as he winced. *Oh, it's been a while. He's enjoyed this in the past.* A wicked grin crossed my face. His hand still wrapped around my neck, squeezing a warning as I slid my hands up his thighs. *How shall this happen? Hmm? Rough and fast? Slow and gentle? Somewhere—*I watched as Raphael began to ease himself down onto my dick. I panted, squeezing his thighs as our eyes locked, and I enjoyed the sensations as his heat took me in slow and hot.

The aggression of our passion written in our gazes was unmistakable. Our love as wild as the wilderness that protected us from prying eyes. I moaned as his ass now rested on my thighs, all of me in his pulsing heat. *Shit, I almost peaked again.* Raphael rocked his hips slowly, and I fought my eyes from rolling back. *Worth the wait...* Again, his breath hitched as my cock jumped as I fought the urge to move or peak. Raphael lifted himself until I almost escaped him before riding my shaft back to his seat, again, slow and agonizing, with his fingers on my neck like the collar I regret not having in this moment between us.

The muscles across my torso tensed each time he rode me down as he repeated the motion again and again. Raphael's other hand was now stroking himself as he recovered from his last release. He suddenly rose and lingered with the tip pressing against his world, tightening on the tip of my cock. With a wicked grin, Raphael squeezed my throat tight until it burned. He slammed down. I peaked with a pleasurable cry. I moaned, eyes rolling back. Raphael rocked as I filled him, breathless from the orgasm he had forced from me. He leaned down, kissing me deeply once more before biting my lip.

His words sent chills over me as he demanded, "Again." Gripping my hand, he placed it on his rock-hard cock once more. "Make me cum again," he purred.

Retreating from where he gripped my neck, he leaned back and braced himself on my thighs. I licked a fang, enjoying the way the muscles in his torso stretched out. My cock throbbed with never-ending excitement inside his tight channel. I stroked him once more, gripping him, sad I couldn't feel him peak with my own cock against him. As Raphael edged closer, he squeezed around my cock, still hilt deep inside him, and I lost it. *Fuck, he's everything I hoped for and more…* Again, I muttered curses as I filled him, flustered at how he made me peak so easily. Agitated, I pushed him off me. *I can't stand it. This won't do. I won't be satisfied if I don't take him how I've been intending.* My aggression won out; I had spun us around. Bending Raphael over a large boulder, I slammed my cock back into him, my cum making him slick as I hammered, growling and moaning as I leaned over him. Raphael panted and shrieked with ecstasy with each hilt-deep slam.

Reaching around, I now had a grip on his throat as I pulled him up, his back against my torso as I grinded hard and deep into him. "You want to cum again?" I snarled into his ear.

"Y-Yes," Raphael's face flushed, clinging to my arms as my other hand cupped his balls. "I want…"

"I expect you to show me." I squeezed his sack, his cock hardening across my wrist as I groaned, slowing down how I grinded against him. "We both know you'll cum because I'm fucking you."

Tilting back, I pulled out until I left him and slid slowly back in. His heart fluttered, his body tensing as I pulled slowly back out once more to repeat the motion. My fingers were tight on his throat while the others were still cupping his balls. I watched as my cock slid in and out of him, felt how his body and cock tensed each time. His body hot as I teased him with my dick, taunting him as I held my prey in place.

"I'll make you cum because you like how I fuck you," I grumbled into his ear, tightening my grip on his neck again. "Be a good Lord." I rode slowly inside; his body taut as he edged dangerously close. "That's a good Lord," I growled. "Cum for me, my lord." Pushing deep inside him, I peaked, filling him thrice, and his breath caught. "Give it to me," I commanded, and he moaned, peaking with me. "That's a good Lord," I cooed, grinding against him as I stroked him, keeping his orgasm lingering as he moaned louder. "Don't stop now, my lord!" I tightened on his neck and began to fuck him hard and fast. "Again," I shouted, and he nutted again with a loud cry of exhilaration. "Good—" I moaned as I surrendered again, caught unaware of how much it impacted me. *Fucking amazing.* We fell forward together onto the boulder, both breathless and exhausted from it. "Fuck."

Raphael swallowed, his words inaudible as he still tightened and moaned from it all before managing to rasp, "Get off."

"I can't," I confessed over his shoulder, both of us gripping the rock.

"Why not?" Raphael panted, catching my reflection in the rippling water at our feet.

"I'll peak again." I laughed, placing my forehead on his shoulder. "You've got me so worked up; I can't stop."

"Have you not run out of room?" Raphael marveled before rocking into me. "Then cum again, fuck me again, if that's what you wish. But this time, pull out afterward," he said, exasperated.

"That was a thought, but," I hummed with the idea before also confessing, "my wound opened back up."

"Fuck, we're a mess," Raphael muttered.

"You started it." I went to pull out and found myself lurching forward. "Fuck." I peaked harder than the other time, and he moaned, cum dripping from where we connected. "S-sorry."

Raphael laughed, shaking his head. "I've lain with so many, but never have I ever had a single man be the one to fill me in—"

"I feel honored to be the one to have surpassed your best orgy, then." I pulled away, splashing down onto my bottom, rinsing myself in the hot waters. "May I go down in Lord Raphael's book of conquests as the best he's ever had and the best to have filled his world properly."

Raphael landed on his knees and looked at the sky above. "Can I confess something to you, Ashton?"

The shift in his tone was sobering, and it made me cringe. "I thought that's why we came out here," I drawled, leaning forward on my knees as my heart thudded loudly. *So eager to ruin a moment between us as always, Golden Boy.*

"It's rare for me to peak." Raphael furrowed his brow. "It's one of the things Cruza and the others held against me as the next heir back before the empire fell. How could I conceive and continue a bloodline if I was unable to sow my seed properly? And so, when the time came, my marriage would be arranged as it had been done for centuries before me. With this singular item, they held me captive. I have sought answers for so long that I had forgotten why I had such a deep interest in the sexual conquests of others."

"Why was it so easy with me?" Raphael's blue gemstones peered over at me, a bittersweet expression on his face. "Don't say it. I understand. You and I are the same in that way."

He splashed around, sitting beside me as the sky began to shift to a peachy tone overhead. "What will we do when we go back across the bridge?"

"We watch one another," I answered easily, despite the heartache the idea of it brought me. "And we don't let them use one another as a means to win, no? Even when they figure out that we have feelings for one another. We know they will, so let's use that to our advantage when the time comes."

"We watch one another, then." Raphael leaned onto my shoulder, a tender side of him he had hidden until now. "I love to watch you. Everything you do, the way

153

you speak and overpower anyone in your way. The intelligence and cleverness that everyone overlooks. What you did for Hodges, and I've heard the stories at the Scarlett House of how often you've helped with no need for money or trade. You've got a tender heart under that asshole exterior. I get why you're so guarded all the time. I can't say I'm much different."

I leaned my cheek on his head as the water stilled, and steam rose up into the cooling air. "I see why you do after watching you. I've learned there's much to be desired about the way someone carries themselves. Well, as I said before, my home is your home."

He chuckled, echoing it with, "My whorehouse is your whorehouse."

Snorting, I sighed as I watched the water pour over the ledge. "At least now we have a place to breathe and prepare for what war awaits us. I can't believe you would throw it all away for me. Missing that meeting puts us back several steps, Golden Boy."

"I'd do it again. I promised myself no one would die in my stead ever again." He huffed. "Not even a feral wolf."

I grunted. No words left to ease his thoughts on the matter or my own. *I, too, feel the same about this.* We sat there in silence until night fell, and the first sign of fireflies drifted between the trees all around like tiny fluttering candles. With no sense of urgency, we took our time to weave back in the dark, the howls of the wolves far away now. Feran snorted and flicked an ear at us as we came through the trees and stumbled exhausted back into the cabin.

The silence was nothing more than the art of unspoken words between us. *We've already confessed all we had kept to ourselves since the day we first met on the field. Now, we move together, aware of who and what we want.* Raphael wrapped my torso with plenty of ointment to ease the pain and recover the damage I had done in my eager lust. Laying down, Raphael twisted to stoke the wood stove, but I pulled him down and into bed, spooning him. Nuzzling his neck, I kissed it, and sleep came easier for the both of us. *Maybe we can just disappear, and the world will just stop self-destructing… maybe we can just stay here and never go back.*

Chapter 33
Stabbing and Shielding

Looking at the rapier, I tossed it from one hand to the other with a scowl. "I don't like this weapon at all," I declared. "It's too thin and bends more than a needle when sewing leather."

"Then don't use it," quipped Raphael, chopping wood.

"But it's all I had that night," I responded, flustered at the memory of how poorly the whole fight had gone. "I should have used my bare hands."

"And you still would have ended up poisoned just the same," reminded Raphael.

"Eh, you're right." I slid the blade back into its sheath.

"What weapon do you prefer?" He paused, thudding the axe into the chopping block and gathering pieces to stack on the stockpile.

"I don't know." I pondered on it. "When I was younger, they tried to teach me hand-to-hand, then the short sword, and lost me to youthful whims with the long sword as my own sword."

"And yet you seem perfectly at home wielding an axe, a hoe, and, I imagine, a scythe and plow aren't far behind those lines." Raphael circled back, pacing back and forth to gather the chopped wood.

"But those aren't weapons," I snorted at the implication.

"You can kill a man with them." Raphael pointed to the axe. "You can relieve a man of his arm with that as much as it can cleave wood."

Furrowing my brow, I gestured. "Go on." *What clever concept are you thinking of, Golden Boy?*

Raphael paused, his eyes rolling up in thought as he continued, "Even a hammer can render a man too broken to fight, if not kill him, when struck in the head with enough power."

"No, I don't like that idea. That's a dreadful thing to do to someone." A shudder shook my shoulders. "How about the hoe?"

"Hoe?" Raphael tilted his head. "But the question is, could you really fight with it? I mean, you did well with the hatchet. Take up an axe. I mean, yes, you can kill someone with a hoe, but I don't think it'll intimidate in a fight, no?"

"Not the hatchet or axe. I was pissed, and the sound it makes isn't something I want to hear again if I can help it." Heaving a sigh, I scratched my cheek. "I can come in looking like the Sacrificial Daughter with a pair of war scissors."

"No, absolutely not." Raphael shook his head. "I'd rather see you with a dagger or short sword. Let's circle back. First off, let's address this need to come in like a charging bull. You can carry a lot of weight, so the question is what type of armor would suit you best: plate mail, chain mail—"

"Leather. I want thick leather and metal plate in only a few places. A hybrid between them all so I can move but something metal here," I motioned across my chest, "maybe back here," twisting, I gestured over my lower back, "and maybe my forearms and shins for good measure."

Sitting down on the chopping block, Raphael nodded as he imagined it. "Yeah, that's rather good for someone who's never been in battle. You have any blacksmiths you can trust?"

"South of here in Liefseid. They're one of the few I know of who don't work with the Farrow clan." Pulling some rabbit skins off the rack, I checked them for wet salts and divided them out so I could move the stabilized ones to be pickled. "Does anyone work with shields anymore?"

"If they take after the fights from the Old Continent, shields aren't allowed. Only wearable armor, a manica on the arm, or buckler attached to a gauntlet at best." Raphael covered his face, groaning over it. "What a farce we will be walking into… we shouldn't have to fight. I wasn't there to vote for or against it."

"Then I don't have to worry about a weapon." Rubbing my scar from the near-death incident, I added, "But I do need some armor. I think I'm going to have to take my part as a Royal Guard who doubles as a valet de chambre a little more seriously when we get back. Don't want a repeat of this fuckery ever again."

Dropping his hands, Raphael leaned on his legs and jested, "At least you won't be able to pleasure yourself behind my back so easily in the future."

"Don't blame me for that." Spreading a few of the rabbit furs out on the worktable, I started to salt them again. "That, too, was your fault."

Pulling away, Raphael went to a tree to relieve himself while he spoke over his shoulder. "How so? I wasn't even watching or doing—"

Stabbing and Shielding

"You were playing with my toys," I interjected. "And when you started playing with my favorites, how could I not get excited?" Raphael turned away, though the red ears told me enough, and I chuckled. "Where is my other cock ring, my lord?"

"Safe." Raphael finished and tucked himself away. "Finish that up, and let's train some more."

Narrowing my eyes, I rolled the hides up and placed them back on the curing rack. With a few pumps, I drew water to wash my hands as he grabbed the wooden swords; he had wrapped leather on one end for handles. Drying my hands on my pants, I caught the training sword he tossed at me with ease. Raphael took his stance, and I copied it. Launching forward, I struggled to deflect the quick jabs. *Why is he so quick on his feet and with his strikes?!* A smack on my arm and knee made me retreat. Temper flaring, I lunged forward for my own flurry of attacks. In comparison, my swings were too wild, too broad, and he deflected them.

Alarm struck me when he stepped in close, knocking me in the chin with the end of the handle. I stumbled back, the heat of my wrath healing the busted mark with ease. Raphael grinned. *He enjoys hitting a feral animal with a stick, does he?* Snorting, I readjusted my stance into my own version. Tightening my movements, I lunged forward once more. The strikes hit harder, and the deflection that had once worked managed to slide down his practice sword. He shifted and side-stepped to compensate, and I gave chase. This time I stepped into him, and he knocked the hilt end into my ribs, and my breath left me.

"You're too big and slow to use that move." Raphael laughed, giving me time to recover and reset. "But much better on the strikes. Making the smaller opponent move more wears us out sooner. Eventually, your uncanny endurance will beat any opponent."

Rubbing my side, I grunted. "You're not being nice about this."

"Let's say I have much anger toward you on several matters and," he puffed out his cheeks, motioning to the bruises on his neck and collarbone before saying, "I'm enjoying beating you with a stick over this."

Licking a fang, I flicked my eyebrows. "You should see the ones I leave on your back as you sleep."

The frown it brought from him made my heart flutter. I charged; the crack and snap of the sticks hitting were thrilling. We were now fighting with intent, the movements quick and instincts burning hot. I swung low to high. His sword caught it, pushing me off as he stepped to the side. I gave chase, letting my blade fall with a new aim instead of resetting as I had done before. Raphael blocked, the force making him bend on his knee. He gave a fiery expression as he recovered and slid farther back. Again, I closed the space only enough for my next flurry of strikes to hit. Snap, Crack, Crack!

I shifted to the side and noticed it canceled his aim. A fanged grin crossed my face, and he swallowed. Another step, strike, sidle, and he was backing up more than in the last sessions. His back hit the cabin wall. With his eyes wide, Raphael blocked the incoming strikes, his movements starting to slow, and arms that had been steady began to tremble with their efforts. I stabbed forward. He deflected over his shoulder, bracing for impact. I stopped, both of us panting with sweat trickling across our bodies. I lowered my weapon as he opened his eyes. For the first time, I saw him fear me… and I hated it. *If it were anyone else, I don't think I would feel such weight in my chest.* I dropped my blade and kissed him before wrapping my arms around him. His heart raced; his body trembled.

"You shouldn't hit a wolf with only a stick," I whispered, and the tension left him.

"You're right. How foolish of me to think he couldn't still bite." Raphael buried his face into my shoulder for a long while, his breath and heart rate slowing. "Sorry, I didn't even notice you were cornering me. I suppose you figured out what I meant, but you caught me off-guard."

"I did." Pulling away, I grabbed the practice sword from him and tossed them both off to the side. "Let's have dinner. We've done this enough."

And I marched into the cabin. *I hate myself so much for thinking it was fun to corner my prey. That prey is my world. Only a fool harms the things he loves most.*

Chapter 34

The Bridge to Nowhere

We stood at the bridge, the early morning rays cutting across the white rapids of the rocky river below. Weeks had gone by, and the time spent at home seemed like a dream. *Is it wrong to want to stay?* I looked at Raphael, and his expression mirrored the thoughts in my mind. *Do we really have to do this? Should we even bother going back at all?* There was an awkwardness as I took a step forward and jolted to a stop. *I don't want to go back.* My fists balled tight, and I turned to face Raphael and Feran.

"I don't…" I choked on my words, chest aching as I looked away in shame. *Why does it feel like the moment I step back over this bridge, it'll be the point of no return for me?* I glanced back at Raphael, who gave me a pitiful expression. *No, it's going to be the point of no return for us both.* My stomach twisted, vomit rolling up into the back of my throat. *Every nerve in me is screaming. Don't go. It's the end for you all.*

"Ashton." Lillian's voice made me turn to where she stood on the bridge. My thoughts had been too distracting to have noticed her approach. "Are you ready? Have you been well?"

Closing my eyes, I swallowed down my fear and instincts, mustering a false smile. "Better than ever."

Raphael grabbed my arm, whispering, "Are you sure? Is this what you want? I will go on without you—"

I shoved his hand off, whispering, "I'm the only thing left standing between Fallen Arbor and my family. I aim to keep it that way."

We crossed the bridge, and something snapped inside me. *Yeah, I'm a wolf who just went against instinct. This will be the death of me. May the Sacrificial Daughter make the cutting of my thread worthy to return to the Mother of Life.* I pulled myself onto Feran, and the horse seemed calmer than before. *Fuck, even this dick of a horse feels it.* Raphael and Lillian rode alongside one another in front of me as I lost myself to thoughts and emotions that I couldn't seem to hold still or give name to. I shook from them as the farm came into view, the once freshly broken field covered in green sprouts.

We were whisked inside, the stable boy blushing at me as he took Feran and the other horses. My father sat at the table; wine and a large meal had been set for us. I blinked, taking it all in. *This isn't a holiday but…* He motioned for us to sit, and we did so. *Shit. He has a serious matter to discuss. I wonder what in the Fates happened while I recovered.* Father hadn't uttered a word, first filling our cups with wine until we sat.

"You look better, Ashton," Father remarked at last, cutting into the meat on his plate.

"What's the occasion?" I asked with a bitter expression.

"I want to send you into war with a proper meal." Germaine glared at me as he shoved the chunk into his mouth.

Oh no, we're not upset or serious. He's fucking mad as hell still. At me? Raphael? Shit, I can't avoid this. I cringed as the conversation unfolded.

Raphael stared at his plate with his shoulders slumped. "What is the situation?"

"The first fight to see who will gain Speaker of the House and lead the council for the season will be happening in a week." Lillian had locked the door and sat down. "Everyone but House Traibon has announced a champion, or so it was implied."

I gulped down my wine until nothing remained in the goblet before demanding, "Who is fighting?" *Did they find out about the crow I sent? Perhaps it never made it, or someone intervened?*

"We don't know." Another aggressive sawing of meat as Father spoke. "And this matter could have been avoided." He shot a heated glare at Raphael, who sat without taking a bite or drink. "But you did save my stubborn son from certain death." He motioned. "Don't insult me. Eat."

Raphael was slow to grab his silverware. "I don't deserve praise. They were meant to kill me."

"No, they weren't," interjected Lillian, taking a bite of food. "Grandmama found out information. They were there for Ashton."

Ah shit. He's mad at me.

With this, Father slammed his silverware down, eyes glowing as he pierced me with his gaze. "Ashton, do you want to elaborate on what this information about Madeleine receiving a Devoted Sister totem is about?"

The Bridge to Nowhere

Raphael sucked on a cheek and looked at me. "That broken, blood-covered totem from before?"

And there goes any chance of making it out to be a rumor. I winced, and the fire in Father's eyes brought him to his feet. "She did not return it in such a state! When? When did this happen?" he roared, demanding the answer.

"She did," I snapped. "I sent it to her. I wanted to know her intent, and she made it known the first moment she could hand deliver it back to me."

"Ashton, how could you?!" Father was furious; his rage lay open for the first time. "We already knew, but this… this you can't take back!"

"In the name of the Knowing Mother, could someone explain to me what in the fuck this is about?" Raphael's voice boomed like a cannon in ceremony, rendering us all silent for a long while.

Do I dare tell him? He'll think it's some foolish superstition…

"It is not my place to say." Father sat, drinking his wine as he looked away.

Lillian glared at me, and I finally confessed, "It's a blood curse."

"Excuse me?" Raphael paled as he took in the grim expressions. "You did what? Is this? I thought there was no magic left in the world?" Again, dodged glares as everyone tensed. "Ashton, tell me what it is you have done to bring on such rage in your own family."

Tapping my fingers on the table, my leg shaking, I let my secret fly. "So, three families were gifted with magic."

"Yes, your grandmama had said something on the matter, and it's why Fallen Arbor…" His words slowed, faltering. "And you? You are one of the bloodlines?"

I held up my hand to declare and corrected, "Two. I have shown signs of two gifts. No one before me has ever acquired more than one gift. The Sacrificial Daughter being the easier one to tell, but after spending time in the wilds with you, I am certain Grandfather's gifts from the Devoted Sister are evident. Granted, this blood curse is a fable, something in old books, and hasn't been done in centuries."

"And what of the totem and curse?" Raphael held onto his silverware tightly.

"Madeleine holds the gift of the Mother of Life. With these three bloodlines, using a Devoted Sister totem is designed as a means for us to challenge one another when magic opposes magic in order to keep the balance." I finally met Raphael's gaze, the distress in those eyes stinging. "It's a blood curse. She can't lay a hand on any of my family until she takes me down, and I can't do the same either. It's only immediate blood. That means my father, Lillian, and even our children are protected by this."

"So that means Philippe is safe from harm by you," Raphael concluded.

"As long as I don't aim with killing intent. I'm not entirely sure how this works, to be honest." Nodding, I shot him a glance. "Blood for blood. It keeps a vendetta between two warring factions between the two individuals who are at odds."

"And if one of you takes the other down?" Raphael pondered, swallowing. "Please tell me there's a way to stop it or break the curse?"

161

"If one defeats the other, they can touch the remaining family." My father answered. "And if someone of their family willingly casts their life in harm's way or takes—"

"Wait!" Interrupted Raphael. "Death is the only way out of this."

Everyone remained silent as I looked away. I didn't want to see the pained expressions on my father, sister, and lover's faces. *Just accept this was the only way to protect you all. I don't want him to know it also protects the ones we love. That after the assassin, I wasn't going to let her have access to take you from me, and that's why I make such silly and bold promises so openly.*

"Why didn't you tell me?" Raphael demanded.

I met his gaze, a scowl on my face as I refused to answer. *He doesn't ever need to know how deep of a curse I have submitted myself to.*

"You didn't have to go that far," Raphael pressed, and I heard his voice falter.

Go ahead, Raphael. Let your heart break all the way. Temper fueling me, I met all their heartbroken expressions with immediate rage and frustration. *I'm as good as dead. Isn't that what you all want to shout at me now?* I looked at the biting of lips and the white-knuckled grips on silverware as their gazes weighed down on me. *Say it! Tell me I'm a dick! An asshole! A monster!* I stood now, leaning on the table, staring them down like a feral beast cornered. *I'm here now. Let it out! Shout at me more about how I'm the fool who let her die.* I shot a fiery glare at Lillian, who looked away. *She thinks it's my fault Mother is now gone deep down, no? And you!* I turned my spite on my father, self-hatred goading me on. *You're only keeping me here because Mother would wish us to remain a family. At heart, we both know it should be her sitting at the table and me buried under that old tree in the yard.* Germaine's face twisted, the rage shifting into pity. *Don't fucking take pity on me. I'm a wounded animal that needs to be put down. I'll handle it myself since no one can stomach it.* Unable to take it anymore, I marched out.

Yanking on the cabin door, I busted the lock off the frame. "I'll be outside when you're ready to leave."

Mother had more to offer this world than I ever could.

Chapter 35

The Traibon Truce

I sat in my chair, brooding. My room no longer a safe place for frivolous memories of being hilt deep in whores and maids, but a reminder of my failure. The carpet had been replaced, but in my mind's eye, I could still see the bodies and smell a hint of blood. My side ached, a reminder that my wound was still not fully healed. Outside the door were guards now; the number had increased tenfold since my near-death experience. We had refused dinner, and the only words spoken between us were nothing more than out of courtesy. For the last several days, we had fitted ourselves with newly tailored suits. Big Hodges was back at the shop alongside his son once again. *At least I did something good before I died.*

Raphael didn't stop there. He insisted on armor, making it to the specs I had only spoken of once with him, weeks before we had even dared leave the forest. It was fashioned with the finest leather and expert blacksmithing imported from Liefseid. Tugging on it, the weight of it on my shoulders and hips grounded me. *How in the hell he got them to rush it in a matter of a week or so is beyond me. Maybe the crafty bastard sent word while we were out there when I was asleep. Clever twat.* I glowered at Raphael as he finished prepping in front of the vanity mirror.

"Stare any harder, and I might be set ablaze," Raphael drawled, meeting my eyes in the mirror.

I broke my glare away, drumming my fingers on the chair's arm. On the bed sat a package. *They finished the fur coat but is he really deserving of it?*

Snorting, Raphael jested, "See, I was right."

"I do not wish to engage in idle chatter," I quipped in annoyance. *He will have to wait.*

Sighing, Raphael finished adjusting his cravat before turning to lean on the vanity. "You can't pleasure yourself behind my back in that." He pushed on with the conversation.

Scoffing, I rose to my feet and headed for the door, opening it to gesture him to go. "Come, we will be late, my lord."

"What about the package?" Raphael nodded to it.

"None of your business," I declared, stone-faced.

Raphael approached, stopping before me as he leaned close to my face. "You can't keep this up forever, you know?"

"Clearly, you underestimate my stubbornness, my lord." With that, Raphael led the way.

Before long, we entered the council room, where everyone sat waiting for us to join. Madeleine glared at me with a wicked grin, the armor in her eyes a small victory from her last attempt. *I suppose the old gods didn't account for the fact that she could hire someone to kill me.* Scanning the room, the invaders seemed excited and jolly, while their daemon counterparts took on haunting expressions. *Of course they are giddy. They don't have to watch people they know get hurt and possibly die.* Unlike before, Philippe wore his own battle armor like a decorated soldier, ready to leave and head to the battlefield. Henri's gaze would not meet my own. *There's a sense of failure here. It's that bad. You two fools can't stand up to the Fanged Lady even with the aid of your own masters? Disgusting.*

"Ah! Welcome, House Traibon!" Cruza was back in his original chair as we approached the opposite end, and Raphael sat. "We are glad to see you and your valet—"

"Royal Guard," corrected Raphael. "And yes, we're both very much alive and well. Thank you for stating what the blind could not see." Raphael's tone rode on a rage I hadn't realized he had come riding into the room with. "Now, I expect an explanation as to why this council would make such an important decision without me, let alone not bother to send word on the rules of engagement. Worse, you disregarded an assassination attempt on a fellow councilman. Do I need to remind you of the follies of my father's fallen empire when they allowed these same mistakes to happen and moved forward for the greed of a single entity?" Raphael's heated sneer landed on Cruza.

"Cruza!" Winston Forestier rose to his feet in alarm. "Did you not say you had discussed it with him? That he's agreed to the matter and that you only needed our reply!"

Raphael was right. This man is worthless, other than as a stepping stone. Who would not press to wait to hear words directly or demand a properly signed and sealed letter in their stead? Foolish twat.

"I don't recall saying that," guffawed Cruza, feigning ignorance with ease. "My head servant Madeleine had sent word. Are you implying we're untrustworthy?" Cruza Vendecci was a snake, and he slithered his way through the councilmen between them with ease. "Perhaps the correspondence was intercepted by Fallen Arbor. After all," he reasoned, "they breached the castle after all."

Ahmed shifted in his chair, his usual aloof demeanor nowhere to be seen. "Yes, I thought it best to wait, but these two fools pressured me into voting."

"You were for it the moment it was offered," scoffed Winston, sitting in his chair, the two bickering with disdain for having not noticed their own puppet strings. "Only because you have the best warrior the daemons have to offer."

"The rules. Does a house have to participate at all?" demanded Raphael. "And let me remind you, I sat there at that table, too, when my father chased this foolish concept, and it brought the empire to its knees in a matter of months before Fallen Arbor was let into the throne room to free him of his head." Now he had their full attention.

Who falls for the same trap twice? They gained a lot from the last time it seems. Here they thought they were out of Fallen Arbor's reach. No, that's not it. I gritted my fangs. *If House Vendecci is working for Fallen Arbor, then the other two got something in exchange for selling out Raphael Traibon or, worse, letting them through the front doors. All three of these men have lain in bed with the dark gods and their underlings. Disgusting.*

"No, no one could have stopped what happened that day." Cruza scowled, the comments striking a nerve with him. "But you can't win Speaker of the House if you don't enter. Why do you inquire about pulling out of the fight?"

"Who cares for such a useless title?" Raphael waved. "We are still equals here, and we should be voting as a whole from this point on."

"Wait! We don't have to participate?" marveled Winston. "I wish to withdraw at once!"

Cruza raised a hand and silenced the old man. "But that's not all. There are more consequences we agreed upon if one doesn't participate." Ahmed looked away, a sense of guilt. "You can't own land if you don't participate."

"Wait, we didn't agree to that." Winston seemed alarmed.

"It was two against one," explained Madeleine before motioning to Ahmed Regius.

"Scoundrels," growled Winston, and Henri pulled him back into his seat.

Worthless twats, I thought bitterly as the farce unfolded before me.

"Does it have to be a fight to the death?" demanded Raphael, giving them a cold glare.

"No." Cruza smirked. "We aren't as uncivilized as your father, the emperor."

"And who is fighting? I hear that you've all chosen your fighters for this." I watched as Raphael laid the questions out as he dodged the remark, knowing full well how to get the details that mattered from them. "I imagine you announced it to one another."

"That is kept secret to prevent foul play." Madeleine's voice cut through the room. "And House Traibon sent word on their champion before your arrival. Did you not know?" She smirked, sliding her gaze from Raphael to me.

He didn't look at me, too quick-witted to not be able to figure out what it was I had done in my brooding silence. "I wanted to make sure the integrity of this folly has some standing. One last inquiry, if I have to play along with this bullshit, I need to know one last rule." Raphael hissed, anger seething in his words, "Can someone challenge the Speaker of the House as often as they want?"

With this, Winston and Ahmed turned to Cruza, who clapped his lips shut tight. The smile and confidence stripped from him, as he hadn't thought it through. *Sure, you said we can hold this seasonally, but you didn't say a duel couldn't be requested or important decisions could be swayed in a Blood Duel. These are influences from Ancient Daemonis culture and the Fanged Lady's own influence you allowed to unfold, Cruza Vendecci.* Cruza turned to Madeleine, who grew excited over the question. As for the other gentlemen, they seemed unsettled, and Winston whispered to Henri.

Raphael peered back at me, and we nodded to one another. *He knew. We had talked about it in passing, but I had shared enough about Madeleine and the bloodlines and ancestors that he had recognized what she had done before I did. Dammit, I should have given him the wolf fur coat. It would have matched that fierce tone and gaze today.*

In a rush, Henri went to the archive doors and, after several moments, returned with the scroll that outlined the rules of engagement. As Henri and Winston paled, the dirty hidden underwriting was unraveled.

"This is unacceptable," muttered Winston, angry as he stared down Cruza, then Regius. "Did you know about this property clause? And this one, on challenging on several accounts. Not only can we challenge for the seat as often as we want, but we can fight to win over a matter of discussion. Worse, this one… this one says if they die in battle…" Winston pulled a handkerchief from a pocket, sitting down as a cold sweat washed over him and he nearly fainted.

Regius smiled, and chills ran across me to see the greed in his eyes. "Yes. If your champion dies, you will lose your property and territory to the winner. But don't worry, you still can sit on the council, but you would need to pay taxes or make arrangements for remaining on the property. Bureaucracy is all, my friend."

Raphael pointed across the table at Cruza, rage erupting from him. "You will be responsible for the death of this country as well. The Blood Advisor and his Fanged Lady will pay for what you aim to do here. Come, Ashton."

I followed him out, and the guards slammed the doors behind us. Raphael rushed down the steps, forfeiting going back to the room. Before I knew it, we were crossing the courtyard, and he was yanking the cravat and jabot out and tossing them to the ground. They opened the gates, and he pulled off his coat and shoved it into the arms of a baffled guard. Confused by the fit of rage, I marched hot on his heels without a word. Down the street we went, as Raphael tugged the laces loose on his shirt. Without hesitation, he marched straight into the doors of the Scarlett House, and my heart caught in my throat. *Why did he practically run off to here?* I looked back, seeing no one of importance, and gave chase inside.

"Beau! Jen!" roared Raphael, snapping his fingers.

"Raphael!" I had to jog to catch up to him in the halls before he stopped to unlock the door to his private bath. "Raphael?"

"Shut your gullet," Raphael warned. The door opened, and he shoved me inside. "Not another word from you." His fist slammed into my jaw, and my eyes took a moment to find themselves straight again, and my jaw ached. "Fuck!" He walked away, holding his hand. "So, fucking hardheaded. If you hadn't sent that damn letter, I had a chance…"

I cracked my jaw, my lip dripping blood where he had busted it. "That was a good one," I remarked smugly.

Raphael turned back and punched me with the other fist. Whack! I stumbled and caught myself on the table, a goblet falling to the floor and shattering. Blinking, I righted my vision, mouth bloody as teeth were knocked loose. *Dammit, he can punch!* I shook my head as he paced and circled, both hands turning purple. *He broke both hands.* Raphael roared, his face blood red with his frustration. Inhaling deeply, I took a seat in the chair as the girls opened the door and froze in the doorway. I opened and closed my jaw; it clicked, and I grunted in annoyance. *Did he break it or knock it loose?*

"Fucking idiot!" At last, Raphael turned and met my gaze. "Why did you do it?"

"I told you. I'll be the one to protect my family, not you," I answered easily. "Who were you planning to send, anyway? Father is too old for this fool's game, and I would hang you by your sack if you even entertained putting my sister in the running."

"I wasn't entering the fight at all," he declared with a broken expression. "I wasn't going to fight. Or find someone else."

"And lose the farm? Even the forest? I think not." I dismissed it easily, and Raphael grew more furious. "We knew before we left that this was the mess we were dealing with. Don't pretend there was ever another way about it all. You know what you did forget to ask that I already know the fucking answer to?" I glowered at him, annoyed at how my jaw ached and clicked. "Once you declare a champion, you can't change until they are dead or unable to stand. That was the clause from the books themselves, and Madeleine wouldn't leave that tiny blood-thirsty item out."

Raphael covered his mouth, glaring down at me with such guilt it made me angry. The top of his hand was purple, and his knuckles were busted and bleeding, but it didn't seem to faze him in the least. *He's hit people hard enough that he's* broken his hand like that before. Raphael turned to the girls and whispered a few things. It was only a matter of minutes before they showed up with a crate of wine bottles and bandages. I abandoned the chair and watched as Raphael drank from the bottle, and they wrapped his hands. The whole time he glared at me, temper untamed.

I've really set something loose. Perhaps we were always both lone wolves who simply wanted to have our peace in the wilds. Snorting, I rubbed my jaw. *Beat your dog down all you want. I'll take it proudly in order to protect all that is mine.*

Chapter 36

Even Tame Beasts Bite

Silently, I watched and waited as the girls tended to his bruised and broken hands. *He did it to himself,* I reasoned. The pang of guilt only pissed me off further. *I need to focus. Shit, who am I going to have to beat damn near to death in a few days?* I leaned on the edge of the tub. No water filled it this time, a sign that he had no intention of going to the Scarlett House at all. *If I face Philippe, what will happen? I don't recall the book saying anything about harming someone, only that I can't kill their blood relatives. I suppose, like everything in my life, I'll just have to learn it the hard way.*

"Have you chosen a weapon?" Raphael seemed back to his cool-toned self as the girls left with the medical kit.

"No." I scanned the room; the assortment of herbs was rather dull in comparison to the apothecary shop or even my father's own private stock. *Ugh, I don't want to discuss this anymore.*

"I can commission or find you one," he offered.

"I know," I said.

"Just let me know what sort of weapon you wish to have. I got you the armor, after all. How does it move for you?" Raphael opened and closed a hand, wincing.

"Fine." My curt replies would only serve to feed both our tempers.

"Very well. I suppose I shall take a page from my father's book to deal with you." There was a sense of assertiveness in his tone as I turned to him.

"Didn't your father hang those who opposed him?" I arched a brow, turning to face him, arms crossed as I leaned against the tub.

"That was his enemies. You are not my enemy," Raphael stated, crossing a leg as he reached over to begin the annoying habit of drinking from a goblet now.

I waited for an answer as Raphael poured his drink. The door opened, and servants were now forcing me to side-step to allow them to pour hot water into the stone tub. Again, I turned to Raphael, yet he continued to drink and refill, glass after glass. Clearing my throat, he stole a glance at me, but Raphael's lips only opened to take in the alcohol, the amount worthy of a sailor's thirst after too long at sea. He finished the bottle and threw it at me. I caught it in my hand, my temper rising as patience waned in the wake of no answer. *How long does he expect me to wait for a reply?* Raphael popped the cork of the next, another refill, and he paid no heed to the glowing eyes I surely wore at the weight of my fury. Throwing the bottle at him, Raphael leaned, and it smashed on the wall behind him as he refilled the cup yet again.

"Are you not going to tell me?" I roared, frustrated with his tightlipped demeanor.

"I owe no explanation to a wild animal." Raphael glowered at me, and a shudder shook me.

Another wave of servants cut between us, the sound of water pouring as Raphael continued to drink. He glowered at me. Unmoved. As if a master pissed at his disobedient dog. *For some godforsaken reason, I can't get my heartbeat to slow. Am I that angry? Or...* I took a step forward, and someone yelped, and I backed up too far, hitting the side of the tub and knocking a jar of rose hips into the water. I fumbled to scoop it up and slammed it back on the shelf. I ignored the fact it had more water than petals in it now as I turned to stare down Raphael.

"And what did your father do with animals like me?" I demanded as they filled the last few inches of the tub before leaving us alone once more.

Raphael smirked. The curve of those lips and resilience in his eyes made me clench my jaw. My wrath bit at me, and I fought the urge to close the gap between us and shake him for the answer. The aching in my jaw reminded me of how hard he had hit me. Not once, but twice. *He's toying with my rage because I pissed him off.* I wanted to shout, to flip the table and smash the bottles at his feet and yoke him up off the chair and roar! But I bit my tongue and stood my ground. Beau and Jen returned and bowed before Raphael.

"Unsaddle my horse," Raphael motioned to me and chuckled.

Jen and Beau looked at one another, grinning, before setting their aim on me. "Go on." I narrowed my eyes at Raphael. "You heard the man. Relieve me of my leather."

Holding out my arms, I waited as they took my armor from me, piece by piece, as Raphael watched in calculated silence. *What game does he play at now?* I listened to the creak of leather, the ting of metal plate, and the thud as it hit the ground. A few times, they struggled to get their fingers onto buckles and straps. The chest plate was pulled off, and it took them both to hold it and carry it away. Underneath laid the thick cloth covered in sweat, and after it came off, I obliged by pulling off the drenched cotton shirt as they tugged my pants down. After kicking off my boots, they fought to pull my pants from my legs and feet. I paid them no heed. My eyes were on the blue gemstones, as cold as ever.

"Bathe him. He reeks." Another refill as the girls pushed me toward the tub.

I paused, waiting for Raphael to say something more. Their hands pressed into me, unable to budge me any further. *Does he really expect me to play along? No. No, I won't.* Twisting, I gripped the side of the tub, looking into the water. I had gotten up to the last step, my eyes glowing. *Fucking so pissed off, and he knows it because my fucking eyes glow every damn time, and I can't tell if he's mad or—* A boot rammed into an ass cheek, and I went crashing down into the water. Gulping water, I rose to my feet in alarm, water waving out, slapping the floor as I sputtered and struggled to breathe. The tub stood half-filled in an instant. Gasping for air, I turned wide-eyed to where Raphael stood aloof, glass in hand, with a smug expression.

"Sorry, ladies, it seems my wolf needed a little push." Raphael turned away, back in his chair, as he seemed unfazed by the rage and growling erupting from me. "Careful, he'll bite and has bitten." Topping off the goblet, he added, "And I expect you ladies to scrub him thoroughly."

"My pleasure." Beau rolled up her sleeves and reached for my hand.

Snatching it out of reach, I barked at Raphael. "Have you lost your mind?"

"I should be asking you that." Raphael motioned with a hand. "Heel boy. Sit and behave."

"Fuck you, Raphael!" A coughing fit flattened the intent, and I inhaled again.

"Once was enough," Raphael jested. "Now sit, or I will act again. I assure you I am done being gentle with a beast who is hellbent on doing everything the hard way, no?"

I opened my mouth, but I couldn't find the words to say or push back. *Did our time in my home mean nothing?* The shock of it all started to take root. I sat, slow and obedient, as the heartache crept in and the hands pulled me into my place where the water was now barely waist deep. *Why am I feeling heartbroken?* I thought bitterly, fuming over the emotions clawing their way forward. *He was supposed to be heartbroken! And why the fuck am I so damn jealous that he can…* I covered my mouth as cloth scrubbed me clean, and fingers unknotted my braid. *Raphael can't do this to me! I don't want to seek out something I can't have and don't deserve. I'm a dead man. I let my mother die, and I am—*

"Your mother chose to fight that day." Raphael's words sent chills across me, and I dared not look at his expression. "Just as you chose not to fight that day. Nothing more, nothing less. Her death is on her own hands. Your life staying intact is yours. Stop mixing the two and guilting your way to the fucking grave, Ashton."

The Champion's Lord

I could hear another pour of wine, the tap of the bottle on the table, and the slosh of water as the girls held their breath as they scrubbed. *Exactly why does he care to discuss what no one has dared—*

"Did you know from the moment I saw you on the farm, I could read you like a book?" Raphael scoffed, water pouring over my head as they ran soap and fingers through my hair like a prized pony. "And I've thought a lot over the matter as to why that is." A tangle caught Jen's fingers, and I didn't flinch as she did her best to comb it out, my scalp aching with her efforts. "It's because we are cut from the same cloth. Our pride and self-hatred unrivaled…" He gulped down the wine, each swallow loud in my ears before the goblet connected with the table. "Well, until we crossed paths, no? After our time in the wilds together, I know what words lingered in your mind that day at the bridge."

"And what words were those?" I asked, knowing it was a dangerous confession for us both.

"We could stay there. Let them burn it all to the ground without us to stop them." Raphael's truth sliced deep.

"You're right," I confirmed. "But I remembered only I can save what I love, and against every instinct, I chose to burn in their place."

"Indeed." Raphael huffed and added, "And know I can never forgive you for this."

"And there it is. The heartache I was fretting at had left you." I licked a fang. "But I suppose my job is to make sure it stays an open wound from here on out?"

"Please, keep it bleeding, my heart, and maybe if we live to see this to the end, I might let you stitch me back together." Raphael relented, frustration riding in his voice. "Bite me, claw me, and maim me. Just let me bleed out these wounds in hopes the poison and its infection might one day let me sleep without hatred or guilt. You owe me that as much as I owe it to you."

"Then, my lord, cut me, beat me, and tie me to your side, if that's what it takes. My leash is yours, after all." I reached across to the shelves, a small knife lying there intended for shaving. "I resign as your Royal Guard." I stood, and the girls glared up at me as I twisted to face Raphael. "You own me now." With my hair tight in one hand, I cut it, leaving no room for even a single knot. *I will become braidless for you if that's what it takes. My life is in your hands, Golden Boy.* I threw the wet rope on the floor between us, and he didn't spare me any reaction. *This is what you wanted after all… that you hold my life in your hands since I refuse to take care of it properly.*

Chapter 37

Run Him into the Ground

Raphael reached down and threw a bottle of wine at me once more, this time full. I caught it, popped the cork, and started to drink it down. Jen and Beau gazed up at me with eyes wide, unsure what to do now that I had shed my right to carry a braid and swore servitude in the old ways to Raphael. The alcohol burned at my core as I broke free to take a breath. Sitting on the far ledge, staring down Raphael, I parted my legs. It was a silent rebellious invitation, and the scowl on his face said he knew what I offered. *He won't do it here. But I shall make him jealous now that I know he is as possessive as I.* My eyes lingered on his neck, remembering how my fingers and lips marked him so easily.

"I expect you to wear him down, even if it takes all night." Raphael's eyes bounced between the two girls, Jen and Beau. "Can you manage?"

"We'll give it our best try," offered Jen, starting to slip off her dress.

"Are you kidding me?" Beau had shed her clothes with haste. Naked and splashing down into the tub, she declared, "I get to go first!"

"Wait, what?" Jen winced as Beau splashed water at her.

"Back off, Jenifer!" Beau hissed.

"Ladies, ladies," I cooed and gave them my full attention for the first time since I had arrived. *Fuck Raphael. May he watch me sow my seed and be jealous!* "I'm not quite ready to start. Perhaps you can change that for me."

Beau had made her way across the swirl of steam and the scent of rose. Her curvy hips swayed as her breasts bounced with each step. The water was barely at her knees, thanks to my epic splash down from earlier. Wrapping her arms around me, she pressed her lips against mine. I deepened the kiss, abandoning my wine bottle on the shelf behind me as I pulled her in. I glanced past Jen as she slid into the tub, meeting Raphael's gaze as my hands slid down Beau's backside to squeeze her ass, pulling her into me. The kiss ended, and her lips suckled at my neck, across my collarbone, and down my torso as I stood there and let her have her way with me. I plucked the wine bottle up, drinking as I stared Raphael down. Beau's lips were hot and silky against the hard planes of my body as she descended to her prize. Her hands glided over my hip, following the muscles until she groped my cock, stroking me slowly. I moaned, her tongue against my shaft, causing me to rise a little.

"Wait," I gruffed and caught Jen's attention before she could join, groping her breast. "My satchel. I brought it this time."

"Oh?" Jen bit her lip and turned to retrace her steps.

"Brought what?" Raphael interjected; face flushed as the alcohol began to settle. "In the satchel, huh?" He dug around inside as he wobbled back to his chair and flopped down. "Oh." He pulled out the black tourmaline cock ring and smirked. "No, don't use this one." He dropped it into the satchel before tossing it on the table. "This one is the correct one, no?" Digging into his pants pocket, he tossed something to me, and I caught it, making the girls yelp and giggle.

"Damn, I didn't even see it." Beau exchanged glances with Jen. "Did you?"

"I can't see shit without my glasses," she remarked as they turned to see what was in my hand.

Glowering at him, I already knew what Raphael had kept and what he wanted to see me use for his own fetish. Opening my hand, the Tiger's eye cock ring lay in my palm. I snorted, taking a huge swig of my wine before putting it down. A grunt escaped me as I pulled it on, even pulling my sack through, wincing at the discomfort. *He doesn't want me to peak fully, or he's trying to make sure I don't peak so easily.* Now both girls came rushing forward, each straddling their own leg of mine, grinding against me. *Shame he doesn't know that I only do that with him, ha.* Lips suckled, licked, and descended down my body once more. My shaft stood erect, the cock ring growing tight, aiding in the hardness. Bare breasts with hardened nipples pressed against my thighs now as Beau and Jen's tongues competed up and down my shaft.

Greed won out as Beau took in my hardened length, moaning as the tip of my cock pressed firmly at the back of her throat. She pulled off, circling the cap before letting me ride her wiggling tongue to the back once more. Watching Raphael as he watched me, I waited eagerly to see some sign of desire. *I want him to get hard watching me.* Jen grew frustrated as Beau pushed her off and knelt between my legs.

Jen changed tactics, spooning Beau from behind, her hands squeezed breasts and pinched nipples. Beau squealed on my cock. *I just want to see him pull that glorious cock out and touch himself while watching me.* Beau pulled off with a pop. Jen slid a hand between Beau's thighs while she shoved Beau down, pushing her back onto my shaft to moan. *Fucking touch yourself with thoughts of what we could be doing right now.* My thoughts pleaded in silence to Raphael as I hit the back of her throat, and my muscles flinched. *Let me see you cum because you want me.* My own frustration peaked as Beau arched, coming from Jen's efforts. Unable to peak because of the cock ring, I shoved them against the other side of the tub, closing some of the distance between Raphael and me. Jen sat on the ledge, Beau between her legs where she stood.

I have it on, and you want to see if I can still keep coming with it on, don't you, Golden Boy? A fanged grin crossed my face as I pushed Beau's legs apart with my knee. *Don't look away from me.* I grunted, pushing hard into her, and she cried out. *This could have been you.* Jen clung to Beau's breasts from behind, but my hand furrowed between them, squeezing Jen's breast. I suckled on Beau's nipple, fucking her as I nibbled and pinched with my teeth.

"I'm going to make you both ascend," I growled, Beau clinging tightly against my body, nails raking across my back muscles as I fucked her hard and fast. She arched, screaming in bliss, before I pulled her off to the side and hungrily hugged Jen into me, my cock slamming into her wet pussy. My hand abandoned her breast, following her body down past her navel to her pink jewel, making her gasp. She yelped with each thrust as I slowly increased the speed of my hammering.

"Slow down," demanded Raphael.

Ignoring him, Jen started to tense and arch. "Fucking cum for me, Jen," I growled. "Show me what I love most."

My words were godlike, and her pussy tightened on my cock. She, too, clawed down my back, howling, her body trembling with her orgasm as she rocked her hips to drive me deeper. *You don't choose when and how I fuck anyone else.* I saw the tightness in his pants, and the excitement sent me over the edge. *Fuck.* I winced, the forceful peaking agonizing as the cock ring kept me from fully releasing. Gathering my wits, I pulled away from Jen, only to turn her and Beau over, both bent down across the tub ledge, hip to hip, as I started my next conquest. *I want you to see the pleasure on their faces as I fuck and play with them.* Now I pressed hilt deep into Beau, my cock hard as a metal rod as she cried in ecstasy. My fingers slid inside Jen's swollen folds, milky and slick with my cum, fucking her with my fingers as she groped at the side of the tub, still sensitive. I could feel them both growing tight as I stared down at Raphael. *Fucking show me that you're turned on by me.* Raphael shifted in his chair, the intense watching adding to my arousal with each thrust of pleasure.

My eyes slid to his crotch, the tent of his pants now evident. *Yes, fucking cum while watching me, asshole.* Catching my gaze, he grunted. Raphael pulled his shirt free, covering the offending and rebellious cock. The girls were tightening and arched again, and I edged dangerously close at the sight of Raphael's shifting. Beau and Jen panted, but I was far from being finished. *He's going to cum for me.* My thoughts were dangerously obsessive now. My cock resting in the crevice where their hips pressed into one another, I rocked and slid against them. Raphael watched, my cock on display on top of curvy flesh for his viewing pleasure.

They were trying to recover, but my fingers were rubbing, enjoying how swollen, hot, and wet my cock had made them. *Touch yourself, Raphael,* I thought, glaring wildly at Raphael as I licked a fang at him. Movement under the shirt, the tensing of the arm that snaked under, showed me what I wanted so badly to see. *That's it. Cum for me. We both know only I can do that for you.* I rocked my hips, fucking them both with my thrusting fingers. I edged closer, wincing as the cock ring made itself known. *Shit.* Raphael grunted; his breath hitched. I pushed forward, and though uncomfortable, I peaked. Cum dribbled slowly from my constricted cock, milky as it ran down my shaft like honey. His shirt fluttered faster now. *Fucking cum already, Raphael.* It was low, too low for the girls' peaking screams to hear as Raphael's eyes closed and he moaned.

Abandoning it all, I was back to sitting in the tub with my cock sore, swooping my wine off the shelf. "You girls catch your breath. There's more where that came from."

"Dammit, Jen," panted Beau as she punched her arm.

"Ouch," Jen whimpered, still trying to catch her breath.

Raphael warned, "Don't think about taking that off, Ashton."

"Wouldn't dream of it," I snarked.

Prepare to cum a few more times while your stallion fucks his way to a good night's rest. Gritting my fangs, I cast a dangerous glare at Raphael, who shifted in reply as if eager to see which of us could outlast the other tonight.

CHAPTER 38

The Bruising of Pride

I awoke on the floor of the castle room, flat on my back, hungover and sore in places that made my stomach turn. *My loins and sword feel like they've been hit by a horse's hoof.* I winced, every slight movement agonizing. "One should never force coming when wearing a cock ring," a Scarlett man named Nick Savage had once told me. I swallowed, and my eyes teared. The drunken mistake had given me a new ring in the most sensitive of places. *I'm a fucking fool.* Panic filled me as I couldn't recall removing the monstrosity I had misused all night. *Dammit.* I sat up, realizing I was in nothing more than a cotton shirt. Part of me was frightened to lift the shirt to see what I had done to myself, while the other half fretted about whether I had had enough sense to remove the fucking cock ring.

"I took it back," grumbled Raphael from the bed, an arm hanging off the edge.

I flopped onto my back as relief washed over me. *I clearly aim to become a eunuch at this rate.*

"I wouldn't look at it," added Raphael, his own hangover matching the growing headache I carried. "Granted, I think it worked."

Furrowing my brow, I pressed, "What worked?"

"My father's technique," Raphael answered.

Looking over, all I could see was the singular arm, unmoving. "And that was?"

"We had a stallion that kept busting up the stables, wrecking fences, and sowing his seed in every mare he caught the scent of." Raphael chuckled, the story bringing back delightful memories. "You see, my father knew horses better than anyone in the empire. It was his secret hobby and something he often made time for more than for me, his half-witted son." Raphael huffed, shuffling to the edge of the bed to meet my gaze on the floor. "So, he took his belt, dared to put himself in striking range of the stallion's mighty kick, and he put a fucking cock ring on it."

I paled as the story went on; his grin was only matched by the sparkle in his eyes.

"He had them take out a mare in heat, let him fuck her until she bruised his pride silly." Raphael rolled away, howling in laughter now. "And the stallion never ran off for another mare nor tore up his master's stable ever again."

"I'll need ointment to relieve the pain," I demanded, unamused to have been compared to his father's equine adventures.

"I have already made arrangements," he chortled. "But will you be able to fight in three days?"

"Both of my prides should be in working order by then," I spat.

I had flashes of the night, of wincing in pain as I foolishly came, knowing the price, but did so anyway in order to antagonize Raphael. *I did make him cum twice before...* My loins throbbed in pain. *Indeed, the alcohol didn't aid in that last moment. Did I pass out?* I sat up and eased onto my legs to scan the room. My pants were tossed to the side not far from me, while the armor and satchel were lovingly placed in my favorite chair on the far side. I took a step and jolted, then grunted in pain. *If I wasn't a daemon with fast healing, this would have proven most frightening.* Plucking my pants from the ground, I eased them on.

"It's bad enough they think me a fool for giving my champion a fill of wine and women before the fight." Raphael changed topics, pushing the matter at hand once more. "Did you choose a weapon?"

"I did." Shoving my armor to the floor, I eased myself into the chair, hissing. "But I don't think you'll approve."

Groaning, Raphael rolled onto his back and threw an arm over his eyes. "You can't be serious?"

"I am," I spoke sternly.

"Fine." Inhaling deeply, he held it in for a moment before blowing it out. "Do you want money or have a custom version made?"

"Money. I'll buy one I feel I can use best," I insisted. "Did we replace the other?"

"No, so buy two while you're at it. No—" Raphael sat up and furrowed his brow. "Sit and lie on the bed and heal. We can give money and instructions to Henri to retrieve them."

"Can we trust him to get us the best ones?" I weighed the option of the bed as my bruised pride continued to punish me for daring to sit.

"How is he to know you intend to take one into battle," drawled Raphael as he threw his covers off, naked, as he left the bed to retrieve a robe. "Now, stop being stubborn. Shed your pants and lay on the bed."

The Bruising of Pride

"I want to hide away what I have done." I eased to my feet, wincing to stand. As the weight of my sack shifted, the pain became horrendous rather than just the usual annoyance of sticking to my thigh. "Fuck me, I knew better…" I scoffed, leaning on my knees.

"Listen, if you wish for aid putting ointment on your purple jewels, I suggest—" I dropped the pants at his words and eased into the soft cushions of the bed. "No, you're right." With a grunt, I managed to get comfortable, covering myself to the waist to hide my shame. "Wake me when the ointment comes."

The covers jerked up and off, and I gripped them to cover my crotch, only to let go as I yelped in pain. "Fuck!"

"You fucking moron." A tall gentleman renowned in Captiva City for his erotic wares known only as N Savage, started to laugh. "I told your ass not to do that. Why the fuck does half your dick look like an eggplant? Didn't fucking listen to me, did you?"

I glowered over at Raphael, who raised his eyebrows and covered the smirk under a hand.

"Why him? He's the last one I wanted to see me like this," I groaned.

"Look, I ain't fucking putting this on him." N Savage dropped the small jar onto the bed beside me. "Remember, boys, this is great for bruises and the back door." He patted my arm, winking. "And definitely invite me back for the next orgy."

"Next orgy?" Raphael knitted his brow, his smile gone. "What orgy?"

"Aw man, you missed it." N Savage hung an arm over Raphael's shoulder, poking his chest as he spoke. "He had this room packed with naked bodies and more bizarre toys than even I have ever seen. In fact," N Savage snapped his fingers before pointing at me as I sniffed the ointment and cringed, "that's when you commissioned all those toys for the stash, right? How'd they…" N Savage stopped short as I cut him a warning glare. "Oh, right. Gotcha, boss. Well, I'm out. Call me back for something fun, and let's not, um, do that again." He motioned to my crotch, laughing and shaking his head. "Fucking crazy."

The door closed behind him, and Raphael snorted. "I see you know my associate."

"Probably better than you." I glared at the jar with a deep look of contemplation on my face.

"Here." Raphael took it from me.

He motioned for me to let him see. Laying back, I opened my thighs, reluctant and swallowing. Closing my eyes, I felt nauseated about what would happen next. *This is going to hurt like hell*—A cooling sensation numbed and tamed the bruising. Raphael's hands were gentle. Closing my eyes, I pulled back all the thoughts I wanted to let loose. *If I get hard, I think I'm going to lose my cock.* The sound of the jar closing brought my attention back, and he pulled the covers up. Raphael had turned away, and I missed the expression on his face.

"How bad is it?" I asked.

"Bad." Clearing his throat, Raphael didn't look back in fear his face would give something away. "Let's not do that again. Now rest."

He blew out the lantern, the low fire in the fireplace the only light as he settled into my chair, arms crossed. "You can lay in bed next to me, you know."

"If someone sees..." Raphael huffed.

"What does it matter?" I opened one eye at him.

Nodding, he relented and climbed back into bed. I smiled. A small victory. Silence fell between us once more. *I hate how easily he tends to tame me after I've even pushed him to the edge. What a couple of fools we are when it comes to jealousy and lust, anger and nurture.*

Chapter 39

The Significance of Threads

The crowds of fools lining the road as we paraded our way to certain death made me ill. *This is just a decorated version of the battle that killed Mother, isn't it? How is this a better option?* The four viceroys rode beside their chosen champions, starting from the castle gates, parading down the main west road and out to where they had fashioned a wooden amphitheater for the event. Feran seemed as tense as me; our girth and height were only matched by one other competitor, Philippe.

I watched him just in front of us; he didn't spare the cheers and waving crowd any attention. Philippe wore a grim expression, eyes straight, like a paladin of the old gods with his silver armor and white fur and leather gear. *He feels the same as I do. This isn't something to celebrate or treat like some festival. These are lives, their lives, on the line, though none of them know it yet.* Snorting, I shifted under the weight of my leather and metal armor and thought bitterly, *they soon will.* I tugged on my left spaulder, hating how decorated it had become while I slept the last few days away, recovering. *I feel like a prized pony. Perhaps Philippe is in—no, he had that armor before they came and wore it often. Warmongers, he and Grandpapa.*

Unlike when I first wore it, the armor plates and leather now had added inlays gilded with gold, worthy of a prince. This was only matched by the encrusted wolf heads with garnet eyes protruding out, snarling and baring their teeth, ready to bite. *It scares me how much this one on the shoulder reminds me of that Alpha that I faced. Granted, I suppose I would rather be a wolf than the emperor's personal stallion.* Even the deep red cape pulled and flapped in the wind as we pushed out the west gate and followed the road to the arena. Beside me, on Ginnie once more, was Raphael. I snorted, the wolf coat grandiose on him with the wolf head hood. The chains rattled under each hoof beat as the teeth and jewels clattered. The was cut long and more of a winter coat, but he wore it. *Cheeky bastard opened my package and took it for himself.*

Viceroy Regius wore an elaborate crown as if he were king of some foreign country as he waved and blew kisses. *Ugh, the ego on that one.* In front of him was Viceroy Forestier, who seemed to share the same sentiment. The daemon beside him was indeed from the Pomeroy clan, from the garments. My stomach knotted. *I wonder if Henri put one of his sons on the line or if one of them insisted. After all, I imagine those three brothers are feeling like Lillian and me. Just want to protect our family and our world at any cost.* The armor looked lacking, despite the wealth the family had. *Granted, they may be counting on agility. It's not a bad tactic, but… this isn't a battlefield. We're caged dogs fighting for our masters. Two of us are wolves feigning not to be wild and feral.* I glanced at Philippe, whose scabbard clanked against the regalia he wore. *And only one of us has tasted a battle and blood. No one here is experienced other than Philippe.*

Leaning, I peered ahead, seeing the youth of a champion from the Farrow clan beside Viceroy Vendecci. He was thin, not even close in age to the rest of us. I swallowed. The smile on his face was unnerving as he spoke to Viceroy Vendecci, who met his little warrior with his own grin. Unlike the rest of us, they had a third person riding along with them. Madeleine dressed in black lace and looked like a phantom or… *is she trying to look like the Sacrificial Daughter? How blasphemous.* With blonde hair, he was a mixed daemon of Farrow and another tribe. *She's using this as a chance to cull the herd. She's always wanted to purify the sacred bloodline and even had the gall once to suggest we should only breed within as a means to gain more power. For what? To rule over and reign over? The wilds? People who wish to be free? Over a continent that knew peace?*

Raphael cleared his throat, and I righted myself. "You shouldn't make it so obvious you are glowering at your competition."

"I'm not glowering." I glowered at Raphael. "I feel bad for the kid up there."

"Yeah, I was thinking it seems strange for them to choose someone like that, but I suppose she's trying not to get her brother killed," reasoned Raphael, pulling Ginnie to ride closer to Feran now so we can talk without the need to shout.

"You mistake her for kind and caring." I paused as the shadow of the amphitheater cast a cool darkness over us all as we traveled through the large gates. "You see, that boy is mixed blood." Soon we met the sun again inside the center of the arena. "She's using the Blood Duels to kill off impure bloodlines in the Farrow clan, and I'm sure we don't know how far her dark intent goes." I looked around, chills running up my spine at seeing statues of the Fates at the three corners of where we were intended to battle for our lives, each holding gilded versions of the ordained items, yet no threads attached between them. "You see this."

"I do, and it feels like they've made this seem like divine intervention." Raphael shifted uncomfortably in his seat. "They did this, too, back in the Old Continent. Fallen Arbor is at play here. I'm sure of it."

"Fallen Arbor is already winning." I locked gazes with Raphael, dread crushing us. "We're too late."

Philippe turned, and he, too, met my gaze. *He feels unsettled by it, too. This is too far, Madeleine. No one but the locals and you would know the significance of what you have done and the message this seeks. And worse, the youth of our people will not know either. How sinister.*

"But shouldn't these have a thread connecting them?" As expected, Raphael was aware of the missing element, unlike his other Old Continent invaders. "What does the lack of threading between them mean? I've never seen all three Fates anywhere without the string passing between them."

"It means that here, the Fates will not give, mend, or protect your threads. Madeleine is giving the youth the impression that they can decide how their fate will be woven here in this arena." I scowled. The roaring excitement as we parceled out into tiny groupings only made my stomach twist. *This farce just will not stop. Either you hope to call the gods here or hope to expel them from your evil deeds, Madeleine.*

"And to you?" Raphael's expression filled with concern, as it called my attention back to him. "What does this really mean? I know you follow the religion to the bone, do you not?"

"Yeah, Philippe and I both have a soft spot for the Fates and the old ways." Glancing at the statues one more time, I answered, "This means they are not welcome here." Raphael flinched, and I chuckled as I explained, "It's rather blasphemous, I know. They are not welcome here, and threads will burn unless they intervene. Though, it's also superstitious in a way and makes me wonder what dark gods and old ways Madeleine is catering to behind closed doors."

"Do you think your beloved Fates will intervene?" Raphael arched a brow. "I know ours didn't lift a fucking finger. In any case, don't be shocked if they fail you today."

"I don't know," I hummed, thinking on it. "I know you don't believe in it, but... seeing that all three bloodlines found themselves here tells me something is up. Madeleine is trying too hard to keep the Fates out, which means she knows something I don't." I stole a glance at Madeleine, and she sneered and turned away. "I hope the goddesses find their own way to crash the party."

"Perhaps that's why you're here," Raphael jested. "Ashton, the feral wolf of the Fates set loose to teach the Fanged Lady a lesson she shall never forget—he bites!"

"Careful," I warned. "They are listening, and if the idea strikes them, they'll tie your thread to that notion with my own, and we'll find ourselves along for a ride we have no more say on."

The Champion's Lord

"Superstitious," Raphael chortled, shaking his head. "I can't decide which you are, a fanatic of the faith or a reasonable man who sees it as a facade for ill-fated people like ourselves."

I opened my mouth to retort something, but the drums started to sound the familiar rhythm of the crier. As if summoned, an overly dolled-up man in bright colors, worthy of festival decorations, appeared on a platform. *Ha, the viceroys made themselves a stage and balcony worthy of kings. I suppose they deserve a front row seat to the horrors they have created for us.* The crowd grew silent as the drums drew near to the end of the small diddly that we all had grown to recognize. The crier took in his audience, inhaling deeply as he prepared himself for the challenge of hitting the ears that sought the words they had come to take in.

"Ladies and gentlemen of Grandemere! Welcome to the first of many battles, a new tradition to show the prowess of our people and seek to bring order to our lands. I wish to welcome you all to the Blood Duel. Today, we will decide who will be this season's Champion Supreme, and their master will take the seat of Speaker of the House on our council!" The crowd exploded in shouts and cheers, the cacophony of it vibrating in my lungs and leaving my eardrums aching. "Let me introduce you to our champions. Fighting for House Vendecci is Brett Warren, a new and upcoming youth from the South Region and Madeleine Farrow's own village."

I winced at the fact. *That crazy bitch is starting close to home. Does she know no mercy for those who she grew up with or watched grow under her family's care?*

"Next, we have a face you surely have seen in town. The youngest son, Fabien Pomeroy, is here on behalf of House Forestier from the East Region." Another roar and whistling as he turned to the next grouping. "House Regius from the West Region is represented by a popular figure you already know well, Lord Knight Philippe Farrow!" Roses came cascading down, women screeching, and the old man didn't even flinch as his horse resettled its hooves. "What an honor we get to see this decorated soldier and Paladin of the Fates in action!" Another barrage of shouts before he, at last, settled on us. "And now, the rare gem as the empire's Heir Apparent has joined the council as House Traibon."

Hushed whispers and distress made vomit roll into my throat. *How much has Madeleine and Fallen Arbor ruined our chances at the people's level? I didn't expect this attack, did Raphael?* I stole a glance at him, but Raphael stood as stern and stoic as Philippe, and my chest ached. *He was even prepared for this, too. Or did he only suspect this outcome when it was clear Fallen Arbor had set the arena up?*

"Their champion is one many of us have had the pleasure knowing, in and out of the sheets." The audience laughed, jeered, and whistled at this notion. "The one and only, the talk of the town, and the wolf of the Scarlett House," I rolled my eyes at the lude introduction, "Ashton Le Denys Thompson!" The crowd found their voices and shouts once more, tipping the scales as flowers and coin landed across the arena floor.

The Significance of Threads

"What do the coins mean? Flowers are a sign of affection and support, but coin?" Raphael arched a brow, curious now.

Ignoring him, I stood in my saddle, waving my arms to demand more. The crowd peaked. More coin hit the floor, earning me scowls from the other champions. Satisfied with the payment that rained down, I sat down and jeered Feran, spurring him to bump against Ginnie. Grabbing Raphael's head, I kissed him before he managed to shove me off. The crowd lurched forward, shouts of names and pointing as they were excited. I had caught onto the game, and more coins fell as they shouted who my next target shall be.

I pointed to Philippe, and they squealed.

Again, I spurred Feran in his direction. His horse spun; a long blade was drawn and pointed at me. The crowd laughed and booed. I looked to my muses with a deep frown and, patting my chest, signaled how heartbroken I was to be denied. Another round of whistles and laughter followed, ensuring I had their full attention and support. I rode back to Raphael, and he palmed my face, earning more laughter and shouts.

From under Raphael's hand, I chortled, "You know, at the Scarlett House, tossing a coin at a man's feet means a nickel for your pickle, Raphael."

Unable to get the crowd back under control, everyone retreated to the hidden war rooms built under the benches where the still rowdy crowd thudded overhead. *At least I earned some favor back. They didn't come here for politics or faith. No, this is entertainment and that, that is something I know well!*

CHAPTER 40

The First of Many Battles

It seemed like ages, waiting for them to call for me. Raphael approached, a scowl on his face. *He hates that I'm going out there and not him.* I shrugged to myself. *He is the better fighter. Too bad. I wasn't going to allow you to go anyhow, Golden Boy.* Raphael tugged on my arm, and I gave him a bewildered expression. For a moment, I got lost in the way the fur coat framed him where he stood, looking more fierce and princely than ever. Pulling his rapier off his side, he tried to hand it to me.

I balled my fist and shook my head.

His eyes widened as he lipped, "Take it!" And shoved it to my chest.

Whispering, I hissed, "No!"

"Take it!" Raphael pushed harder. "It's yours." His wrath was written across his face.

Grabbing the rapier, I shoved it hard back into his chest. Raphael's face flushed red as he shoved it into my chest yet again, the sound of the hilt pinging off my chest plate. I threw my arms out, hands fisted like a child, refusing to move on the matter.

"Fucking take it!" Raphael shouted, unable to keep his temper in check.

"No." I smirked at the idea that my temper didn't best me for once. "I have my weapon."

"That's not a weapon," he hissed.

The First of Many Battles

"Look, weren't you the one who said anything can be a weapon?" Raphael winced as I pushed his own words back onto him, and he covered his face in shame. "I promise I'm not being a fool. I have a plan."

"Says the man who paid for his armor with coins off the arena floor because the crowd wants to pay you for sexual favors," Raphael reprimanded me on my feat.

"Don't be jealous," I cooed, pushing his rapier back to him and walking away to retrieve what I had picked out for the occasion. "Besides, I have the most experience with this. I love using this thing. It can take a hit."

"It's a farming tool, Ashton." Raphael flung an arm at the arena door. "They all have weapons, swords made for cleaving men's arms off. Weapons specifically designed for battle."

"No offense, but I didn't come here to maim or kill anyone." Holding the long wooden handle, I grinned like a fool to see the leather gripping that helped me find the center. "This hoe should do the trick. Besides, folks want to be entertained, and I need to do something to improve your reputation."

"You do realize the silence is because it was more of a shock that a local businessman and known hermit had such a prestigious standing this whole time?" Raphael groaned, rubbing his forehead. "I appreciate you think my ego is wounded, but I can assure you that is not the case, my wolf."

Scoffing, I tugged at the cape. "Do I really need to wear this blasted thing? It's going to get me killed."

Inhaling deeply, Raphael finally glared at me before smirking and cooing, "Folks want to be entertained." He leaned his head onto my shoulder, whispering, "Come back in one piece."

The arena door opened, and a servant motioned for me to exit. Behind them, the sun lit the dirt floor of the arena like a brazier of white ash. I tugged one last time on all my buckles, thumping heavy-handedly across the panels to make sure it was all in the right place. *Last thing I want is a piece to cut loose or pinch the shit out of me.* Satisfied it was in working order, I marched for the door.

Raphael had cut between me and the doorway. He planted his lips firmly on mine as he deepened the kiss. *Fool, now they know about us...* I could hear the crowd whistling and women shrieking as I pulled him in to deepen it further. *I can't say I wasn't hoping for one more before battle in case it would be my last.* I pulled away, the blue gemstones ensnaring me.

Raphael warned, "Come back alive, or I'll personally hunt down the Fates myself."

"Promise?" I jested, and he walked away, out the door that led to the platforms. *I'll take that as a yes, then.*

Stepping out into the arena, I squinted. *Today's a shit day for summer to start. Hot weather while in armor is a bitch.* I blinked a few times, my eyes adjusting, and before me was Fabien Pomeroy. The breeze sent my cape flapping in the wind, dust pluming up between us. *Damn, he looks just like Henri when he was younger.* Dark skin, tall, and athletic build. Fabien glared with his maroon eyes glowing as he stood far away. Overhead the crowd roared, the crier spouting gibberish, but I paid no heed to the fools who pitched us against one another like fighting dogs. Instead, I focused on Fabien, taking in the lack of armor, the clenched teeth, fangs long, and lastly, the weapon hidden in the sash around his narrow waist. I sighed, putting a hand on my hip as I looked up at the waving fans. *Damn, this doesn't feel right.*

"You sure about this, Fabien?" I asked, casting a serious glare.

"What choice do we have?" Fabien retorted.

"Where's your armor, then?" My words made him tense, and I smiled, knowing full well what Henri would have told his prideful son. "I see. Henri asked you to turn down the fight. And, as collateral, took your armor from you to ensure you wouldn't make an attempt." Sliding my gaze downward, we circled one another, and the sun caught the metal poorly hidden in the sash. "Does he know you brought a dagger out here?"

Fabien pulled it out, and the crowd roared, goading him on. "My father told me you ran away from the battle that day."

"I did." I watched him, just as the wolves had watched me. *He's trembling. His grip is shit. And, like me, he's just as naked as I was that day.* "But don't take my cowardice to mean that I don't know how to fight."

Fabien pointed his blade at me, spouting rumors and ill-intended words. "They said you were supposed to be your mother's shield, and you let her die alone on the battlefield!"

Gasps and silence filled the crowd as the trumpets blasted for the battle to start. Sucking on my cheek, I squinted up at the platform where Raphael's golden braid swayed in the wind, catching my focus. *Why'd he have to bring that up?* I spun the hoe, swirling it in my hand as I began contemplating what I wanted to do. My anger was growing, and I landed my glare on Fabien. *His shaking is starting to slow, but that's the adrenaline of the horns and start.* Wiping sweat from my brow, I flicked it onto the dirt and licked a fang. *One more chance. Then I bust Fabien in the mouth for talking about my mother. Yeah, that feels right…*

"Stand down, Fabien." I stopped where I stood. "Don't make me do this because I'm sure no one wants to say they lost to Ashton the Ashamed." *Yeah, I know what they call me behind my back, kid.*

"You don't even have a weapon," Fabien admonished, baffled by the hoe in my hand.

"Oh, this is a weapon," I reassured. "If you want, I'll show you."

Fabien scoffed, "You really have gone off the deep end. Father said you've gone mad with grief."

"And your father's right." I gripped the handle with both hands, widening my stance.

Fabien glanced at his blade and took a more offensive pose. He serpentined the blade in the air, a show that he was very familiar with the weapon he had brought. I stepped forward, and Fabien backed away. With a fanged grin, I flicked my eyebrows up and gave Fabien a look that said, "Really?" Anger seethed forward in his

The First of Many Battles

eyes, and he roared, charging at me. Fabien swung wide, and I hooked the blade with the metal of the hoe and thrust downward. Shocked, he pulled the blade back and jabbed it forward once again. Pushing down on the handle, I blocked and stepped back. Fabien ran forward, and I sidestepped, his wild swing missing. His eyes shut as he lunged in for a close attack. *He's so scared he can't keep his eyes open.*

I hooked the hoe on a leg and yanked. Fabien's leg left him, and he went tumbling to the ground. Backing off, I gave him a moment to sputter the dirt from his mouth and grab the blade that had left his hand so easily. Climbing back to his feet, Fabien wore a soured expression. I twirled the hoe a few times before letting it rest casually on my shoulder. Shaking off the fall, he adjusted his grip on the blade. Another shout and rush forward. With a huff, I jabbed the handle end into his foot before rolling out of his fall range. Again, he faceplanted into the dirt and the dagger scattered. I glanced up to the platform where Henri stood next to Raphael, making idle chatter. *They are wondering if I will end this or do harm to Fabien, I imagine.* Looking back to the youth, I put the hoe back on my shoulder and the other hand on my hip.

"Do you admit defeat?" I asked, watching Fabien stand again, chin bleeding from a scrape.

Fabien panicked, scrambling to yoke his dagger from the ground. "I can do this all day!" he roared. "It's not like you can kill someone with a hoe."

My temper flared. "Fabien, stand down." Rubbing the back of my head, the lack of a braid reminded me that my intent could no longer be my own. *Raphael would insist on reminding the boy anything can kill if that's the intent.* "I will not go easy if you strike me again."

Fabien ran at me, his eyes more focused, his grip surer. *Now it's a more serious fight. But there's still too wide of a gap of experience between us.* Fabien charged in. I aimed for his foot, and he jumped back. *Good, he's not closing his eyes anymore and is being more attentive. Consider this your first lesson from me, boy.* Gripping the handle with both hands, I blocked the next two swings, the dagger scraping the wood and clinking against the hoe. Drawing back, I jabbed forward, popping Fabien dead center in his face with the flat of the hoe. The dagger fell, and he stumbled back, holding his face. Blood dripped across the ground, but I didn't stop there. Hooking his leg, Fabien landed on his back with a loud thud and wheezed as air rushed from his lungs. With uncanny accuracy, I brought the sharp edge down, aiming for his head.

Fabien screamed; the hoe so close to his ear it cut his braid. "Do you admit defeat?" I growled. "Or the next time I bring this hoe to the ground, it'll do so through your skull, Fabien."

"Defeat!" he shrieked.

He crawled from me, blood covering his face and his nose broken. The crowd roared, but I didn't celebrate. *There's nothing to celebrate about a grown-ass man beating the shit out of a clueless boy.*

CHAPTER 41

Blood and Threads

I sat on the bench watching as Philippe faced off with the youth from his own village. What words they exchanged were too far off and muted to hear. *Philippe and I will face off. He looks like he's doing the same as I did against Fabien. Now we will see which of our pupils heeds our advice.* Again, the experience and age seemed centuries apart between the mismatched opponents. *There was no drawing of names, as they implied. They pitched us both against the youth and saved the real fight for last. So, the question is, what does the scroll say on this note? Sadly, Fabien and Brett will have to keep facing us in fight until death or rendered too crippled.*

It was over, fast and hard. *Maybe it's not the same. The Paladin of the Fates isn't going to humor this folly.* Philippe didn't draw his blade, deflecting with his gauntlets and scabbard before beating Brett down with one powerful punch. *Ouch.* Blood arched as Brett's feet locked onto one another, and he thudded to the ground. Brett didn't move. The audience, who seemed so happy over the fights, fell silent, gasping audibly. *Now they realize our lives are on the line. Was that why he took him down so quickly? That he will not entertain as I had done?*

"Kill him!" Madeleine screeched, and the arena gasped once more. "Kill him, Philippe, as your master demands of you! The Fates are not welcome here, and all sins are forgiven!"

Blood and Threads

Cruza was quick to tug her back, paling at the outcry before slapping her. Madeleine held her face as she fell back into her chair. *Bloodlust will outrun her master's needs, I see.* The rage on Cruza Vendecci's face said it all. How dare his trusted servant imply he give his property away so easily? Losing a chance at Speaker of the House was more than enough. Philippe marched for the exit; his stone-faced expression said nothing of his sister's demands on her twin. Ahmed Regius shifted in his chair, a serious look across his face. *He, too, wanted the boy to die for the sake of his own greed. I suppose it's come to our fight.* Standing where I sat on the front bench, I jumped the wall and let out a loud whistle, sharp as an eagle's cry. Philippe stopped in his steps.

"Let's get this over with, Philippe!" I shouted.

Philippe turned back, narrowing his eyes at me. "Yes, let's just end this sooner and not drag it out."

The crowd roared with excitement as Philippe doubled-back. Servants dragged Brett from the arena as we circled one another like two animals, ready to strike. A servant ran out, handing me my hoe. The crowd laughed and whistled in acknowledgment. Philippe knitted his brow, matching me as we paced and stepped in sync with one another. The hiss of his blade leaving the scabbard made the hairs on the back of my neck stand on end. *He's going to take this seriously and either kill me or give me the first real ass-whooping of my life.* Swallowing, I held my hoe in both hands, unsure when the fight would take off. *I can't be careless. Not with him.*

"Why take Brett down so fast?" I pressed, very aware any words said here were free from prying ears.

"Mercy." Philippe glanced at the blood painting his gauntlet. "He's a dear friend of my daughter."

"He's a little young for Francesca," I humored. "Isn't she my age?"

"She watched over him as a baby on more than one occasion. Watching him die would be like losing a child." Philippe swapped the longsword from one hand to the other. "Shall I use my strong hand, or weak hand, to defeat you today?"

"Are you really still mad about that?" I blinked, recognizing the tone and intent. *Last time he said that to me, it was…* "You are!" A grin crossed my face, and I relaxed. "You're still pissed about—"

"Shut your whore mouth," Philippe hissed, choosing his weak hand. "I will beat you over the head with your pitiful farming tool. This isn't a joke, Ashton Le Denys Thompson! Perhaps I can relieve you of your fingers and other appendages to render you useless at the Scarlett House!"

"Oh, come now, Philippe," I chortled. "She's nearly a good hundred years old."

"She is my daughter," he spat.

"I suppose you've been wanting to fight me over the matter for a while." I scratched my jaw and shot a glance at Raphael, who wore a serious expression. "Just leave something for my lord, no? He's rather fond of my … services."

The horns filled the air, and Philippe came in striking hard. Unlike Fabien, his strikes left deep cuts in the handle, chips and splinters flaking off. Each block jarred my hands, and the joints in my wrists, elbows, and shoulders ached with my efforts not to let go. *Shit! He hits like the rocks I catch on a bad day in the field!* Sweat dripped down my temple as I gritted my fangs. The speed and rhythm of his blows was uncanny and only matched the ferocity of the wolves from before. Anger rose inside me, and I managed to shift my defense. I drew down the hoe and broke his drumming swings. I aimed to jab forward, but Philippe rolled under and was on his feet by the time I steadied my own stance.

Sliding my hand down the shaft, the shards of wood bit at me. *If this keeps up, he's going to cut through it, and me, all with his weaker hand. Fucking monster!* Ignoring the splinters, I added length to the hoe and went on the offense. Swinging down on him, I kept my distance and forfeited on powerful strikes to save my hide. Philippe blocked with a gauntlet, and I pulled him forward; the surprise in his eyes a small victory. He knocked the pommel of the sword into my gut as he shouldered the hoe off his gauntlet. Coughing, I wheezed, backing away. In horror, I watched him change hands. *Not the good hand.*

"I should have run you through, but I'm not as well practiced with my left hand." Philippe smirked, rolling both shoulders. "I must say, you did catch me off guard. For the first time in a long while, I'm enjoying myself."

"Warmonger," I croaked, finally drawing in a deep breath. "Why are you swapping hands?"

"Well, it seems you're not as bad as I had thought." Philippe dropped into a pose. "I'll give you the attack this time."

I stood there with the weight of his invitation squashing what confidence I had at ever besting him. Scanning him over, neither of us was panting, meaning this fight hadn't gotten far at all. *He's definitely going to kick my ass.* I stared down at my gnarled wooden handle, the splinters making my hands sting and bleed. *No time to fret over small matters. He might kill me over fucking Francesca in his bed when he went to Winter's Perch that year.* I repositioned my hands to give myself more reach at the furthest end to the head of the hoe. *I can't get close. If he has a chance, I'm getting stabbed just for the fun of it. Psycho.* I drew a breath, steadying my nerves. I focused on Philippe; he seemed impassable. *There's no way I'm winning.* Scoffing, every muscle ached and burned under the tension I carried. *But I can see how far I can push myself.*

Raising the hoe overhead, I launched straight ahead at Philippe. His pose shifted, the movements graceful and agile. *He's aiming to deflect!* Some fleeting instinct drove my next actions. I let the handle slide, splinters clawing my palms as I returned to a higher, more powerful grip closer to the metal. Dropping to my knees, the momentum and sand frictionless as I slid past Philippe to the side. I hooked his leg, and he dropped to one knee, spinning with an amused expression. My heart pounded louder than the screams and whistles that poured down upon us both. I launched to my feet, running back to him. This time I let the handle claw into me the other direction, then reached back as I swung. Philippe raised the sword to block the end of the hoe. The collision was just enough to send sparks before denting his pauldron and bouncing off.

The force of it helped me push the bulk of my body back to where I aimed to stay, mimicking the blind spot as the wolves had done with me. I barely managed to retrieve and reset my grip for the powerful one as Philippe lunged forward. Swinging again from the opposite side of his sword, he was too angled to get a solid strike. I aimed for his shoulder again and found it gone. I blinked as my body twisted, and I lost my footing. *Fuck! I thought I had him and overshot and didn't think about what if I missed—ugh!* A boot connected with my ribs from under where I fell. The crack and pop made me scream as the world slowed. My eyes were wide with pain and surprise, my thoughts grasping what had transpired in a matter of seconds. *He fucking dropped to the ground flat on his back!*

I bounced and rolled across the dirt, my side on fire and bruising with the broken rib. Spitting blood, I was on my feet. Philippe jumped to his feet and ran at me with a wild grin and a glow in his eyes. *He's enjoying this.* Holding the handle tightly, I could feel the heat of my blood and sweat dripping from my hands, down my forearms, and off my elbows. Blood dribbled from my mouth, dirt clinging and crusting across half my face. *Now I'm pissed off. That was dirty, Old Man.* My temper rose, a pop making it easier to breathe, and his grin faltered a second before I rose the hoe to block the two-handed downward strike.

The blade cut the wood better than any axe could have dreamed of doing. Tossing the wooden end at Philippe's head only bought me enough time to block the next two-handed blow with the metal of the hoe. We stood there, two bulls gridlocked against one another. *Which of us has more power?* I pushed, and Philippe slid slightly. It was enough to prompt Philippe to counter by sliding the sword, though he grunted as it failed. Again, that uncanny drive for survival goaded me. Kneeing the pommel, I brought him back to where I had the advantage, and he scoffed. With a throwing motion, I executed a defensive maneuver and broke away safely. Philippe glanced down to marvel that I had mustered enough power to succeed.

We paused, panting.

Wiping blood from my chin, I spat more across the sand. The shorter hoe was still viable to use, but I had lost the advantage of being able to attack from afar. *Shit.* Philippe shook out his hands and again gripped the hilt with both hands. I winced, although my broken rib had healed the moment I had found my wrath. *I need to feel more pissed off if I have a chance. The uncanny ability to heal quickly when pissed off was made for the battlefield, wasn't it?* I glanced at the statue of the Devoted Sister, the protector of threads and the one who bestowed the men of Le Denys with the ability, and she met my gaze. The sun made the weapon in her grip glisten and strike across his eyes. *A sword big enough to be a shield. Perhaps...*

The distraction prompted Philippe to launch his next attack. A breeze yoked on the cape, and I misstepped and flinched. I barely managed to meet his strike with my own, the weight of it jarring the hoe from my hands. Rage filled me, the cape still snapping in the wind and clinging to me like the sails on a ship. *This fucking thing.* Managing to duck under the strike, I tore the offending garment from my armor and cast it like a fishing net at Philippe. It caught his blade, tangling with it instead of being cleaved into shreds. *Thank the Fates!* I turned, my anger fueling me to heal just enough to break into full stride across the arena. *Fucking cape!* The crowd lost it; shouts and the beating of feet on benches drummed alongside the stampede of my heartbeat.

Slamming into the Devoted Sister statue, I tugged at her wrists. The sword she carried was almost my height, but I didn't care. *Anything is better than no weapon!* Cracks formed at her wrists. *Come the fuck on. BREAK!* The silver and gold ornate blade had every indication of having been made in the old ways of forging but was made too monstrous for practical use. Looking at the statue's face, I froze. The Devoted Sister's eyes glowed and blinked before a smile crawled across her face. *I've finally gone mad!* She looked down at the blade, and I followed her gaze. Her fingers let go, opening to set the blade free. I stumbled back, dragging the blade with both hands.

"ASHTON!" Philippe roared as he ripped the last of my cape from his blade.

I looked at Philippe but turned back to the statue of the Devoted Sister, stammering, "As you wish, I'll carry your blade and become a shield for the threads and fates of our people."

The hilt fit like it was intended for me and me alone. I tried to lift the huge flat sword, muscles aching under the strain. *Why in the fuck give me something I can't fucking lift?!* Wrath filled me. *She gave it to me! It's mine and mine alone to wield.* I changed my stance, widening it, and brought the blade up. *I don't care if I break myself doing it.* It was every bit as wide as I was shoulder to shoulder. If stabbed in the ground like a gravestone, the pommel would be just a palm's width higher than me.

The crowd fell silent, murmuring hisses like an ill-fated wind as Philippe charged forward. *Come, let's see how far my faith can carry me where no threads are welcomed and are replaced with the spilling of blood!*

Chapter 42
The First Champion Supreme

Philippe closed the gap quickly, sword lunging forward. I swung my newfound weapon. Our blades connected, and Philippe was pushed back several steps. Roaring, I let my muscles stretch as I braced to counter with a backswing, single-handed now. The crowd shrieked, but it only fed the anger building in me. *They are so focused on the battle before them that they failed to see the miracle that unfolded. I hope you didn't miss it. Madeleine. We're fucking coming for you!* Philippe deflected, and he backstepped and circled around. I dropped back into the low stance and held the blade with both hands, inhaling deeply as my body burned with adrenaline.

Coming from the side, I swooped a leg as I swung, using the weight of the blade to turn to face Philippe. Again, our blades connected. The grunt and growl escaped him as, once more, Philippe was shoved across the way and forced to retreat. I reset my stance; the movements coming to me naturally as sweat dripped off my chin, mixing with the sand and blood. Philippe circled me like the wolves, and my temper flared. *I dare you to try. You're only one.* Philippe settled in front of me. He steadied himself, calming his breath and temper. With two hands on the hilt, he launched forward. I waited, my gut tightening in anticipation of the calculated attack. Philippe raised his longsword overhead, but my gaze stayed on him. Sliding on his knees, he aimed to glide under me once more, wanting to distract me with his swing. I didn't budge. His gaze meeting mine, the world slowing down around us, and his sword sliced downward. I hadn't swung as his blade connected with mine, sparking down the length as he skidded underneath.

I let go of the behemoth blade in my hands.

The monstrous hunk of metal falling was enough for Philippe to abandon his own blade and aim to guard with his gauntlets. I lifted him up, pulling him out of the way as my blade thudded and lodged into the ground like an axe on the chopping block. I stood, lifting him as my temper peaked. I wanted to tear him to shreds, but I blinked, coming back to myself enough to drop him at my feet. Sand and dust plumed all around from our efforts. My blood painted the arena floor, the crowd's roar sounding perverse in the moment. Philippe sat on the ground, looking up at me in wonder. *Fuck, I'm exhausted.* I spat blood and wiped the sweat from my brow under the searing sunlight.

"Do you," I panted, swallowing to catch my breath to finish asking, "do you surrender?"

Philippe fell to his back and scoffed, "All that, and this is the great thing you have to say to me?"

I leaned on my knees, my side still tender from where he had cracked it despite my temper having healed it. "Tell me something, fellow worshipper of the Fates, I think I've gone mad."

"What?" Philippe squinted at me, just as winded as I had found myself.

"The sword." We both looked to the claymore with the blue inlays and gold gilding. "Did I break it from her hands, or did she give it to me?"

Philippe's eyes widened, and he twisted to peer at the statue. "She…" His words halted as his eyes fell upon cracked wrists and open hands before they fell to the ground in a pile of rubble before him. "She gave it to you. By the Fates, you were chosen."

"Fuck me." I covered my face. "I told Raphael he would invoke something when he said…" With my hands on my hips, I started to pace back and forth, sick to my stomach. *What else will they make me do?*

Philippe managed to kneel on the ground; bowing before me, he shouted so all who could hear. "I surrender!"

Closing my eyes, the battle over not easing the panic in my chest. "Philippe, say nothing about the statue."

"As you wish." Philippe sat up as I turned to glare down at him.

"Drinks later?" I offered.

Philippe laughed, pulling to his feet. "If that's where you think we can talk about the old gods and the Fates, then yes." He paused, looking at the blade before retrieving his own. "How the hell do you even wield something that weighs as much as a loaded wagon?" Philippe marveled, shaking his head in disbelief. "What was it that Raphael said that you think called their eyes to you?"

I licked a fang and confessed, "Ashton, the feral wolf the Fates set loose to teach the world a lesson they shall never forget—he bites!"

The First Champion Supreme

Philippe started laughing, slowly at first, and it built into a great roar.

"Come on. It makes no sense." I yanked my newfound sword from the ground. "Dammit, this thing is heavy." I scowled at the Devoted Sister statue, complaining, "We couldn't pick something more practical?" I dragged it behind me, unable to shoulder it as Philippe joined me in my march to the underbelly of the bleachers.

"I suppose, now I don't feel so angry." Philippe threw an arm over my shoulders, his mood more spirited than I had seen in a long while. "You're a better fighter, good instincts."

"Angry about losing?" I questioned, body sore and aching more with each step as the adrenaline started to fade.

"Francesca losing her flower to such a loyal servant to the Fates." I choked at his words. "What? Too much?" Philippe asked.

Shaking my head, I couldn't look the poor man in the face as I announced, "That flower was plucked and lost a long time before I came."

"Are you implying my daughter is a whore?" Philippe retreated his arm and scowled.

Cringing, I thought on the word and asked, "If you define someone who spends most of their time and money at the Scarlett House fucking… as a whore…"

"She does not." The shadow of the amphitheater brought cool air and relief from the sun.

I collapsed on the bench as Raphael burst into the room, and I motioned, "Ask the owner himself if you don't believe me."

Raphael flinched, catching the heated glare of Philippe, and paused to add, "Ask the owner what?"

Philippe snorted and turned away without another word. I met Raphael's gaze and waved it off. Raphael knelt in front of me; the relief across his face said it all. *He thought I was good as dead, too.* I pulled his forehead to my own, simply happy to be alive. My breathing had slowed, my heart thumping back to a normal range. My body trembled in the wake of the battle. Everything between Philippe and me on the battlefield seemed to have unfolded in a matter of minutes, though it felt as if I had been stuck for eons.

"You didn't have to win," Raphael spoke at last.

"I wasn't aiming to win," I snorted.

"You smell horrendous," he announced.

"I know. And I'm fucking tired as hell," I declared.

A servant approached, bowing deeply. "They wish for you to join everyone on the platform so we can declare you Speaker of the House and Champion Supreme for the season."

Nodding, Raphael clasped hands with me, pulling me to my feet. Gripping the sword, I lugged it onto a shoulder at last with a grunt. *So much heavier than the hoe.* Following them, we weaved through the many hidden rooms until we were led to the stairs. As we came to the top, the sun slammed into me. I blinked. The roaring crowd stood in praise of their first Champion Supreme. The bitter expressions on the faces of the viceroys and their advisors came with murderous intent. *Good, fuck you guys, too!* The underdog had come out on top despite the calamity that had unfolded. *It doesn't matter. None of you saw the Devoted Sister intervene.* My gaze slid to Madeleine, where she sat glowering, fingers drumming on her chair. *What have you done to force the gods to join in this ill-fated turn of events? What other dark rituals have you and Fallen Arbor performed that will bring Grandemere to its knees before we see an end to it all?*

"Ashton?" Raphael's words brought me back. "They said the sword is yours."

"Yes, let the sword be the symbol of Champion Supreme," offered Cruza Vendecci.

Casting my stare down to the Devoted Sister, I retorted, "Since this is the blade of my goddess, I guess that means," my eyes cut through him, glowing with the rise of my temper, "I can't allow anyone to ever defeat me."

"Philippe says he didn't know you had battle experience," interjected Ahmed Regius. "Where on earth did you acquire such skills?" he pressed, the suspicion in the eyes of all the viceroys weighing down on me.

I smiled, unbuckling my own gauntlet to show the scars on my arm, and answered, "Have you ever fought wolves while naked?"

Forestier gasped at the marks. "You must be joking?"

"Beware of where you bathe and nap on the border of the Forest of Wayward Souls." I pushed the gauntlet into Raphael, meeting his gaze. "Let's go. I wish to bathe and nap before my celebration party."

I turned, and the Fanged Lady stood in the way of the exit, her false smile unsettling. "Do you mind if I take the sword to have my smiths clean it and make a holder for—"

"No." I searched her face, curious now. "Who put the threadless Fates in the arena?"

"Oh, Madeleine thought it would honor the warriors and the local believers," offered Cruza Vendecci.

"I see. And the blade?" I asked, ignoring the viceroy, and glared at Madeleine.

"Well, I don't recall a real weapon being placed in their hands, so I think whoever was so clever to do so," she narrowed her eyes and stepped out of my way, "was rather clever to think that far ahead."

I laughed, shaking my head as I stole a glance back at her and the rest of the derelicts before me. "You give me too much credit. I'm an animal who just aims to breathe and breed for one more day. Whoever placed those weapons there aimed to have divine intervention unfold where it was made unwelcome. I hope you're ready for the wrath you will bring down upon us all, Madeleine."

"Superstitious dribble," she hissed.

"Let's go." Raphael shoved me forward.

As we made our way back, I fought the sleep nipping at me. *This is it; this is how my life and the fate of those I love ends. I can't let her and Fallen Arbor do this.* Looking at Raphael, my heart broke. *I have only myself to blame. Instead of pursuing*

The First Champion Supreme

a life, I went after things I desired and never took one thing seriously, not even when love presented itself to me on more than one occasion.

This is how legends and martyrs are born.

A god's intervention, even the slightest act, can send the realm of mortals spinning. I pray I find a means to use this blade I carry on my shoulder to protect all I hold dear.

May the wolf of the Fates stay strong against those who dare to bring magic back into this world.

"Ashton, are you alright?" Raphael had cupped my face, searching my eyes. "When did you learn to use the claymore?"

Scanning the room, I realized I was sitting in my chair in the room, unaware of the time that had passed as I dozed in and out. "I didn't." I searched his eyes. "You…" I swallowed the words I intended and kissed him deeply. "Let's just keep breathing. I'm tired and not in the mood for a party."

Raphael laughed. "Understood, my wolf. We have council tomorrow, and then—"

"Home," I demanded. "Take me back home after that."

Raphael frowned. "What's the matter?"

"I think I've been chosen by the Fates, and I can't shake this feeling that it's only going to spiral for us both from here."

"You so…" His words faltered. "I suppose I did give them the idea after all." *The nonbeliever at last believes.* "I did see her let go of the sword, did she not?"

I nodded. "Indeed."

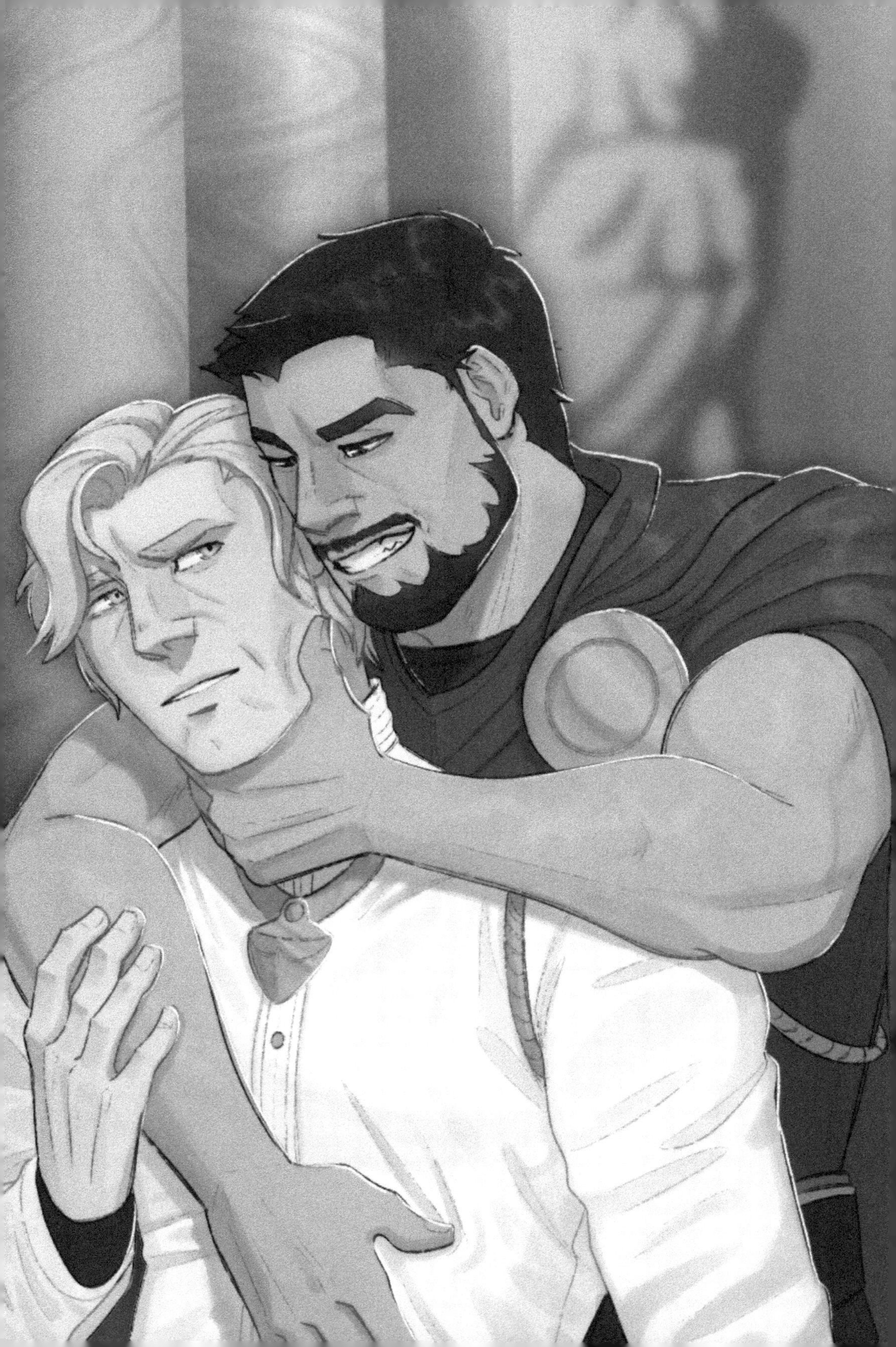

About the Author

Valerie Willis is the Chief Operating Officer for 4 Horsemen Publications, Inc., an expert digital typesetter, and a fantasy romance author based out of Central Florida. When writing, she loves crafting novels with elements inspired by mythology, legends, folklore, fairy tales, and history. As COO, she oversees the design of all books including covers, typesets, and author branding where she pulls in creative print design while making versatile eBooks.

You can find her hosting workshops or attending as a guest speaker at many events (MegaCon, DragonCon, OCLS Writers Conference, Florida Writers Conference, SavvyAuthors, Women in Publishing Summit, etc.). She's been on panels with best-selling authors from Peter David to Delilah Dawson sharing her expertise in writing, research, worldbuilding, character development, book design, reader immersion, and more. You can also find her co-hosting on the Drinking with Authors Podcast speaking with Jonathan Maberry, Heather Graham, Charles Gannon, and many more on their own journeys as an author! Or talking about the spooky stuff over on Eerie Travels with topics such as big foots, mermaids, and even Bloody Mary!

Her award-winning dark fantasy paranormal romance, *The Cedric Series*, is a blend of genres that appeals to a wide range of readers who describe it as "dramatic, lustful, and fantasy fulfilling." The motto here is: "No immortal is beyond the ailments of man" that includes powerful creatures, demons, witches, and deities! Many of the monsters are derived from Medieval Bestiaries adding a fun flavor of new yet deeply-rooted assortment such as Coin Iotair, Shag Foal, Cynocephali, and more.

Like many authors, her writing journey started in grade school and carried her through high school. Many who grew up with her talk often of the traveling binders that were often kept safe in their lockers. This was the precursor to the now complete young adult dark urban fantasy of the *Tattooed Angels Trilogy* starting with *Rebirth*. This alternative historic piece about immortals and a failed reincarnation Hotan covers a wide variety of life lessons such as whether to follow your own lifepath or the one chosen for you, breaking toxic traditions, and the obligations of cleaning up our family's mistakes and destruction. Inspired by her own life tribulations, it has been the beacon to keep her moving toward the world of books and writing even now.

For readers of fantasy MM romance, check out her pen name V.C. Willis with the Traibon Family Saga starting with books *The Prince's Priest* and *The Priest's Assassin*. If you are looking for steamy paranormal erotica, chase down Urban Legends and modern retellings of fairy tales with Honey Cummings. Many have found themselves laughing out loud and fanning themselves while reading *Sleeping with Sasquatch* and *Wanton Woman in White*.

In 2021, she left her day job to join 4 Horsemen Publications, Inc. full time to bring over a decade of typesetting skills and industry knowledge to the table. Nothing is more rewarding for her than making fellow author's dreams come to life in physical format so they may share them with readers. Designing and writing books has been a longtime passion since childhood of hers and she continues to inspire and encourage authors around the world whenever possible, indulging whenever she can to chat about the books folks are reading and writing.

Keep in touch and keep reading!

WWW.WILLISAUTHOR.COM

LINKTR.EE/WILLISAUTHOR

More Books as VC Willis

Dante's Ascension

The Prince's Priest
The Priest's Assassin
The Assassin's Saint
The Saint's Bloodeater
More to come!

The Fall of Ashton

The Champion's Lord: YONDER webnovel
Champion's Love: KU short story

The First Champion Supreme
Writing as Valerie Willis

Cedric: The Demonic Knight
Romasanta: Father of Werewolves
The Oracle: Keeper of the Gaea's Gate
Artemis: Eye of Gaea
King Incubus: A New Reign
Queen Succubus: Holder of the Crown

Val's House of Musings: A Mixed Genre Short Story Collection

Rebirth
Judgment
Death
Writer's Bane: Research 101
Writer's Bane: Formatting

ANTHOLOGIES & COLLECTIONS

A World of Their Own
Work of Hearts Magazine Release
How I Met My Other: True Stories, True Love
It Was Always You: A Thrill of the Heart Anthology

Demonic Wildlife: A Fantastically Funny Adventure
Demonic Household: See Owner's Manual
Demonic Carnival: First Ticket's Free

The Hunted—Thrill of the Hunt 3
Urban Legends Reimagined—Thrill of the Hunt 4
Buried Alive—Thrill of the Hunt 5

PUBLIC DOMAIN REMAKES

Bulfinch's Mythology with Illustrations
Book of Werewolves
The Fairy Faith of Celtic Countries

The Champion's Lord

Writing as Honey Cummings

Sleeping with Sasquatch
Cuddling with Chupacabra
Naked with New Jersey Devil
The Erotic Cryptid Collection

Laying with the Lady in Blue
Wanton Woman in White
Beating it with Bloody Mary
The Erotic Ghosts Collection

Beau and Professor Bestialora
The Goat's Gruff
Goldie and Her Three Beards
Pied Piper's Pipe
Princess Pea's Bed
Pinocchio and the Blow Up Doll
Jack's Beanstalk
Pulling Rapunzel's Hair
The Urban Erotica Fairy Tale Collection

Curses & Crushes: KU short story

Queen's Incubus: YONDER webnovel

Book Club Discussion Questions

1. Ashton has a lot of things he feels guilty for, including his mother's death and how the noble houses managed to overthrow the Grandemere Council. Do you think his guilt is justified? Why or why not?

2. In an instant, Ashton is fascinated by Raphael Traibon. Do you think this is raw physical attraction? Or perhaps he sees himself in the vagabond prince from the Old Continent? Do you think his reasons for his attraction to Raphael shift throughout the story?

3. Clan Thompson is joining the fray rather late. Do you think Clan Chief Germaine did this to protect himself? Protect his family? Or does he predict nothing good will come of these alliances or contracts of servitude?

4. Do you think Raphael shared a similar instant attraction to Ashton when they met? What makes you think he did or did not? What impression were you left with about Raphael's form of desires in the first visit to the Scarlett House?

5. There are several saucy scenes between Ashton and Raphael throughout the novel. Do you think there's significance in how rarely they went all the way with each other? Do you think their locations influenced how far they went? Or do you think their actions were a lustful way of punishing each other for feeling a certain way?

6. Philippe Farrow seems to hold a grudge against Ashton, but at the same time, there's a silent hint of respect for him. Do you think there's more to their relationship or history with one another that is off the table to talk about? We know Ashton slept with Philippe's daughter, but how does this hint how close they were to each other in the past?

7. We only get fleeting moments with Ashton's sister Lillian. What impression do you have of her through her actions and dialogue? What impression does Ashton give you from his internal thoughts and reactions?

8. Ashton finds himself in compromising situations often, from fighting wolves naked to finding his assumptions horribly inaccurate, especially when it comes to Raphael. What does this say about his character? Do you think it's due to bad luck? Or do these things come about because of his ego? Or the implication he's not thinking far enough ahead at any given time?

9. When Ashton finds himself being cared for by Raphael after nearly dying, what does this reveal about their relationship (despite neither of them addressing it fully before this point)? Were Raphael's actions worth throwing away their chance to keep House Vendecci in check and creating a scenario that cost them control?

10. Mad Madeleine is the twin sister of Philippe Farrow, a Paladin of the Fates. How do the two differ from one another? Do you think she takes advantage or manipulates Philippe? Or does he tolerate it in his own way? How did it make you feel when she pitted him against Brett Warren, a childhood friend of his daughter?

11. Ashton reveals on more than one occasion that he is a devout believer in the Fates, the daemon deities that control everyone's life threads. When the Devoted Sister comes to the rescue, he seems more distraught than excited. Do you think this is the right reaction for a believer seeing their god come to life? Or do you think he understands the deeper meaning of catching a god's gaze?

12. At which point in the story do you feel Ashton and Raphael were being the most honest with their feelings for the other? At what point did each of them self-sabotage to not just aim to deny themselves of being worthy of love but attempt to force the other to abandon the other? Who do you think has the greatest amount of self-hatred?

Discover more at
4HorsemenPublications.com

10% off using HORSEMEN10